PROJECT DATE

"You never said what kind of name Rio is."

"It's short for Riordan. I suppose we've never officially met." He stuck his hand out. "Riordan McKenna."

"Philomena Donovan." As I slipped my hand into his, goose bumps crawled up and down my arms. Then I frowned as his words registered. "That sounds like an Irish name."

"My dad's Irish but my mom's Puerto Rican. I get my coloring from her. My eyes and my name come from my dad." He grinned. "Mom says my eyes were wasted on me, but she's just jealous."

I looked into said eyes. Definitely not a waste.

"Do you have any brothers?"

"No. Just me and my dad."

I nodded. If Rio's dad were anything like him, I could believe it.

"Go out with me again."

I blinked. "Excuse me."

"Go out with me." He rubbed my knuckles and smiled in an adorably boyish way that seemed like it should be at odds with his manly exterior. "Please."

Staring into his eyes, I realized I'd forgotten all about Barry, Daphne's party, and my parents breathing down my back. At this moment, all that mattered was the touch of his hands on me and his earnest look that showed just how much he wanted to see me again . . .

D0837470

Books by Kate Perry

PROJECT DADDY

PROJECT DATE

Published by Zebra Books

Project Date

Kate Perry

ZEBRA BOOKS
Kensington Publishing Corp.
www.kensingtonbooks.com

ZEBRA BOOKS are published by

Kensington Publishing Corp.
850 Third Avenue
New York, NY 10022

Copyright © 2007 by Kathia Zolfaghari

All rights reserved. No part of this book may be reproduced
in any form or by any means without the prior written con-
sent of the Publisher, excepting brief quotes used in reviews.

If you purchased this book without a cover you should be
aware that this book is stolen property. It was reported as
"unsold and destroyed" to the Publisher and neither the Author
nor the Publisher has received any payment for this "stripped
book."

All Kensington titles, imprints, and distributed lines are available at special quantity discounts for bulk purchases for sales
promotion, premiums, fund-raising, educational, or institu-
tional use.

Special book excerpts or customized printings can also be created to fit specific needs. For details, write or phone the office
of the Kensington Special Sales Manager: Attn. Special Sales
Department. Kensington Publishing Corp., 850 Third Avenue,
New York, NY 10022. Phone: 1-800-221-2647.

Zebra and the Z logo Reg. U.S. Pat. & TM Off.

ISBN-13: 978-0-8217-8029-9
ISBN-10: 0-8217-8029-8

First Printing: September 2007
10 9 8 7 6 5 4 3 2 1

Printed in the United States of America

To Suzie.
Even though she's disgruntled that I
still haven't written her cats,
Samantha and Tigger, into a story.

And to Nate.
Because when I ask him if he loves me despite it all,
he always says there's nothing to despite.

Kudos to . . .

Nate Perry-Thistle, for augmenting my meager technical knowledge. All mistakes are my own.

Misa Ramirez and Susan Hatler, for support beyond the call of duty.

Parisa Zolfaghari, my favorite sister and number-one fan. Not to mention my Portland liaison.

Julie Linker, who always puts everything into unique perspective. I shudder to think what I'd do without her.

Suzie McSherry, who deserves several pages of thanks. Suffice it to say, Suzie rocks.

Nate Perry-Thistle, for knowing when to force me to write and when to force me to play hooky.

Betsy Fasbinder, my fairy godmother of all writing stuff.

Afra Afsharipour, Allison Brennan, Floyd and Joy Perry-Thistle, Diego Valderrama, Behrooz Zolfaghari, and everyone else who's been so supportive.

The Kung Fu gang, because they kick ass (figuratively as well as literally).

And finally, Nate Perry-Thistle, who listens carefully to all my frustrated tirades and then soothes me with kisses.

Chapter One

To Do:

> *Add hard drives to personal server*
> *Compile and install new Linux kernel at work*
> *Remind Matt about class tomorrow*
> *Buy tampons*
> *Dump Barry (for real this time)*

I didn't have to wait by Barry's black BMW long before he strolled out of the gym and toward his car.

His eyes lit up when he saw me, and he hurried over eagerly. "Mena, I thought I was supposed to pick you up for our date. Am I late?"

"No." He was never late. Actually, he was quite predictable, which was part of the problem. "I just needed to see you and I couldn't wait—"

"I know what you mean." He dropped his gym bag and grabbed me by the waist. "I've been thinking about you all day."

"Barry—" Before I could say another word he plastered me to his chest and laid a big wet one on my mouth.

I sighed in resignation and tried to give the kiss a chance. But it did nothing for me—not even the smallest tingle of warmth. It was too soppy, too limp. Utterly uninspiring and, well, gross.

As much as I wanted to blame his kisses, that wasn't why I needed to break up with him. Fact of the matter, we just weren't right together. Yes, he was convenient and my parents liked him but, truthfully, we didn't really get along. We didn't *click*.

And the more I hung out with Barry, the more I realized I couldn't settle. I wanted a soulmate. I wanted someone to understand me and like me despite that.

Barry deserved someone who liked him more deeply than I did. He was a great guy, for the most part. He deserved to be loved as much as I did. Just not by me.

The problem was that even if we broke up, the chances that we'd get back together were high. Precedence had been set—in the year we'd been dating, we'd separated and hooked up again dozens of times (like I said, it was convenient), and that was doing us both a huge disservice.

So this time I was calling it quits for good. I'd been thinking about it for days, and I'd plotted just the way to end the madness.

Trying not to gag as he slopped his tongue all around the outside of my lips (his specialty), I pushed on his chest and pried myself loose. "Barry!"

He lifted his head and frowned. "Huh?"

"Stop." Wiping my mouth, I took a step back. I'd procrastinated long enough. It was now or never. "Barry, we need to talk."

"Talk?" He combed his hair with his fingers. Like always, his blond hair flopped back into place perfectly.

Actually, everything about Barrington Emery Wallace III was perfect—his looks, his clothes, his job, and his background. He was a Ken doll come to life.

A Ken doll who kissed like a Saint Bernard.

With renewed purpose, I took another step back so I

was pressed against the passenger door of his car. "Yeah, I have something I want to say."

"I'm all ears." He gave me the crooked grin that had attracted me to him in the first place.

Oh, this was going to be tough. "I think we should stop dating."

His grin widened and he reached for me again. "I think you should come over here and give me another kiss."

"Barry, I'm serious."

"So am I." He took a step toward me. "Come on, Mena. Let's skip breaking up and get on to making up."

I held my hand out to hold him back. "No. We're breaking up for good this time."

"We always break up for good. It's our favorite game," he said, taking my outstretched hand and crowding me against the car. "Did I tell you how beautiful you look tonight?"

Beautiful? I looked down at the rags I'd put on instead of my usual colorful, funky clothes. A potato sack would have been more flattering.

"And your hair." He fingered a lock that'd slipped loose from my intentionally messy ponytail. "Like spun wheat."

I didn't think wheat could be spun, but that was beside the point. Batting his hand away, I said, "Barry . . ."

"I love it when you get impassioned. Your eyes get stormy." He leaned in. "Are they blue-gray or gray-blue?"

"Barry!" Damn him, why wasn't he listening? I tugged my hand out of his and shoved him back. "I'm totally serious. This is it. We're over."

His grin faded and he crossed his arms. "Why?"

I blinked. Usually when we broke up, we respected the other's wishes. It was clean with a minimum of fuss. Barry questioning the process was a new phenomenon. "This isn't working. We aren't working out."

"Why not?"

"Because," I grabbed the first excuse that came to mind, "I can't stand your kisses."

He frowned. "Excuse me?"

"Your kisses. I hate the way you slobber all over my face. They gross me out." Then I thought I should clarify. "Just the mouth-to-mouth ones. When you kiss anywhere else it's fine."

"Good to know."

He sounded shell-shocked, but I wanted to make sure I nipped this relationship in the bud, so I went on. "And we don't rock each other's boats. Essentially, you, um, don't turn me on."

His face drained in shock.

I crossed my arms to keep the guilt at bay (no, it didn't work) and considered what to say next. It had to be something that would bruise his ego enough to never come back to me. I took a deep breath, told myself that this was in Barry's best interest, and went in for the kill. "When we have sex, I think of other men to get excited."

"What other men?"

"MacGyver," I blurted without thinking.

Actually, that wasn't far from the truth. I've had a wicked crush on MacGyver since I was eight. MacGyver is my idol. A guy who can solve any problem with a paper clip and a stick of gum? Shiver.

Barry would believe it too. My best friend Matt always teased me about the posters of Richard Dean Anderson I had pinned all over my office.

"I have to confess, Barry, I agreed to go out with you because you kind of look like him." Outright lie. He didn't look anything like MacGyver. "Only you lack the, um, inventiveness. In bed."

He frowned. "How do you know what MacGyver's like in bed?"

"Oh, I know. It's all in the hands." I glanced disdainfully

at Barry's. At least I hoped it was disdainful—I'm not a great actress. "Your hands are kind of, um, small. And you're not spontaneous. I mean, don't you think it's overkill to lay out all your clothes for the week? What if the weather changes? You know how mercurial the weather is in Portland. And why do we have to go to the same restaurant all the time? I know the food at Hurley's is supposed to be the best in Portland, but there are hundreds of other restaurants we never go to. What if I feel like Lebanese for a change? What if I want McDonald's?"

Even though it seemed like I'd given him enough reasons for never seeing me again, I was on a roll and it was impossible to stop. Before I could control my mouth, I heard myself say, "And your feet smell."

Barry blinked and staggered back.

I'd never been deliberately mean in my life. Well, okay, except for the time I washed all my sister Daphne's whites with a red T-shirt. On purpose. Oh, and that time in high school when Aaron Jackson (who I'd had a crush on) called to ask Daphne (who was visiting from college) to the winter formal and I "accidentally" lost the message.

I tried not to feel bad over how I was undoubtedly making Barry feel. I was justified—this was for his own good. And if I told myself that another, oh, couple of hundred times, I might actually believe it.

"You know what, Mena? I think you may be right."

I tripped, which was no small feat considering I was standing still. "I am?"

"Yes." He nodded. "I've been thinking the exact same thing."

"Oh, you have, have you?" Then why did he look so angry?

He must have missed the doubt in my voice. "I've been thinking of breaking things off myself. You're a great woman, Mena, but the sex *is* rather lackluster between us, isn't it? I've found myself fantasizing a time or two myself. About, uh, Cameron Diaz."

Which is why two seconds ago you were trying to give my face a tongue bath? Can we say defense mechanism? And I was positive he picked Cameron Diaz because he knew I couldn't stand her. "At least MacGyver has brains."

"Cameron's got ingenuity," he countered. "Like in that movie when she used sperm for hair gel. You couldn't come up with something like that."

Well, he had me there. If that was the difference between inventive and unimaginative, guess which I'd take.

But that was beside the point. This was *my* breakup scene. He had his turn the last time. I glared at him. "Can't you have any original thoughts?"

His brow furrowed. "What?"

"You're just repeating everything I've been saying to you. Haven't you been listening?"

Barry's eyes narrowed. "No need to get snippy. Can't we end this on a friendly note?"

I gaped at him. He wanted to end this on a friendly note? He'd just told me I was boring in bed. *No one* had ever said that to me. In fact, I'd been complimented a time or two. Not to brag, but I've got skills.

I was just about to give him a piece of my mind when I realized my objective had been achieved. Barry and I were on the same page. There was no chance we'd get back together in a weak moment. Not after these revelations.

Somewhat appeased now that I had the situation in hand once again, I blinked hard enough that my eyes teared. I looked up, pouting a little. "Fine."

"Fine." He stared at me. "Will you be okay?"

"Yeah. Sure."

He looked like he didn't believe me but he nodded.

"Is everything okay here?"

I looked up to see Barry's friend and boxing instructor, Rio, not two feet away and watching us with concern.

I didn't know Rio except in passing, and I was glad he hadn't arrived sooner because I didn't want him to get the wrong impression of me. I really wasn't heartless. Or sexually unexciting.

Not that I liked Rio or anything. I mean, sure, he was Latino-hot with thick ropey muscles, latte skin, and sky blue eyes. Not to mention his melted Snickers voice. But he was Barry's friend and, therefore, out of bounds. Plus, he wasn't my type. I went for brainy, not brawny.

My eyes drifted down to the bag Rio held in his hands. *MacGyver hands.* I blinked. How come I'd never noticed before? Maybe I needed to take brawn out for a test drive.

Barry cleared his throat. "We're fine," he said. "Just talking."

Rio nodded. "See you tomorrow evening then, Barry."

With another searching look at both of us, he continued around the building to the back parking lot. I supposed that was where the employees parked. Not that I cared beyond the fact it gave me the opportunity to ogle his jeans-clad butt as he walked away.

"Can I walk you to your car?"

"Huh? Uh, no." I gave Rio's retreating figure one last look and turned to Barry. "I'll be fine. I'm just a couple of cars down."

He nodded. "Goodnight then, Mena."

"See you, Barry." I took the keys out of my pocket as I strode to my Prius, unlocked the door, and headed home.

My house was in a trendy part of Portland, off NW 23rd. The entrance to my home was on the porch level, but then you had to walk up a flight of stairs to get to my spacious, sunlit flat. I rented out the ground floor (an almost subterranean unit).

The first thing I did when I got in was call my best friend Matt.

It rang three times before he picked up, breathless. "'Lo?"

"You aren't masturbating to Tomb Raider again, are you?" He had a full-blown framed poster of Lara Croft wearing a skimpy bikini—the video game Lara, not the Angelina Jolie one—in his cave (aka home office).

"I just walked in from racquetball. And I've never masturbated to Tomb Raider."

"Liar."

"Although I'm not saying Lara Croft isn't hot."

I grinned at the smile in his voice. "You're such a geek."

"You're one to talk. So why are you calling me? Shouldn't you be breaking Barrington's heart right about now?"

"Mission accomplished. It wasn't as bad as I thought it was going to be." I winced thinking of the mean things I said to Barry. Then I pictured Rio's hands again and felt my face flush. Well, it was where I pictured them that made me burn.

"Am I to understand he wasn't crushed by the thought of never again touching your fair skin?"

"He said sex with me was lackluster!"

Matt chuckled. "You can't be *that* bad."

I held the receiver out and crossed my eyes at him.

When I put it back to my ear, he was laughing. "Doc, didn't your mother ever tell you your face could freeze like that?"

I harrumphed. "How'd you know what I was doing?"

"I know you."

True. Matthew Turner and I had been best friends since junior high. We'd had computer lab together. He'd been patronizing, implying that I didn't know half what he knew about computers. To show him, I cracked into the school system and changed his D in P.E. to a B. We'd been friends ever since.

And he's called me Doc from that day on. I'd thought he had a Bugs Bunny fetish but it turned out he was just shortening my name, Philomena Donovan (no, I have no idea what my parents were thinking), to PhD. Ergo, Doc. Yeah, he's odd.

"So what happened?" he asked me.

I gave him all the details, including the slimy tongue down the throat just to giggle at his reaction. When I was done, he simply said, "You got what you wanted."

I knew that. Still.

"You did what you thought you had to do. Get over it, Doc."

"Jeez. Thanks for the compassion."

"Any time." He chuckled. "You want to come over?"

"Tempting. But I think I'm going to stay in. It's late and I have to be at work early tomorrow."

"When? At ten?"

Wise ass. "So I don't like to wake up at dawn."

"Nothing wrong with that." He sighed. "But I was hoping you'd bring takeout with you."

Notice how he didn't ask me to cook for him. Boiling water taxes my culinary abilities. "Sorry. You're on your own."

"Damn. I'm hungry."

As he was always hungry, I didn't feel any real sympathy for him. "Order a pizza. You know you'll be happier not sharing with me. I'll see you tomorrow, right? At class?"

"Class?"

I sighed. Sometimes I was tempted to pin notes to his clothes. "Yeah. Remember? Kung Fu?"

"That's tomorrow night?"

"I'm surprised you remember to put on clothes before you leave the apartment."

"I can't help it. I have important things on my mind."

I could concede that point. He designed software for an aeronautics firm. Sometimes in the middle of a conversation he'd drift off and you knew he was working on whatever bit of code was giving him trouble at the moment.

"And I didn't forget about class. I just didn't realize tomorrow was Wednesday."

"Uh-huh." Likely story. But before I could rag on him some more, my call waiting went off. I moved my cell phone away from my ear and looked at the screen. Wince. My mom. "I gotta go, Matt. My mom's on the other line."

"See you tomorrow, Doc."

Taking a deep breath, I switched to my mom's call. "Hey, Mom."

"How are you, Philomena?"

"Fine." She was the only person who called me by my whole name. "How was Belize? You're back, right?"

"I had a good time. I did some work at an orphanage while your father was hunting for his beetle." She sighed. "He didn't find it."

Uh-oh. "He didn't cause any kind of national incident, did he?"

My parents often headed out to weird locations so my dad could hunt down an elusive bug. The whole bug collecting business had always struck me as odd. My parents were the ultra-earth conscious, grow-your-own-organic-veggies, make-a-difference types. They lived outside of Portland in the Willamette Valley and had a practically self-sustained farm. Collecting rare insects seemed like an oxymoron to me, but when I'd point this out to my dad, he'd reply that he was actually protecting them from the environmentally callous.

On top of it all, Dad didn't take failure well. The last time they went on a bug hunting expedition, he was foiled from capturing his specimen because his guide— a hapless boy barely out of puberty—handed him a net that had a hole from a mishap the previous day. Fortunately, the boy was a great runner and managed to escape. I don't think it comes as a surprise that Dad isn't allowed entrance into that African province any more.

Mom sighed again. "I managed to convince him a Central American jail wasn't a place he wanted to spend any amount of time. But that's not why I called. Have you talked to Daphne?"

Daphne is my nemesis. And my sister, but that's secondary.

"Not in a few days," I said guardedly, even though it was more like a few weeks.

"I've been trying to reach her all day but she's not answering. I'm worried about her."

Of course this was about Daphne. It was always about Daphne. I should have known my mom didn't call to talk about me. I wanted to say maybe their precious angel didn't answer because she was getting laid, but that sounded implausible even to me. Daphne didn't have casual liaisons. Actually, Daphne didn't have any liaisons— she was too busy saving the world. So I just muttered "Hmm."

"When did you say you'd last spoken with her?"

I didn't. "I'm sure she's fine, Mom. She's probably all wrapped up in work. You know how she gets."

My mom harrumphed. "Sometimes I wish she were less driven about her work. Like you, Philomena."

Backhanded compliments were a fact of life with my parents where I was concerned. And it generally led to a list of all the areas where I lacked in comparison to Daphne. I walked into the living room and flopped onto the couch. At least I could be comfortable while she ragged on me.

But instead of launching into a tirade about my job (she hates that I'm a sys admin instead of doing something worthwhile, like researching childhood diabetes), she said, "Her thirtieth birthday is coming up. I was thinking of throwing her a big party. What do you think?"

Hours listening to my parents' friends rave about how great Daphne is? Terrible idea. "Is she coming home?"

"She'll come home," Mom said confidently.

I couldn't help but remember six months ago when Daphne came back to Portland for Christmas. Pure hell. All I heard was Daphne this and Daphne that. I knew my sister was perfect—I didn't need it crammed down my throat.

I'd been ecstatic when she went off to California for college and stayed there. I'd thought, finally I wouldn't be crowded by her enormous shadow anymore.

What happened, though, was kind of like when a rock star dies at the height of his fame—instant immortality. I had to live with the specter of Daphne hanging over my shoulder, at home, and at school. Thank God we hadn't attended the same university—I think that saved my sanity. It was bad enough that I wasn't out to save the world like Daphne; at least I didn't have teachers comparing my mediocre intelligence to her brilliance.

I won't even touch the fact that I dropped out of college after the first year and the furor *that* caused.

"Philomena? Are you there?"

I shook my head and relaxed my too-tight grip on my cell phone. "Yeah."

"What do you think?"

"Uh—" I had the distinct impression I'd missed something. "Sounds great."

"You weren't listening to what I was saying, were you?"

"No, actually." I winced, but I didn't bother to deny it. Lenora Donovan had Spidey sense where her daughters were concerned.

"I was saying that, while it's great that Daphne is so dedicated to her work, she needs balance in her life. How long has it been since she's had a boyfriend?"

Was this a rhetorical question? "Not sure."

"That's what I mean. Daphne should take a page out of your book and find herself a nice man like Barry."

I didn't want a nice man. And I certainly didn't want Barry. My mind flashed on Rio's capable, MacGyver hands, and I shook my head. "Mom, Barry and I—"

My mouth snapped shut as her words registered. Holding the phone out, I rubbed a finger in my ear. Did my mom just say Daphne needed to be more like me?

"I have to tell you, Philomena, I think Barry is absolutely wonderful. He's respectful and does good work for the environment. Even your father approves, despite the fact that Barry drives a BMW."

When I brought the phone back to my ear, she was still talking, oblivious to my stunned silence. "I can't tell you how happy I am that you've found such a great man. If only Daphne would too. She should be more like you, Philomena."

Be more like me? Twilight Zone alert.

Mom went on like the world wasn't spinning off its axis. "I haven't always understood your choices, Philomena, but I can't approve of Barry more. You've done really well this time. He's the son your father and I always wanted."

I felt a familiar sharp pang in my chest. I was a very successful sys admin, owned a house, and was a third degree black belt in Kung Fu, but to my mom my best accomplishment was the guy I was dating. Who I wasn't dating as of twenty minutes ago. "Mom, listen. About Barry—"

"I have to admit that having Daphne come here for a party is only secondary to having her here so I can show her how well you've done for yourself with Barry. Maybe you'll rub off on her."

My mouth clamped shut. I couldn't believe it. Me, a role model for perfect Daphne. For the first time EVER.

"Maybe you and Barry can come to dinner later this week."

I needed to tell Mom I'd broken up with Barry,

but the words *role model* and *rub off on Daphne* swirled in my mind.

But it was now or never. She'd given me the perfect opening. So I took a deep breath and said, "Sure, Mom."

Wince. Not exactly the right words.

"Okay, honey. I'll call you to arrange dinner. And to let you know the date for the party."

"Right." I hung up and stared at the ceiling.

I really should have told Mom I'd broken up with Barry, but I could just hear the tirade—how I always messed up things in my life. Like college. My career choice. And now the perfect man (gag).

But, to tell the truth, the most intoxicating part was that Mom (and Dad, by default) finally acknowledged that Daphne wasn't so great and I was. Sure, it wasn't for the most optimal reasons, but beggars couldn't be picky. I'd been waiting for this moment for twenty-eight years. No way was I going to let it pass by.

That I'd broken up with Barry the night before? Minor technicality. I could fix anything. MacGyver wasn't my idol for nothing.

Chapter Two

"Another day, a whole new set of possibilities."
—*MacGyver, "Slow Death" Episode #19*

Rrrep. Rrrep. Rrrep.

I slammed my fist down on the shrieking alarm clock four times before it shut up.

Damn alarm. Who in their right mind woke up to one, much less got up predawn? Because eight-thirty was predawn in my book. I covered my head with my comforter and tried to find that warm spot to snooze for a few more minutes.

Oh yeah, right there. I snuggled down and closed my eyes . . .

Rrrep. Rrrep.

I shoved the covers off me, picked up the devil's appliance, and threw it across the room. When it hit the wall, I heard the faint snap of plastic breaking.

"Shit. Now I'll have to fix that," I muttered as I stumbled out of bed. First things first. I needed caffeine, and I needed it fast. I pulled my robe on, flipped the hood up, and headed to the kitchen.

I felt human after two cups of coffee. However, I

probably still shouldn't have answered my cell phone when it rang. Especially since the screen read *Daphne*.

But I did. "What?"

"Mom's left a dozen messages for me in the last twenty-four hours." Her low, calm voice set me on edge. "Are they back?"

I refrained from saying that, as their favorite daughter, she really should have a better grip on their schedule. Yeah, I've been working on my self-control. "They came back yesterday."

"Hmm."

I pictured her lower lip sticking out and her long, graceful finger tapping it like she always did when she was thinking. It should have made her look dorky, but on Daphne everything looked good.

It just killed me.

Daphne was the Road Runner to my Wile E. Coyote. My greatest efforts never paid off, and she could do no wrong. While she didn't intentionally try to foil my every move, it still worked out that way.

I'd concluded she was genetically superior years ago. She was taller, curvier, and smarter. Everything about her was shinier. For example, we'd inherited the same blond hair from our mom—technically. But Daphne's was shiny honey blond and somehow mine just looked dirty.

As if that wasn't enough, she was also a do-gooder—she worked on finding cures for bizarre childhood diseases at Stanford—so resenting her took extra work. But younger sisters were supposed to resent their older sisters, right?

Blame it on the caffeine kicking in, but I decided to make an effort to reach out. "So, how's it going?"

"Okay."

I frowned. Something in her voice said that was far from the truth. "Are you sure?"

Instead of answering, she neatly diverted the conversation. "How are you doing?"

I try to be a caring sister and she doesn't respond. Typical. "Pretty good. I got a raise at work."

"You're saving your money, aren't you? Do you have some kind of retirement plan at work?"

I wasn't even twenty-nine and she wanted me to worry about retiring? At least *I* owned a house; Daphne only rented a condo. (My parents were quick to point out houses cost a fortune in Palo Alto. Excuses, excuses.) "I'm doing okay."

"Because you can't depend on other people," she said bitterly.

I frowned. Daphne, cynical? Not natural. One of her most unattractive traits is her never-ending optimism. She makes Mary Poppins look dour. "What's wrong?"

"Nothing." Even she realized she didn't sound convincing, so she repeated it more forcefully. "Nothing. Really."

"You sure?"

"Yes." She sounded like she was forcing a smile. Then she sighed again. "I have to get back to work—I'll let you go. Talk to you later, Mena."

"Right," I murmured, totally confused, listening to the dial tone. This probably wasn't one of those presuicidal calls. But if it was, I hoped she left me the denim jacket she got in Paris. Daphne had godawful taste in clothes, but that jacket was awesome.

Nah. I shook my head, flipped the phone closed, and tossed it aside. Daphne would never hurt herself. She was too conscious of other people's feelings. Her empathy made her the ideal research scientist. Our parents always bragged about how brilliant and altruistic she was.

Like being a systems administrator wasn't noble. I'll have them know that without me, a whole lot of people would be without Internet access. And imagine where humanity would be then.

I figured out what I was going to do about Barry and my parents that afternoon at work. I was deeply engaged in an illicit game of Grand Theft Auto (the latest version kicked ass) against one of the guys in Sales when the answer came to me.

Mom wanted someone charming, handsome, and successful as bait for Daphne. Barry was just a convenient body, someone at hand who fit the bill. But I could get any other guy with those qualifications. What did it matter whether or not it was actually Barry? A rose by any other name and all that. There had to be any number of men who would pass muster.

I ran my idea by Matt as we were sparring in Kung Fu that evening.

"What?" He stopped with my arm leveraged behind my back, a fist wrapped in my hair, arching my neck uncomfortably.

"My mom only wants me to bring some guy whom she deems as perfect to push Daphne into a relationship." I tried to wiggle my arm out of the figure-four lock but he held strong. "It doesn't matter who it is."

"You're missing one key element to this equation, Doc."

I looked at him. My head was torqued so I didn't have to do more than move my eyeballs. "What element?"

"Your mom wants Daphne to see a well-matched couple and the benefits of settling down. She's not going to be happy if you bring Bill Gates to dinner if you don't care about him." He kicked my feet out from under me so I landed on my back, breaking my shoulder and arm and causing head trauma. In theory. In reality, he let go of me so I could break my fall.

I frowned up at him from the mat. "I still don't see how that's going to be a problem."

Matt held out his hand to help me up. "So you're going to find a guy you're genuinely interested in to the point of love in the next week-and-a-half."

"Why a week-and-a-half?" I took his hand, hopped up, and promptly used it to leverage him down to his knees.

"Because Daphne's birthday is in three weeks and you need to introduce this paragon of manhood to your parents well enough beforehand so they actually believe you care about him. Jesus, Doc, ease up on my wrist. I'm a software engineer. I need it to type."

"Oh. Sorry." I let go of his hand, and then because our instructor, Dwight, was giving us dirty looks (we weren't supposed to chat while we worked out), I finished Matt off with an outside crescent kick to his head that sent him flying. Well, I grazed by his face and smacked his open palm, which he'd held up as a target for me. But otherwise he would have gone flying.

"Why are you doing this?" Matt asked as he got to his feet.

I blinked demurely, trying to stifle a grin. "I'm being a good role model for my older sister."

"In other words, you want to rub it in Daphne's face."

I frowned. Was that wrong? "You'd do the same in my shoes."

He snorted as he pulled out the rag from his belt and mopped his face. "No, I wouldn't. And she's only thirteen months older than you. You're practically the same age."

Fortunately Dwight signaled the end of class so I didn't have to reply. Grabbing my water bottle, I took a long drink while Dwight went over what he wanted us to study this week. He loved giving homework, from stuff like practicing nonjudgment to breathing. And I liked doing it. I was all for personal growth.

This month, we were supposed to be aware of opportunities, no matter what guise they presented themselves in. Piece of cake. I was always open.

I headed to the changing room to get my bag before the guys started disrobing. Usually, they let the women have the room first (there was only one changing area) but tonight I was the only woman who showed up for class so I had to fend for myself. I didn't really mind changing with them—I was all for naked male flesh— but Matt would be in there and that was just too weird. I mean, I'd seen his bare chest plenty of times. But seeing him in his skivvies? Totally disgusting.

In his defense, Matt *did* have a nice body. He looked kind of scrawny in clothes, gangly and all gawky arms and legs, but he was nicely sculpted. Thin with long muscles. Surprising, really—you wouldn't expect it by just looking at him.

But then, Matt was full of surprises. I mean, he was a superb coder of software, a third degree black belt, and played violin in a way that could make the most cynical person weep.

There was a space of about twelve minutes in high school when I thought Matt was perfect and that we might be more than friends, but then we kissed. To me, kissing him was like kissing a brother: just plain wrong. I still thought he was perfect, but for someone else.

As if my thoughts had conjured him, I ran into him on my way out of the changing room. "Hey, Doc, want to grab a Guinness?" he said.

"Kells?" I asked rhetorically. Kells was my favorite Irish pub in Portland. The atmosphere was relaxed, the food was good, and the Guinness was sweet and creamy. "Meet you outside?"

"Wait for me by the door. My car's down the street."

I rolled my eyes and headed to the bathroom to change. I was a third degree black belt too, but his vein of chivalry ran so deep he still insisted on walking me around when it was dark.

Matt finished dressing first and was waiting for me, leaning against the front door. "Ready?" he asked, bending down to pick up his Kung Fu bag.

"Let's go."

Because it was a weeknight, we found parking practically right in front of the bar. I waited in the rain while Matt secured his Mercedes Jeep with The Club and then we walked inside.

I headed toward two empty seats at the far end of the bar, running my hand along the gleaming dark wood of the bar top. Kells was classier than the typical Irish pub but, like I said before, the Guinness was really the shining star here.

Matt ordered for us as he took a seat.

I hopped up next to him. "Guess who I saw this morning."

"Who?" he asked absently as he pulled out his wallet.

"Are you paying?"

"First round. Second round is yours."

He always said that, but we never ordered a second round. Oh, well—I'd get it next time.

"So who'd you see?"

"Magda." Magda was my tenant and an enigma I was always trying to decipher. I didn't understand why a woman like Magda wanted to live in the dark basement space I rented out. She was strikingly beautiful and expensive looking—the type of woman who belonged in a penthouse in New York instead of a musty cave.

He stopped riffling through his wallet and looked up. "No way."

"For real."

"Where's she been? It's been a long time since there was a Magda sighting." He nodded to the bartender, who set our drinks in front of us, and handed over a bill.

"I didn't ask her where she's been. Not that she'd tell me. That woman has secrets." This was one of our favorite games: speculating about Magda's life. She was so private. And mysterious. In the Employer section of her renter's paperwork she'd printed: self-employed. "I can tell you she had a black case with her. And when she saw me, she tried to hide it."

"A black case? What do you think she had in there?"

"Sex toys," I said confidently.

Matt choked on his beer. I leaned close, waiting to see if it would shoot out his nostrils, but he pushed me back. "You aren't still waiting for me to gush liquid out of my nose, are you?"

"Hell, yeah." The one time it happened back in high school had been incredibly entertaining.

Smart man, he changed the subject. "Why do you think Magda has sex toys in her bag?"

I shrugged. "I know we thought she was a spy—"

"Or a hitman."

"Right. But I think we were wrong."

Matt glanced at me curiously. "What does she do then?"

"She's a high-priced call girl."

"Have sex, will travel?"

I nodded. "Exactly."

He scrunched his face in that way he does when he's considering a complex algorithm. "You might have something with that theory," he said finally.

"I know. The way she comes and goes at all hours of the day. The way she's gone for days—" I snapped my fingers. "I bet she gets hired by rich men to pleasure them for weeks at a time."

"She does like to wear leather," Matt said slowly, getting into the game.

"Maybe she's a part-time dominatrix."

"What kind of sex toys do you think she has in her case?"

I thought about what I'd put into my bag of tricks if I were a high-priced working girl. "Vibrators. Lots of them in all sizes. And whipped cream. And that oil stuff that you blow on and it makes your skin feel hot."

Matt blinked at me. "You've given this some thought."

I felt my face flush. "I just have a fertile imagination."

"Do you have her phone number?"

"Yeah." I frowned. "Why?"

"If she has anything like what you just mentioned, maybe I should make an appointment with her."

"Oh, gross!" I whacked his shoulder. "That's disgusting. She's my tenant."

"It wouldn't be like we'd have sex under your roof. We'll go to my place. Or a hotel so that oil stuff doesn't stain my sheets."

I punched him again.

"Ow." He rubbed his shoulder. Then he grinned. "Had you going, didn't I?"

"Now every time I see her I'm going to imagine your scrawny ass on top of her."

"No, I'd let her be on top."

I glared at him but he just laughed. Abruptly he sobered and said, "Are you sure about this, Doc?"

"About Magda being a call girl?"

"No. About this Daphne thing. It's not a very nice thing to do to your sister."

"I'm not doing anything to my sister." I took a swig of beer to stifle the guilt that swelled around my heart. Then I thought about all those years living in the black void created by Daphne's dazzling being; my spine stiffened and my lip protruded. "What's so wrong, Matt? It's not like I'm hurting anyone. I just want a little—" I paused to find the right word.

"Revenge?" he offered helpfully.

"No. Just a little attention from my parents."

Matt shook his head. "Sounds like revenge to me."

I decided to try another tack. I leaned closer to him and grabbed his forearm. "Don't you remember what it was like for me? Everyone comparing me to Daphne, asking me why I didn't get as good grades or why I didn't apply myself like Daphne. Why I wasn't serious like Daphne. How it was unfortunate I wasn't as pretty."

He covered my hand with his. "Yeah, but it wasn't as bad as you think."

"My parents didn't come to my high school graduation because of Daphne."

"She was getting that special science award." He frowned at me. "You know that was a big deal for someone so young."

"Still," I said stubbornly. "I was never good enough. Even now, even though I'm damn brilliant at what I do, do I get any recognition? No. Why? Because she's out saving orphans. No one realizes without people like me, the networks and computers they need for their work wouldn't be available."

He studied me in that kind, all-knowing way he'd had since he was a pimply kid. Finally, he said, "I just want you to be happy."

"I'll be happy when I prove I can do something better than Daphne." I smiled, hoping it reached my eyes.

Matt looked like he wanted to say something more but he didn't. Thank God.

I diverted our conversation back to Magda, only speculating on her career wasn't as much fun anymore.

Chapter Three

"Maybe it's about time I expanded the realm of possibilities around here."

—MacGyver, "The Escape" Episode #20

I stole a glance around the doorjamb of my server room. All clear. Before anyone saw me, I closed the door and slid the lock home.

I grinned. "Free at last."

Plopping down on the floor, I pulled out a lime green pad of sticky notes and a pen. I tapped the pen against my lips. Where to start?

Because Matt was right—if my plan was going to work, I had to make my parents believe I was head over heels for the Barry-substitute. The catch: I didn't have much time.

Actually, this was a good way to start on my new mission to find a soulmate as well. What if the Barry-substitute turned out to be fantastic and exciting and creative and thought the sun and moon revolved around me? It'd be very convenient.

So, best choices on top, or start off with the least viable ones?

"Best choices first," I murmured. I didn't have time to

fool around. Hooking the pen on my bottom lip, I let it dangle while I mentally ran through all the men I knew. Then I weeded out the geeks (I knew lots—occupational hazard) and the unemployed (the tech industry has had its ups and downs). And I tossed out Matt, because that'd be like dating my brother (blech).

Rio flashed through my mind, and I started to add him to the list. But even as my heart sped up at the idea of going out with him, I froze mid-letter. He wasn't exactly viable. I doubted my parents would be thrilled if I told them I dumped Barry and started to date a guy who teaches people to beat other people up for a living.

With a pout, I crossed him out and surveyed what I'd come up with.

Hm. I scowled. Not promising. I let my head thunk backward against the wall, hoping the impact would knock an idea loose.

Nothing.

Maybe if I whittled down my criteria. Did it matter if he was handsome? That was icing on the cake, but the cake could still be delicious even plain.

"Okay. Successful with good manners." I had to know someone like that.

Rehooking the pen, I wiggled my lip so it tapped my chin. Then I balanced the sticky notes on top of my head.

Still nothing.

Someone banged on the door. I startled and bumped my head against one of the servers.

"Mena! You in there?"

Shit—it was Lewis, my intern. He was the reason I was locked in the server closet. Him and the fact that when I'm at my desk, people stop by to tell me their computer woes. I needed some sanctuary to get this list done, and the server room seemed the most optimal place.

I debated not answering, but Lewis was persistent. It was one of his most infuriating traits. Why couldn't he be like any other punk teenager and shirk his duties by playing video games?

"Mena!" He pounded harder on the door.

Shit. I got up, unlocked the door, and swung it open. "What?"

Then I realized I still had the pen dangling from my lip. I snatched it off and gave Lewis a look that said he'd better not comment. "What?" I barked again.

He pointed. "You have a pad of sticky notes on your head."

I narrowed my eyes at him and reached for the pad. It pulled a few strands of my hair. I grimaced and tried to lift it off gingerly.

"Do you need help? I can help you."

"I got it," I said quickly. "Thanks, though."

He looked disappointed for a split second, but then he bounced back to his normal puppy eagerness. "I finished dusting all those computer cases. I'm ready for my next assignment." He looked around the server room. "Is there something wrong in here? I can take a look around. Want me to straighten all the cables? I bought these really cool cord organizers. They're corrugated tubes that are color coordinated—"

"Lewis," I interrupted, "have you taken lunch yet? Maybe you should take a break."

"A break?" His brow furrowed. Two seconds later his expression cleared. I could almost see a light turn on inside his head. "Do *you* want lunch? I can get you lunch."

"Um. No, thanks. I'm fine."

"I can get you something. What would you like? I have my bike." He looked at me with adoring eyes. "I'd go anywhere for you."

Oh, God. I patted his arm—briefly, so he wouldn't

turn into a puddle of mush at my feet. "Thanks. I'm fine though. Let's go find you something to do."

Lewis monopolized the rest of my afternoon. Spending it with a pimply nineteen-year-old wasn't the way I'd envisioned it, but at some point while I was showing him the finer points of coding in Perl I got inspired. I knew just who to call up and ask for a date: Johnny Morgan.

Several times during the day I picked up the phone to give him a call, but I stalled. Was it a good idea to talk to him at work? Though I had to—I didn't know his home number and he was unlisted. But what if he had clients with him? What if his secretary wouldn't patch me through? What if he was busy?

Oh, hell—what if he had a girlfriend?

"Get a grip," I finally told myself. Resolutely, I picked up the phone and dialed.

"This is Johnny."

Where the hell was his secretary? I glanced at the time and realized it was well past seven. She'd probably gone home.

I entertained the idea of hanging up for only a second before I cleared my throat and said, "Hi, Johnny. This is Philomena Donovan. The sys admin?"

Did I mention Johnny was the VP of Business Development for the same company I worked for?

I knew I probably should have thought twice before asking out a coworker. That never seems to end well. But we were on opposite spectrums in the work chain, so I didn't think anything bad could come of it. Worse case scenario: He'd laugh at my question and then I could avoid him for the rest of my life by hiding in the server room. (It's a multipurpose room, really.)

There was a long pause after I said who I was—significant enough that I felt I needed to fill it. "You know, Philomena, the woman who helps you out every time you have trouble accessing your email?"

"Oh, yes! Of course." Then he groaned. "Don't tell me the network is going down. I have an urgent proposal to finish for the Japanese next week. I need Web access."

"Oh." I shook my head, stopping abruptly when I realized he couldn't see me. "No, the network's fine. Great, in fact. We haven't had to send out any Saint Bernards for lost packets in days." I chuckled at my little joke. I loved tech humor.

"Uh, right." He coughed. "Well, what can I do for you, then?"

The moment of truth. I rubbed the tip of my nose and blurted it out. "I was wondering if you'd like to go out sometime."

Silence.

Oh, shit. I closed my eyes, wondering if I could build some kind of time machine to go back and erase this call. I think MacGyver once built one out of a cardboard box and a couple of Q-Tips.

The silence on the other end was so great I could hear the seconds tick by. I opened my mouth to take the offer back—I could find someone else to take me out. I wasn't beautiful like Daphne but I had merits. And I wasn't desperate (at least, not yet). I could find another guy, no problem. "Well, I just—"

"You're the one with the long blond hair, right? Athletic looking with the great legs?"

I glanced down at the legs in question. "I think so."

"And you're kind of bohemian in the way you dress, with those colorful *tight* T-shirts."

"Um—"

"And you have that Catholic schoolgirl outfit with the short skirt and the thigh-high socks!" He whistled. "Sure, I remember you."

Maybe calling him wasn't such a great idea. "Well, I've gotta go—"

"I'd love to go out with you."

"You would? I mean, okay." I grinned.

"How about Saturday?" I heard him flip some pages. A calendar? How novel. I didn't know anyone who still kept a paper calendar. "I play tennis at four, so how about if I pick you up at eight? We can go to Hurley's for dinner and take it from there."

Hurley's? I stifled a groan. "That'd be great."

"I need to get your address."

I considered telling him I'd meet him for drinks and we could go from there. But then I thought if he picked me up I could check out his car. (My parents' philosophy on cars was too complicated to get into.) So I gave him quick directions and got off the phone before I could embarrass myself in any way.

I sat back in my chair and tapped a pen against my lips. Then I grinned, wide and hard. "Damn, I'm good."

Where the hell were they? I pushed aside my clunky Steve Madden boots and delved deeper into the abyss (otherwise known as my closet). The shoes had to be in here somewhere.

Daphne would say (after a slow shake of her head) that it was amazing someone who was a compulsive list-maker (i.e., me) could live in such disorder.

Daphne, of course, is one of those freaks who's always put together, from her hair to the last spoon in her kitchen drawer. So it stood to reason that she wouldn't understand my organization methods. Ask me where anything I owned was and I could find it in two seconds flat. Except for my cell phone. And the damn Via Spiga heels.

"They have to be here." I crawled into the void and began tossing things over my shoulder into the bedroom. Eventually I'd get to the shoes.

I did. They were at the bottom of the pile. Probably

because I hadn't worn them in eight months or so, since the last time it'd been warm enough (sandals don't get much play in Portland, as it rains nine months out of the year).

Slipping them on, I turned my feet this way and that to admire the pedicure I got this afternoon. The woman who did my feet assured me Baghdad Nights was my color. I never realized nights in Baghdad were purple.

I got up and glanced at the alarm clock that was once again on the nightstand next to my bed. I'd attached the broken piece with the only thing I'd had on hand—strawberry bubble gum. The clock tilted to one side drunkenly, but at least it worked.

Sort of. No amount of gum could repair the digital numbers, and I noticed the hour number had a light bar missing. It read six o'clock, but I had a feeling it was really eight. I scrounged around for my cell phone to double-check, just in case.

Johnny was due to arrive any second, so with one last look in the mirror, I winked at myself, grabbed my handbag (no jacket because it was unseasonably warm today), and went to the living room to wait.

The doorbell rang precisely fifteen minutes later. When I answered it, Johnny was leaning against the door. "Wow."

I tried to look demurely modest. I may not have been angelically beautiful like Daphne, or stunning like Magda, but when I made an effort, guys noticed. And tonight I'd made an effort: short black skirt, red tank with a sequined dragon circling one breast, my hair à la Nicole Kidman, lips to match the top. And the shoes.

"For you, Philomena." He held out a perfect red rose.

Props to me for not rolling my eyes. I smiled sweetly, said "Thank you," and tossed the flower onto the staircase behind me.

I realized that might have been the wrong thing to

do when I turned around and saw he was frowning. But I flashed him my most flirtatious smile and his frown cleared right up.

The cheesy rose aside, I was glad to see him. He looked good. He wore black slacks, a dress shirt, and a blazer. I tried to picture Rio dressed like this, but I could imagine him in only a torn wife-beater and jeans that were dangerously worn in strategic places.

"You look hot. Damn hot," he said, doing that blatant, all-over perusal guys do.

I didn't mind. I wanted him to find me irresistible. I gave him a siren smile—or what I hoped was a siren smile. As I turned to lock the door, I bent slightly at the hips and stuck a leg out. I was no dummy—if he liked my legs, I was going to shamelessly use them to my advantage. It worked, too; I felt his gaze like a brand on my bare skin.

When I turned around, I could read the anticipation in his eyes. I waited for that little part inside me to tingle in response. Nothing. So why was it one glance at Rio's hands and I was panting for his touch?

I shrugged mentally. It'd come. It was sure to. Johnny was a stud. He kind of looked like Brad Pitt (who my mom adored) and if half the stories I'd overheard about him in the restrooms at work were true, I was in for a good time.

"Shall we go?" He took my elbow and guided me down the porch steps.

I thought we'd walk since Hurley's is only three blocks from my place, so I was surprised when he stopped at the curb in front of his car.

A Jaguar. I almost groaned. My parents were *not* going to like that. I could almost hear their lecture on disrespecting the environment with a gas-guzzling hog.

And then it occurred to me that my parents weren't

going to like what he did for a living either. *Biz dev* equaled *capitalist pig* in their book.

Maybe this date wasn't such a great idea after all.

"Here you go." He opened the door and handed me down into the passenger seat.

I waited till he settled in on his side before I said, "We could have walked. It's not very far."

"Walk?" His eyebrows twitched like he was trying to understand a foreign concept.

Ah. I nodded. "Are you from Los Angeles?"

"Originally, yes." He smiled quizzically at me. "How did you know?"

I hid my grin by looking out the window. In college I had a friend from L.A. who would have been happy if she could have driven from class to class instead of walking. "Just a lucky guess."

"Here we are," Johnny said as he pulled into the narrow parking lot two seconds later. Literally.

I got out of the car. It didn't occur to me to wait for him to open my door until I saw the dismayed expression on his face. Oops. To make up for it, I smiled really big and said, "I've been really looking forward to tonight."

He brightened right up and took my arm. "Me too. I was surprised when you called me."

"Oh?" Was that a good thing?

"We don't interact at work much. Of course, I'd noticed you—" his grin was only slightly lecherous "—but I never considered asking you out."

"Why not?"

"It wasn't obvious."

I frowned. I didn't get a chance to ask what the hell that meant because he opened the door to Hurley's and the maitre d' swooped down on us. "Ms. Donovan. A pleasure to see you again. You look lovely this evening."

"Hello, Jean." His name was really Jose but that was a closely guarded secret.

Jean-Jose glanced at Johnny before returning his gaze to me. "Do you have a reservation this evening?"

I had to give him credit for not batting an eye. I'd been coming here at least twice a week with Barry for the past year (off and on). It must have been a shock (and somewhat scandalous) to see me with another man days after he'd seen me with my boyfriend.

Johnny cleared his throat. "Yes. Under Morgan."

Jean-Jose nodded without looking at the reservation book. "Right this way." He led us to the front dining room. I usually didn't care where I sat, but tonight I was relieved to be where we were, right next to the gleaming oak bar. If the date went bad, at least I wouldn't have to wait long for a drink. I could even get up and mix one myself if I got desperate.

But maybe I was wrong. The date started off rocky, but that didn't mean it was going to tank. Johnny was still an okay candidate to present to Mom and Dad; I'd just have to get creative with his job description. And we'd have to take my Prius when we went to my parents'.

Jean-Jose pulled out my chair and waited patiently for me to sit. "Can I get you anything to drink while you peruse the menu?"

I wanted to order a beer—they carried Chimay here, which was right up there with Guinness—but Johnny beat me to it. "A bottle of champagne, please."

"Excellent, sir." Jean-Jose raised his brows at me, but didn't say anything when I gave him a weak smile. Not letting it slip that I hated champagne, he went to obediently fulfill Johnny's order. Good man, him. I briefly wondered if he was attached.

"I love champagne, don't you?" my companion asked in happy anticipation.

"Hmm." I smiled and widened my eyes in what I thought would look like excited agreement.

His brow wrinkled. "Are you okay?"

"Yeah. Why?"

"For a moment you looked like you might be sick."

Maybe I needed to take acting lessons.

Before he could make any more inquiries about my health, I asked Johnny a question of my own. "What did you mean when you said going out with me wasn't obvious?"

He shrugged and opened his menu. "Just that it wouldn't have occurred to me."

"Why not?"

"You're not my type." He seemed to have realized he made a slight faux pas (my glare might have tipped him off), because he quickly appended his statement. "You're hot, Mena, don't get me wrong. But I usually go out with more conservative-looking women."

I glanced down at myself. Conservative I was not.

"But then you asked me out and I thought what the hell." He grinned suggestively. "I'm looking forward to my walk on the wild side."

Oh, God. I rolled my eyes, snapped open my menu, and studied it like there was a quiz at the end of the evening. Johnny took my cue and lifted his as well.

Our waiter came with a couple of flutes cradled in one hand and the bottle cupped in the other. He chatted amiably about the specials while he popped the cork, poured us each a glass, took our order, and left us to enjoy our bubbly.

Johnny and I both took a tentative sip. Okay, actually I pretended to take a sip. I tilted the glass until the vile stuff touched my lips, but I didn't open my mouth.

"This is great stuff. The right way to start off a beautiful evening with a beautiful girl." Johnny raised his glass. "To us."

Unimaginative, but I guessed it worked. I felt like I should say something too, but I didn't know what. When in doubt, you could never go wrong by quoting Mac-Gyver. "'Water's funny stuff.'"

He stared at me blankly.

Sigh. "Never mind." I clinked my glass against his and pretended to take another drink.

Despite the champagne (and that fiendish comment that I wasn't his type—I almost expected him to say I was lacking in bed too), I still had hopes that Johnny would be my new and improved Barry, so I tried to dazzle him with my clever wit. "Do you know why they call it hypertext?"

His brow furrowed as he thought about it. "Why?"

"Too much JAVA." I burst out laughing, holding my stomach. I couldn't help it—that joke always cracked me up. At least I didn't fall off my seat this time.

I dabbed the tears at the corners of my eyes and smiled up at Johnny, expecting to see him sharing my mirth. I sobered when I caught him gawking at me like I was insane.

Okay, so he didn't appreciate my humor. Not promising, but it was hardly a relationship breaker. I was sure we could connect on other levels. "So, Johnny, what time do you wake up in the mornings?"

He blinked at me and then downed his entire glass of champagne. He reached for the bottle to refill it. "Not too early."

"I knew it." I grinned, watching him pour the champagne to the very brim without spilling a drop over the side. Talented. "Me either. Mornings were intended for sleeping."

"I know." He flashed his Colgate smile at me. "I sleep in until about five-thirty and then I go for a run. Six if I'm feeling really lazy."

"Six?" I choked on my spit, which meant I had to down some of the fizzy wine.

"I know. It's decadent staying in bed that late."

"You probably have a special alarm clock you take with you when you travel," I accused him with narrowed eyes.

"I *never* leave home without my Sharper Image alarm clock."

Shudder.

I was saved from having to reply by our waiter, who arrived with dinner. Johnny kept up a casual stream of conversation as we ate and, aside from the occasional question and intermittent nod, it didn't require much effort on my part.

While we waited for our after-dinner espressos, I escaped to—I mean, excused myself to the restroom. I opened the door that hid the hallway to the bathrooms and promptly walked into someone. Someone who smelled delicious. (Though it might have been the scent of food from the kitchen.)

Large hands caught me before I ricocheted back into the dining area. "Steady there."

I looked up and bit my lip so I wouldn't say *hubba hubba*, because the man I'd walked into was a stud. Outdoorsy tanned, a great smile, and eyes that twinkled in mischief. Great body too—solid (I knew that because I'd bounced off it).

He stared at me, forehead wrinkled in concern. "Are you okay?"

I heard Dwight, my Kung Fu teacher, whisper in my mind. *Be aware of all opportunities this week.*

I appraised my victim. Maybe I asked Johnny out so I would be right here at this moment to meet this man. This was the universe teaching me. Far be it from me to callously disregard fate. So I grinned and batted my eyes at him.

His lips stretched slowly into a wide smile. "I guess you're doing okay."

I hoped my smile was suitably mysterious.

He slipped something into his pocket and took my hand. "Tell me, are you free for drinks in—" he glanced at his watch "—a couple of hours? We can meet at the Benson Hotel."

I was about to shout *Yes* when I saw the tan line on the third finger of his left hand. What guy wore a ring on his third finger if he weren't married? And the line was stark, so either he got divorced yesterday or what he slipped into his pocket was his wedding band.

The bastard.

Lowering my eyelids coquettishly, I plastered myself to his side, trailed my finger down the open vee of his shirt, and in a sex-heavy voice said, "At the Benson? I guess that means you really want to get to know me."

His free hand skimmed over my ass. "Intimately."

"That can be arranged." My smile was slow and laden with promise.

Promise of retribution. Before he could make another slimy move, I thrust my knee, hard, right into his crotch.

Taking Kung Fu has a lot of advantages. One of the most important: learning how to nail a guy in the groin. You can aim anywhere in that region and get satisfaction, but for maximum damage, you need to hit under the balls in an upward motion (like you're driving his package up into his body). Do that and the guy is down for the count.

This loser was no different. The second I drove my knee into him, he doubled over with a girlish squeal.

Unfortunately, my elbow *happened* to be in the way as he bent over so his nose ran into it.

I blinked innocently. "Oops. Sorry." I shoved him aside and went on to the restroom.

I took my time in the restroom collecting myself. The cold towel I applied to the back of my neck did wonders for cooling me off, and in minutes I felt ready to go back to Johnny.

When I walked out of the restroom, I noticed my new friend sitting at a table with a skinny blonde who sported a whopping diamond on her finger. He was hunched over, clutching his lap, while the woman whispered at him with a mix of confusion and impatience. The ring was back on his finger.

The bastard. As I passed him, I caught his eye and made a grab-squeeze-twist motion with my hand. The color drained from his face and he looked away. Fast.

Suddenly, Barry didn't seem so bad. He may not have been very interesting, but I doubted he'd hit on another woman behind my back.

But I was here with Johnny and determined to make a decent go of it. Even if he was a little dull.

So when I sank into my seat again, I favored him with a big smile. "Hey."

He stared at my mouth so intently I thought I had a huge crumb or something on it. I was about to ask him what was wrong when he said, "What do you say we get out of here?"

I shrugged. "Sure."

He paid the bill while I downed my espresso. Jean-Jose thanked us as we walked out the door and around the corner to the car.

"What did you want to do next?" I asked, eyes on the uneven sidewalk to keep from tripping. There was a band playing at a bar down the street from my house. A rock band. A loud rock band. Loud music equaled no conversation; a big plus at this point.

Johnny stopped suddenly and yanked my arm.

"Oof!" I collided with his chest, which knocked the breath out of me.

And then his mouth was on mine.

I stared at his intently scrunched face. This wasn't exactly what I'd planned, but it wasn't a bad idea. Might as well know how he kisses. So I closed my eyes and gave myself up to it.

His technique was good. Not an overwhelming amount of tongue. Not too much saliva.

But his lips . . . They were kind of mushy. It was like kissing the back of an old woman's arm—the flabby part that swings when she waves. I frowned and tried to get past that, but the image was vivid and once it was in my head I couldn't shake it.

On top of that, I was woozy from lack of air (he was like a Hoover), so I pushed on his chest and took a step back.

"I've wanted to do that all night." Johnny stepped forward and tried to nuzzle my neck.

Tried, because I scrunched my shoulder and wormed my way out of his embrace. "Johnny, this is—" Wrong? Gross? I settled for, "Too soon."

Hey, that was good. I mentally patted myself on the back and tried to look virginal.

"Too soon?" Johnny frowned and stepped back. "You're kidding, right?"

"No." I shook my head mournfully. Really, I wanted to grin. "This is our first date, and I want you to respect me."

He cocked his eyebrows as he pointedly stared at my outfit. I was sure there was a culture somewhere in the world where a miniskirt and tank top were old-fashioned, so I stayed quietly righteous.

"I should probably take you home, then," he said slowly.

I nodded. "That'd be best."

We walked another couple of feet, not touching. Then Johnny whirled to face me again. "What isn't too soon?"

I had the distinct impression I was a challenge now. But I still needed a new Barry to impress my parents with, and until I found someone better, I couldn't rule Johnny out. I remembered his kiss (without gagging), and then I heard Dwight whisper *opportunities* again. So I said, "A couple of dates?"

He grinned. "What are you doing tomorrow?"

Looking up lip-muscle-firming exercises online. But I kept that to myself, smiled enigmatically (I hoped), and let him take me home.

Chapter Four

Lessons Learned from MacGyver
#124
Computer nerds can be attractive underneath their glasses.

Rrpp. Rrpp. Rrpp.

What the hell?

I lifted my head from underneath the down comforter and glared at the alarm clock. It mocked me, sitting there defiantly crooked.

Why the hell was it ringing? It was Sunday. Either six forty-five or eight forty-five, probably the latter. Better be the latter.

Rrpp. Rrpp.

I scooted over and whacked it once, hard. The plastic part I'd stuck back on with gum flew off, but the alarm still shrilled. So I did what anyone would do: I yanked it so the cord came out of the socket and let it drop to the floor.

Unfortunately, it hit the hardwood floor instead of the rug next to my bed. I heard a crack and a metallic ping.

Looking over the side of the bed, I groaned. The volume knob had broken off. No sign of metal, which meant it was probably something on the inside.

I groaned again. "Shit."

I pulled the covers over my head and scrunched my eyes closed. I *would* sleep another couple of hours.

Ten minutes later I decided it was futile so I dragged my carcass out of bed. I "accidentally" kicked the clock on my way to the closet to get my robe, after which I shuffled into the kitchen to make myself a large pot of coffee.

The first cup I downed like medicine. The second I savored. By the third I felt human enough to call Matt.

He answered on the second ring. "Hello?"

"I need advice."

Silence. "Doc?"

"Yeah." I frowned. "Who else would it be?"

"Exactly. It's not even ten yet."

"Don't remind me." I felt proud that I managed not to punctuate my statement with a growl. The coffee had mellowed me out.

"I'm just shocked." He paused. "You do know it's Sunday, right?"

This time I did growl.

"Have you had coffee yet?"

"Three cups."

I could hear his thoughts loud and clear: *and still you're surly?* But he wisely backed off. "What kind of advice do you need?"

"I went out with Johnny last night—"

"Johnny?"

"Johnny Morgan. The VP of biz dev at work."

Matt groaned. "Doc, never shit where you eat."

"Huh?"

"You don't date guys you work with," he said succinctly. "It makes it awkward after you break up."

"I don't work with him."

"You just said he was from work."

"Yeah, but I don't actually work *with* him. His office is on a completely different floor."

Matt sighed. I could picture him rubbing his neck like he does when he's exasperated. "So what advice do you need?"

"Should I go out with him again?"

"Was your date fun?"

Fun? I wrinkled my nose. That wasn't exactly how I'd put it. Though kneeing that guy in his privates was pretty entertaining. "Um, it was okay."

"Was he a good kisser?"

I almost gagged, remembering. "His technique was good, but his lips . . ."

"Then don't waste your time. You know how you are about kisses."

I frowned. "How am I?"

"Particular."

My frown deepened. "I am not."

"Are too."

"Am not."

"Are too." He chuckled. "But don't worry I think it's because Barry and the half-dozen guys before him weren't right for you."

Oh. Yeah, that was true. For a second I thought Matt was saying it was my fault their kisses sucked. Kind of like Barry saying I was boring in bed. (Yeah, that still loomed large in my mind.)

"Once you find a guy that's right for you, you'll like his kisses," Matt said sagely.

"Do you find kissing women repulsive?"

He snorted. "Hell, no."

"So you think I shouldn't go out with Johnny again?" He'd been a good candidate, except for his kiss. And his car. Oh, and his job.

"I think you should come to my soccer game today."

I pursed my lips. "Are there going to be single men there?"

"Dozens of them."

"Okay."

An hour later I was showered and dressed in a pair of old Levi's, a wife-beater, and my red Diesel tennis shoes. Hair in a ponytail and a swipe of lip gloss and I was good to go.

Because of the continuing gorgeous weather, I went down to sit on my stoop while I waited. I couldn't waste more time on Johnny. Matt was the one to say it: I had to *like* the guy I took home. If I didn't, my parents would be able to tell.

I didn't think I'd be able to like Johnny enough to fool my parents. His kisses just . . . Shudder.

So, sitting there, I compiled a mental list of options.

1) Find the love of my life (might be somewhat difficult given the time constraints)
2) Find someone I was in lust with (if I was hot enough for a guy it might fool my parents into thinking I was in love)
3) Pretend to like someone (unfeasible—I can't act)
4) Take acting lessons (hmm, definite possibility)
5) Track down Richard Dean Anderson and convince him we were fated to be together

Of all my options, E seemed the most viable solution.

Matt arrived late. Not surprising. I was impressed he remembered to pick me up.

I hopped down the steps and jumped into his car. "Hey."

He smiled. "Hey, yourself. Ready?"

"Yeah. Guess what?"

"What?" he asked, checking his blind spot before pulling out into the street.

"Magda left a note for me that she was going to be out of town for the next week. Just an FYI."

He glanced at me. "Where do you think she went?"

"A sex worker convention," I replied instantly.

"Do you think they have seminars at those kinds of conventions?"

I pursed my lips in thought. "If they do, I bet Magda conducts one."

Matt smirked. "*How to Give Your John the Most for His Money?*"

"Or *It's Not About the Size.*"

"*What to Expect When You're Hooking?*"

"*You and Your Whip: Forming a Mutually Fulfilling Relationship.*"

"*Improving Your Oral Skills.*" He glanced over, daring me to top that one.

It took me a moment, but I got it right as we arrived. "*Thriving Under Pressure: What to Do When They're Just Too Big.*"

We parked, and I got out and went around to his side of the car to wait for him. He was rooting around in the back seat, God knows for what. I took the time to look around (never know who might be hanging out in the parking lot).

"Here. Make yourself useful." Matt shoved a bag at me.

I lifted it experimentally. It was small but surprisingly heavy. "What's in here?"

"Lunch." He grabbed his gym bag and closed the door. "Come on. The game's starting any minute."

I wanted to point out I wasn't the one who was running late, but I didn't want to antagonize my ride. And I was looking forward to meeting one or two of his teammates (guys who played soccer had great legs).

I followed Matt to the field. There were two groups of players on either side along with the friends and families who'd come to cheer. We headed toward the motlier bunch of people.

"Matt, quick," I whispered. "Point out which guys are single."

He glanced down at me. "Tell me you aren't serious about this."

"Hell, yeah, I'm serious. We've already had this conversation." I studied the men in the lineup. There were a surprising number of women playing on Matt's team too, and for a moment I entertained the idea of adding 6) *Give up men and find a lesbian lover* to my list. But kissing a woman? I wouldn't want someone else's lipstick smeared on me.

So I pain-punched Matt in the ribs. "Just point out the ones who are especially successful."

"Ow! Doc—"

"And who don't drive gas-guzzlers." I shrugged at his frown. "You know how environmentally conscious Mom and Dad are."

"Oh, well then, that makes the choice easy," he said facetiously, rubbing his side. "You want Ian."

I followed the jerk of his chin to two guys who stood on the fringe of the group, talking quietly. One was tall and fairly good-looking with blondish hair and a lanky body. The other had glasses and unkempt hair that looked like it needed a good stylist.

I focused all my attention on the blond. "Ian's cute."

"Ian's the one with the glasses."

"Oh."

"Ian owns a software company that does a lot of pro bono work for education. And he drives a Prius."

"*Oh.*" I studied Ian again. He didn't look so bad. He didn't have striking looks, but he seemed like he had an okay body at least (it was hard to tell with his baggy sweats). If he played soccer, he had to be in decent shape.

"I didn't know you had this mercenary streak in you," Matt said.

I scowled at him. "I don't."

He just stared at me.

"I don't." But I winced internally. He was right.

Heartless, that's what I was. And shallow. I picked Johnny based on his looks and see how that turned out? Maybe Ian was just the kind of guy I needed. A socially conscious programmer. I bet we'd have a lot in common. Maybe that's why I hadn't met my soulmate yet, because I was picking the wrong sort of guys.

Not this time. I took a deep breath and opened myself to the possibilities.

Fortunately, Matt didn't say another word because we'd joined the group. He did a quick round of introductions (like I was going to remember everyone's names) and then deposited me next to Ian. That's what a great friend Matt is. He supports me even when he doesn't agree with my methods.

Ian blinked owlishly at me, like I'd suddenly materialized into the space next to him.

No problem. I didn't mind being the forward one. I held out my hand. "Hi. I'm Mena."

"Yeah, that's what Matt said." He reluctantly took my hand, shook it once, and dropped it.

I tried not to frown. "Do you play soccer often?"

"Yeah."

"You must be good."

Shoulder shrug.

"Have you played long?"

Another shrug.

Huh. I stared at him. Maybe he wasn't interested.

No—he was a guy. He had to be interested. Unless he was gay.

I studied him some more. He didn't look gay.

Then he took off his glasses and stowed them in their case. Underneath the Coke-bottle lenses he was actually decent-looking. Certainly not in the same caliber as Barry or Johnny—and not even close to Rio—but definitely interesting.

So I tried with renewed enthusiasm. "I was wondering

if sometime you'd like to get together for a drink or coffee or something."

He narrowed his eyes at me. Whether it was in suspicion or because he couldn't see me, I didn't know. "Why?"

I guess I had my answer. I pursed my lips and tried to come up with a truthful answer. "You looked interesting."

Not bad, Philomena Donovan. Not bad.

He watched me suspiciously for at least another twenty seconds (while I tried to look fetching) before he said, "Fine. Drinks. Tuesday. Seven o'clock."

"Great." I smiled.

He grunted and joined his team out on the field.

I went to where Matt dropped his stuff and sat on the ground by his bag to watch the game. I couldn't keep the satisfied smile off my face. I had a good feeling about Ian. Sure, he was kind of terse, but that was understandable. He was probably just shy; a lot of computer nerds were. Matt was (except around me, but I didn't count because we'd known each other forever).

Once I got a drink into him I was sure Ian would loosen up. And if he didn't, no biggie. I didn't mind a man of few words. I perked up and grinned. There could be advantages to that.

"Hey."

I glanced up and blinked. "Rio?"

He grinned. "I was running and noticed you over here so I thought I'd say hi."

It was like one of my in-the-dark-of-the-night fantasies come to life. He wore shorts, a loose tank top that did little to cover his chest, and a glistening layer of sweat that showed off the definition of all his muscles.

Yummy.

I cleared my throat and tried not to stare at certain parts of his body that were eye level from my seat on the ground. "Um, hi."

He chuckled. "Hi." Then he nodded toward the game. "You play soccer?"

"Oh, no." I couldn't help it—I sneaked a look at those certain parts. I wasn't disappointed. "Chasing a ball isn't my thing. I'm just here to cheer on my best friend."

"Mind if I join you for a few minutes?"

"Go ahead," I said, though I wasn't sure why.

Rio dropped to the ground next to me, so close I could feel the heat radiating off his skin. "It was nice seeing you the other night. Barry should bring you by more often."

Ha! Barry would love that. "Actually, Barry and I aren't dating." *For the moment,* I added silently. But I figured I should be honest with Rio because Barry might talk to him.

"Really?"

Was it me, or did he sound kind of happy about that? I turned to look at him and, sure enough, he watched me with interest, kind of like he was wondering what I kissed like.

Okay, that might have been projection on my part.

I cleared my throat. "So how long have you taught at the gym?"

Rio didn't seem to notice how lame my attempt at conversation was. He smiled and said, "I started teaching eight years ago, when I moved to Portland. I met Barry about that same time."

I ignored Barry's name and asked, "You didn't grow up here?"

"No." He shook his head. "We lived in Germany until I was ten and then Connecticut. My dad was career military but he retired and took a post teaching at West Point."

"Oh." I perked up. The military part was unfortunate, but my parents thought teaching was a noble profession. "What does he teach?"

"History of warfare and battle tactics."

Oh. Somehow I doubted they'd find teaching the art of war noble. "What made you move out here?"

"I followed a woman." He smiled ruefully.

The thought of him liking someone enough to move across the country with her didn't sit well with me. Which totally didn't make sense. I frowned. "Barry never mentioned your girlfriend."

Not that Barry mentioned anything about any of his friends, but Rio didn't have to know that. I was just fishing for information.

"No girlfriend." He gazed at me for a drawn-out moment before he turned back to watch the game. "Lisa just needed me to help bankroll the move to Portland. I broke up with her shortly after the move once I realized what was going on."

Ouch. I winced in sympathy, unable to imagine anyone using a guy like Rio. Aside from being absolutely droolworthy, he was smart, attentive, and interesting. He did seem a little under-motivated in his career, but no one was perfect.

"And I've dated since, but I haven't found anyone special." He flashed me that look again.

What did it mean?

Before I could ask him, he got up and dusted his shorts off. "You should come by the gym sometime, Phil. Ask for me."

"Uh. Right."

He smiled. "I hope I see you."

Frowning, I stared at him as he jogged away. Was that a pickup, or was he just drumming up attendance for his lessons?

"Too bad he isn't the right kind of guy," I murmured, because I wouldn't mind him teaching me a thing or two.

I shook my head. I should have kissed him—surefire way of getting over this infatuation. He probably kissed like a fish. But as he faded in the distance, I had a hard time making myself believe that.

Chapter Five

Biggest Mistakes of My Life: The Annotated List

1) *Selling the '67 Mustang I rebuilt in high school to pay for college—too bad I only attended for one year*
2) *Not kissing Aaron Jackson while I had the chance, even if he liked Daphne better*
3) *My prom dress—what kind of crack was I smoking??*
4) *Turning down the job offer from pre-IPO Google—dumb, dumb, dumb*
5) *Going out with Ian*
6) *Dumping Barry prematurely*

I was in purgatory, and I had no one to blame but myself. And maybe Matt because he was the one who introduced me to Ian, though I felt fairly certain he'd deny all responsibility.

"Hey." Ian nudged me. "Want some?"

I looked down at the basket of pretzels he offered and shook my head. "No, thank you."

He turned to his left. "Want some?"

George, Ian's friend, nodded and grabbed a fistful. "Thanks."

Ian acknowledged the gratitude with an upward jerk of his chin before turning around. "How 'bout you?"

"Yeah. Thanks, man." Chili, another one of his friends, took the outstretched basket and tipped it to pour some directly into his mouth. He chewed, downed half his pint, and belched so loud my beer glass vibrated.

Why he and George arrived with Ian, I had no idea. I asked Ian out for a drink. It never occurred to me that he'd bring friends. Idiot friends at that.

George slammed his pint down on the bar. "I've got a joke for you guys."

I smothered a groan in my beer. Not another one.

"Two old ladies are standing outside their nursing home smoking when it starts to rain. The first lady pulls out a condom, cuts off the end, covers her cigarette, and continues to smoke.

"The second lady asks her what that is. Lady One says it's a condom and that you can get them at the drugstore.

"The next day Lady Two goes to the drugstore and announces to the pharmacist that she wants a box of condoms. The guy's embarrassed—she's friggin' eighty years old—but he delicately asks her what brand she'd like.

"The old lady says, 'I don't care, sonny, as long as it fits a Camel.'"

Can we say junior high? But the three of them high-fived, laughing it up like it was the most hilarious thing they'd ever heard.

It seemed like I should make an effort to get to know Ian (and, consequently, his friends). The only way to make any headway with them was to play along. So I said, "Guys, I have a joke for you."

The sudden silence was deafening.

Mental shrug. They'd be believers after they heard my joke. I was already grinning just thinking about it. "How do you keep a programmer in the shower all day?"

Ian scratched his head (the most he'd reacted to

anything I'd said all night—already this was a success).
Chili and George exchanged frowns and then simultaneously asked, "How?"

"Give him a bottle of shampoo that says lather, rinse,
and repeat." I started laughing even before I finished the
punch line. Oh, I cracked myself up. I stuck my hand in
the air, ready for my high-five.

When nothing happened, I wiped the tears clouding
my eyes and looked at them to see what the deal was.
They all gaped at me like baboons.

I frowned. "Get it? Lather, rinse, and *repeat*." They
were programmers, for God's sake—they should get it. I
waited for it to strike them.

Nothing.

George coughed. "I've got another joke for ya."

This time I did groan, but they didn't hear me over
the eager exclamations from Chili and Ian.

"Three dickless guys walk into a bar—"

I squeezed my eyes shut and prayed for lightning to
strike me now before it was too late.

Having no vision affected my hearing because I completely missed the middle and end of George's joke.
Thank God. I opened my eyes in time to see the three
guys chortling and exchanging high-fives. Again.

That was when I noticed Ian's stained T-shirt had a
hole in the right armpit. The hole itself didn't bother
me. (Though he knew he was going on a date with me.
Couldn't he have worn a clean T-shirt without any
holes?) What disturbed me was the pale skin I saw
through the hole. No hair.

I choked on my beer.

Chili whacked me on the back. "Ease up there, man."

I nodded my thanks, not bothering to point out he
had the wrong gender.

My mind whirred. The fact that Ian had no armpit
hair bugged me. Big time. I forgot all about getting the

guys to high-five me and instead thought about Ian's armpits. Did he shave them or wax them? Why?

And how could I surreptitiously find out? I felt insanely curious about his preferred depilatory method.

George draped his arm over my shoulder. "So, Marta—"

"Mena," I corrected automatically.

"Yeah, that's what I said. You ever had cybersex?"

Cybersex was a favorite topic with these boys. It'd taken me only five minutes in their company to figure that out. It wasn't a big surprise though—I was beginning to suspect that none of them had ever touched a woman who wasn't inflated. "Can't say that I have."

"I've been thinking of making a suit you slip on that's connected to software on your computer. Say there's a woman you like—" George frowned. "Well, not *you*. Unless you're into that sort of thing?" he asked hopefully.

"Ah, no."

"Oh." He looked crestfallen for an instant before he continued. "Well, she has the software on her machine too, and she can control your suit through her console. Kind of like online gaming, get it?"

Chili shook his head in awe. "That's genius, man."

"What about the woman?"

They all gawked at me.

I shrugged and picked up my glass. "Why doesn't the woman get a suit too? I wouldn't want to play along if I didn't have a suit."

"You'd play along?"

George's question was a little too eager, so I was careful about how I answered it. "No. I just mean that if a woman did want to play along, she should have her own suit."

George's face scrunched up. "I'll need to think about that."

What was there to think about? It was logical. But I just rolled my eyes and signaled the bartender for another beer.

"My company can distribute the software if you want," Ian offered.

George beamed. "Really?"

"Sure." Ian held up his hand for a high-five.

Here was my chance. I leaned closer to the bar. If I got low enough, I was sure I'd be able to see through the hole in his shirt.

Shit—it was too dark. I wondered if I had a pen light in my purse.

"Dude, you okay?"

I looked up to find all three guys frowning at me. I tried to smile like there was nothing out of the ordinary going on. "Of course."

They didn't look like they believed it. They kept glancing at me while they discussed the details of their virtual sex suit.

I snorted as I picked up my glass. Like I was the weird one here.

When they started debating what color to make the suit (guess what color Chili wanted), I decided it was time to make a move. "So, Ian."

Ian jerked and glanced up like a deer in headlights. "Huh?"

I smiled coquettishly. "Besides marketing cybersex suits, what do you like to do?"

He blinked several times. Then he shrugged. "Stuff."

"Uh. Cool." I hoped my smile didn't look sickly. Maybe he was into martial arts. "What do you think of Jet Li?"

"Dude, I never fly," was Chili's response. George and Ian nodded in agreement.

Okay, maybe I should try another joke. My last one didn't pan out, but I had one that was sure to get a laugh out of them. I started to chuckle just thinking of it. "How many programmers does it take to change a lightbulb?"

All three guys goggled at me.

"Two, in case one leaves in the middle of the project."

Laughing, I slapped my hand on my knee. Freakin' side-splitting, I tell you. I was sure to get a high-five for that one. Looking up, I put my hand in the air.

The guys were staring at me with puzzled expressions on their faces. Then Chili said, "Dude, programming jokes are lame."

George turned to the guys, stroking his chin in thought. "I think the cyber suit should be purple."

"Why purple?" Ian asked.

"Because the sexiest man on earth is Prince and his color is purple."

I found logic in that, so I knew it was time for me to call it a night. Ian obviously didn't want to engage, and I flirted with insanity for a second by considering asking George or Chili out.

"Guys, it's time for me to head out." I slipped off the barstool. "Good luck on the sex suit. I'll see you around."

George clapped me on the shoulder. "Hey, Mona, we'll take you home."

Chili nodded. "No prob, man. It's like on our way."

I wasn't sure how he knew that since I hadn't told them where I lived. "Thanks, but it's not necessary—"

"Get off your ass, Ian." George cuffed him on the back of the head. "Your date wants to go home. Be a gentleman."

"Yeah, man." Chili nodded again.

Ian frowned at his friends. "She can make it home on her own."

Oh, the chivalry. Be still, my heart.

"Quit being a dickhead and let's take the woman home." George pulled Ian off the barstool and lugged him out of the bar. "Didn't your mom teach you anything?"

"Really, guys. I can make it home on my own," I said, dragging my feet after them.

George shook his head. "The streets aren't safe."

Portland was hardly Harlem, and I was a third degree black belt. But they (George and Chili) were so intent on taking me home, I figured I'd just go with it. I didn't relish waiting for a bus anyway.

They shoved Ian in the back seat. I followed. George drove and Chili sat shotgun.

George cranked the ignition and turned around. "You guys can make out if you want to. We won't look."

Chili nodded enthusiastically. I wasn't sure if he was agreeing with the making out part or that he wouldn't look. I thought the former.

I bared my teeth in a smile. "That's awfully thoughtful."

"Yeah, and if you want to take your top off, that's okay too," George added.

"I'll keep that in mind," I murmured.

Ian scooted closer to his door and gripped the handle like it was a life preserver.

The ride home was abnormally quiet. I was conscious of George's furtive glances in the rearview mirror, as if he was hoping to find Ian and me groping like teenagers. Ian glared at me accusingly and hugged his door harder. Chili didn't bother with subtlety—he faced backward for the first ten minutes until it became apparent nothing was going to happen.

I sighed. In a deeper, Richard Dean Anderson voice, I said, "'You may not believe this, but there have been times when I've had a lot more fun in the back seat of a car.'"

Chili whirled around. I wouldn't have been surprised if he had whiplash in the morning. "Dude, you into Mac-Gyver? MacGyver rocks. When I grow up, I want to blow shit up with soy sauce."

"Admirable goal," I said.

"You know when he disarmed a missile with a paperclip?" Chili shook his head reverently. "My favorite episode, man."

George shook his head. "Nah. The best episode was when he rode a casket like a jet ski. Bitchin'. I never get to do shit like that."

Ian spoke up. Finally. "MacGyver's the man."

George stuck his hand over his shoulder. Chili and Ian stretched to meet him, but they paused short of touching and looked at me.

I shook my head. "I'm not taking my clothes off."

Chili rolled his eyes. "Dude, get your hand up here."

"Oh. *Oh.*" Finally. I leaned forward and the four of us high-fived.

It was as satisfying as I thought it'd be. Except for their sticky palms. But I'd wash my hands when I got home. For now, I just basked in their unexpected acceptance.

"I've come to a realization."

"That you should stop chatting before Dwight kicks you out of class?"

I crossed my eyes at Matt as I bowed to him. I figured the bow, which we do before we spar, negated the disrespect with the eye thing.

"Real adult there, Doc," he said, also bowing. "You want to go first, or you want me to?"

Usually the highest rank goes first. Since Matt and I are the same belt, we arbitrarily decide who gets beat first. This evening I was feeling magnanimous, so I volunteered.

"So what was your realization?" he asked after he traumatized my nervous system with a pain punch and broke my neck.

"That maybe I dumped Barry too soon." I yielded and sidestepped when he lunged at me. As he flew by me, I kicked him in the back, which sent him flying into the wall. I finished with a couple of strikes to his kidneys and his spine.

When I stopped beating him, Matt turned around and asked, "What happened to Ian?"

"Ian sucked." I scowled and punched him.

He blocked and countered with a punch to the lower sternum to break my ribs. "He's a man of few words."

"And few manners. His only redeeming quality was his reverence for MacGyver." I folded into his strike. He followed it up with an elbow to the same spot, which would drive the broken ribs into my lung or, worst-case scenario, into my heart.

Usually I would have admired such economy of movement—moves that debilitate with a minimum of fuss excite me—but I wasn't feeling charitable tonight. "Did you know he brought along a couple of friends?"

"Not George and Chili." He palmed my nose and then flipped me over his back and slammed me into the floor. "Yes. You know them?"

"Just from soccer." He kicked me twice for good measure before stepping back. "They come and cheer us on sometimes."

"Did you know Ian has no armpit hair?" I asked as I hopped up from the mat.

"Excuse me?"

I nodded as I straightened my gi and retied my belt. "I know. How weird is that? I can't date a guy who has no pit hair. What's up with that? Does he have leg hair?"

"Can't say I've ever checked out his legs."

"All night he kept trying to get away from me. And he barely talked to me. I'm not that repulsive, am I?"

Matt grinned. "Why do you leave yourself wide open like that?"

"It was like I was back in second grade and he thought I had cooties." I frowned at him accusingly. "You didn't warn me."

"I didn't know you had cooties."

My glare promised retribution. Painful retribution.

His grin widened. "I didn't know about his pits. And I figured you'd noticed he was a little shy."

"A little shy—ha!" I threw him a right hook, which he ducked. Then he elbowed my liver, punched my kidney, and broke my back over his leg before letting me fall to the floor.

I lay there for a full minute, staring up at the ceiling, before got to my feet. "So what am I supposed to do now?"

"Abandon this plan and live your life for yourself instead of your parents."

"Ha!" I didn't wait for him to throw me a punch. I attacked with a kick to the groin.

Thwak! I connected soundly with his cup (that's gotta be one of the greatest sounds in the world). I wanted to take a moment to revel in the beauty of it, but I quickly followed it up with a crescent kick to his face and then brought the same heel down at the base of his skull.

"Jeez, Doc." Matt picked himself off the floor, adjusting his cup. "You didn't have to kick the jewels so hard. I have future generations of Turners to think about."

"What exactly am I supposed to do now?" I demanded. "I don't have that much time left. Daphne's party is coming up. Fast."

"Be a liberated woman and go by yourself."

Only fourteen years of friendship kept me from hammering his teeth in. For real.

"Dwight's giving us evil looks." Matt jerked his chin toward the corner of the studio.

I didn't have to look to know Dwight was staring at us. Dwight's gaze is freaky. His eyes can convey any number of things, and you would have to be an idiot not to know he was telling us to stop fooling around and start fighting.

Grr. I narrowed my eyes at Matt. "Throw me a damn punch or something."

He kicked me—Matt never does the expected. I slipped it and took a couple of steps in as I brought the heel of my hand up to jam his nose into his head. Then I stuck my fingers in his eye sockets, put my foot behind his left ankle, and drove his head into the floor. I kicked his side to break his ribs and stomped on his chest to drive it into his lungs.

As I waited for him to pick himself off the floor

(I guess I took him down harder than I meant—oops), I realized what I'd have to do. "I have to call Jeremy."

Jeremy was a friend of mine from college. Actually, for two months ten years ago he'd been more than a friend, but we'd quickly realized the only thing we had in common was our love for beer.

Matt frowned as he got to his feet. "I think you must've driven my head harder into the mat than I thought, because I swear I just heard you say you were going to call Jeremy."

"I did."

He stopped stretching his neck and stared at me. Then he slowly exclaimed, "Are you out of your *mind*?"

On the inside, I agreed with him. Jeremy wasn't an ideal choice. But he was the only one at this point. I shrugged. "Jeremy isn't obvious, but—"

"Jeremy's a freak."

"He's not. He's just—" I struggled for the right word "—different."

Matt snorted.

"Jeremy's quite entertaining."

"Yeah. Freaks tend to be."

I put my hands on my hips. "I'm out of options here, so unless you have a bright idea I have to call up Jeremy." It was a sad day when you realized all the available men you knew were unendearingly geeky.

Matt shrugged. "Do what you want, Doc. I'm just saying Jeremy is not the one for you."

"Why not?"

"He has a great mind and he may be funny, but you need someone whose idea of fun isn't sitting in front of the TV and speculating on whether Bill O'Reilly wears a hairpiece. And do you really want to be involved with someone who was fated to be Unabomber II at birth?"

I pouted. Matt had a point. "So what am I supposed to do?"

"Forget this scheme."

I pictured the disappointment on my mom's face

when she found out I'd broken up with Barry. She'd say "Oh, Philomena," her voice heavy with resignation like I'd let her down big time. Again.

Then I pictured my angelic sister languishing in the shadows while everyone exclaimed how accomplished I was now with my great job and great house and great boyfriend.

Like there was any debate which vision was better.

So I emailed Jeremy first thing when Matt dropped me off at home after class.

To: god@jeremylitton.com
From: me@philomena.com
Subject: hey

hey jeremy—want to go out sometime?

phil

I knew I'd drive myself insane if I sat there and waited for him to reply, so I went into my bedroom, stripped out of my sweaty gi, and hopped in the shower.

As the hot water scalded my skin, I wondered what Jeremy looked like these days. I hadn't actually seen him since college, and back then he was kind of scruffy-looking. I frowned as I realized Matt was right—Jeremy did look like he'd spent a considerable amount of time in a one-room shack in the woods. And there were those diaries he always scribbled in. . . .

"That was almost ten years ago," I told myself for re-assurance. I'd definitely changed in that time period. It was a given that he had too.

I hoped.

As I raided my closet for a robe, I glanced at the clock. I was distracted by its apocalyptic look—I'd wound duct tape around it a couple of times to keep the plastic casing intact. The rattle was still there, but who cared as long as no one shook it? It told time and that's all that mattered. Right now, it glowed S thirty-five, which I figured meant nine thirty-five.

I doubted he'd emailed me yet. Not everyone has the email etiquette Matt and I have: respond quickly and often. That's what email is all about—immediate gratification.

I jiggled my trackball as I sat at my desk and put in my password. Yes, my screensaver at home is password-protected. You can never be too careful.

"Oh," I gasped when my email terminal popped up. He'd responded.

To: me@philomena.com
From: god@jeremylitton.com
Subject: Re: hey

Philomena Donovan??

Frowning, my fingers flew over the keyboard.

To: god@jeremylitton.com
From: me@philomena.com
Subject: Re: Re: hey

how many philomenas do you know?

His reply arrived ten seconds later.

To: me@philomena.com
From: god@jeremylitton.com
Subject: Re: Re: Re: hey

Only one. Thank God. I can't imagine the world with more than one of you in it.

Jeremy had always thought he was more clever than he really was.

To: god@jeremylitton.com
From: me@philomena.com
Subject: well?

so you want to go out or what?

I tapped my foot against the leg of the chair while I waited.

My nerves were jittery. What was up with that? This was just Jeremy. I couldn't even blame it on excessive caffeine because I hadn't had any since my second cup of coffee in the morning. I knew desperation when I felt it.

Fortunately, I didn't have to wait long.

To: me@philomena.com
From: god@jeremylitton.com
Subject: Re: well?

Why?

I pursed my lips and wondered how he'd take it if I told him because I was looking for my soulmate, or at least a good facsimile.

Exactly. So I sugarcoated it.

To: god@jeremylitton.com
From: me@philomena.com
Subject: Re: Re: well?

i was just thinking about you and thought it'd be nice to rekindle what we once had.

I reread my email before I sent it and grinned. Philomena Donovan: master of flattery.

Jeremy's response arrived a split second later.

To: me@philomena.com
From: god@jeremylitton.com
Subject: Re: Re: Re: well?

ROTFL

Frickin' hilarious, Donovan, considering we didn't have anything
but joint ownership of a bottle of aspirin for hangovers.

I scowled and typed furiously.

To: god@jeremylitton.com
From: me@philomena.com
Subject: Re: Re: Re: Re: well?

i could give you a list of all the stuff we had in common.

Two seconds later:

To: me@philomena.com
From: god@jeremylitton.com
Subject: Go ahead . . .

Give me your list.

I rubbed the tip of my nose, thought about it, and
began tapping at the keys.

To: god@jeremylitton.com
From: me@philomena.com
Subject: what p & j have in common: a brief list

beer
darts
salty peanuts

"Ha! Take that, Mr. Doubting Jeremy." I sent it and
waited.

To: me@philomena.com
From: god@jeremylitton.com
Subject: Pathetic List

Great, Phil. When I decide to open up a bar, I'll give you a call.
Until then, I think I'm safe in saying we don't have much of a
future together.

But, hey—I'm flattered you thought of me. Maybe I'll dedicate
a blog posting to you.

Take care. And thanks for the laugh.

I glared at the screen. Bastard. I can't believe I
thought he'd be an adequate choice. I considered kicking his computer off the Internet (yeah, I can do that—
I've got skills). There's a certain joy in booting a person
off his connection, watching him reconnect, and then
booting him again. I admit, it's a perverse joy, but a joy
nevertheless.

I didn't do it. Instead, I put the first season of Mac-
Gyver into my DVD player and wondered how to get in
touch with Richard Dean Anderson. And if he still had
all his teeth. (How old was he, anyway?)

Chapter Six

"I think I should get an unlisted phone number."
—MacGyver, "Trumbo's World" Episode #6

The door to the server room clicked shut behind me. Frowning, I started to turn as an arm snaked around my waist. Without thinking, I grabbed a fistful of shirt and bent my knees to chuck my attacker over my shoulder.

"Whoa, gorgeous. It's me."

"Johnny?" I tried to turn around. He'd never know how close he'd come to being flipped onto the ground.

His arms held me in place so he could nuzzle my neck. "I've missed you this week. Did you get my messages?"

"Um—" I admit it, I'd been dodging his calls. "You called?"

"Yeah. A few times. Let's go out tonight." His hand crept up.

I peeled it off me before he reached my boobs. "Johnny! We're at work."

"I know." He didn't sound contrite. "Maybe one day we can have a quickie in here."

Gross. Not even in his dreams. Of course, if he were Rio it'd be a different story.

I wedged myself out of his embrace and pushed him away. "You know how I feel about that."

"I know." He grinned. "This virginal stuff turns me on."

Fantastic. "Johnny—"

"Where do you want to go tonight?"

"Home."

Wrong answer. I swear I saw his ears perk up like a cocker spaniel. "That sounds great."

"No, I'm going home alone. All by myself," I added just in case he didn't get my drift.

Watching the enthusiasm drain from him was painful. "Oh."

I almost felt bad—*almost* being the key word there. "Sorry."

"No problem. I understand."

His tone said the opposite, and I felt compelled to make an excuse to make him feel better. "It's just that it's been a long week and I'm really tired."

"I can rub your feet," he offered eagerly.

I was tempted for a split second, maybe less than that. "Thanks, but I'll take a raincheck."

As soon as it came out of my mouth I wanted to smack my forehead. Idiot. What was I thinking, encouraging him?

But it did the trick. He smiled brilliantly. "Great. I'll give you a call tomorrow."

I hoped my smile didn't look sickly. "Um. Right."

"Rest well, Mena. I want you nice and fresh this weekend." He wiggled his eyebrows and let himself out of the server room.

I banged my head against a machine. Stupid stupid stupid. What was I thinking? I'd never get rid of him this way.

"Hey, Mena. You okay?"

I looked up to see Lewis pop his head in, a concerned frown on his face. I sighed and tried to smile. "I'm fine. Just a headache."

His frown deepened. "Hitting your head against the computers probably isn't the best cure." He threw his hands in the air. "But you're the boss. You know best, of course."

At least he had some intelligence.

"I could give you a shoulder massage," he said eagerly. "And neck. Your muscles are probably tight."

"No, thanks." What was it with guys offering me massages today? Before he could deflate on me, I said, "But you could go buy me a bottle of Advil and a Coke."

"Okay!" He raced off before I could give him any money.

I rolled my eyes. At least I'd gotten a reprieve from him.

Two seconds after I got back to my desk, the phone rang. I picked it up without thought. "Mena speaking."

"Philomena, it's your mother."

Damn. What good is caller ID if you don't check it? "Hey, Mom. What's up?"

"I talked to your sister."

Goody for you. "Oh, really?"

"We set the date for her birthday party."

My lungs seized, and for a moment I thought I was going to hyperventilate. Please please please let it be postponed for a month. Or five.

But my mom dashed my hopes. "It'll be on the twenty-first."

Considering that was Daphne's actual birthdate, I wasn't especially shocked. But how was I going to find a viable temporary boyfriend, much less a soulmate, before then?

However, I was surprised on one count. "That's in two weeks. Can Daphne get the time off right away?"

"When I spoke with her last night she said it'd be no trouble. Have you talked to her?"

"Yes." I didn't tell her it'd been a week. I wasn't in the

mood to hear the lecture on keeping in touch with my only sister.

Actually, I wasn't in the mood to deal with any of this. It'd been a tough week, starting with Ian, peaking with Jeremy, and ending with Johnny.

Johnny. Shudder. I had to nip that in the bud.

All I wanted was a good workout and some time to myself. Searching for your soulmate—or even a temporary stand-in—was tiring work.

". . . number so maybe you could extend the invitation for me. In fact, how about if you two come to dinner this weekend?"

I shook my head. "What was that, Mom?"

She sighed. "Focus, Philomena."

"One of my employees needed my signature," I lied. I hated it when she got that disappointed tone in her voice. The only thing that'd distract her was reminding her how important I was.

"I was saying that I don't know how to get in touch with Barry."

I stifled the instant panic in my chest and asked, "Why do you need to get in touch with Barry?"

"Weren't you listening at all, Philomena?" She didn't bother to wait for the answer. I guess she already knew. "I wanted to personally invite him to Daphne's party. And also to dinner this weekend."

Yikes! "He can't make it this weekend, Mom."

Pause. "Why not?"

"Um, he's out of town. On business." Thank God she wasn't here in person—I'd never have gotten away with the lie.

"Oh." She sounded immediately appeased (no one turned down an imperial summons, even by proxy). "Well, that's too bad. Maybe sometime next week."

I've taken Kung Fu for over nine years. I'm trained to recognize openings and opportunities.

This moment was one of them.

I knew if I was ever going to tell my mother that I'd broken up with Barry, this was the moment. The path was open and clear—I just had to seize it. "Listen, Mom. About Barry . . ."

"I can't tell you how proud I am that you've found someone like him."

I grimaced. "Right. Um, Mom?"

"I wish Daphne were more like you in that regard. She never talks about her personal life. Does she tell you if she's dating anyone?"

"Well, no." Daphne and I had never been open with each other, despite the fact we were only thirteen months apart. Besides, Daphne wasn't a dater. Her work defined who she was; nothing else was important. "But about Barry—"

"I'm so happy about the balance you have in your life, Philomena. I hope on this trip Daphne sees how well-adjusted you are and decides to take your example."

Sigh or growl? It was a toss up; I could have gone either way. "Listen, Mom. I have to go. The production environment for one of the Web sites went down and I need to check the error logs."

"Okay, honey. I'll talk to you later."

Always worked. Talk tech and my mom was so outta there. I said my goodbyes and hung up.

Then I growled.

The guys around me frowned at me from behind their monitors. I heard one of them mumble, "Someone get a leash."

I opened my mouth to tell him what he could do with the leash when the phone rang again.

Never say I don't learn from my mistakes. I checked the caller ID this time, but I didn't recognize the number so I picked it up, figuring it had to be a vendor or something.

It wasn't. "Hello, Mena. It's me."

Me, as in my archrival.

I was about to ream Daphne for calling me at work. (What did my family think? That I lounged around and ate bonbons all day?) But then I realized she never called me at work. Ever.

"What's wrong?" I asked.

"I wanted to ask you a favor." I could see her twisting a lock of her perfect hair around her finger like she did when she was unsure. Which wasn't often.

"What?" If she wanted to borrow a dress for the party, I could tell her right now her boobs were too big to fit into anything I owned. Not that I could blame her for trying—my wardrobe *was* more fashionable than hers.

"I was wondering if I could stay with you while I'm visiting."

"Excuse me?" I wiggled a finger in my ear. I thought for sure she had asked me if she could stay with me.

"Can I stay over at your place?"

I narrowed my eyes at the receiver. Suspicious. "Why?"

"Mom's going to drive me crazy with this party thing. She hasn't let up on me since she's been back." Daphne's voice took an accusatory tone. "She keeps saying how great this guy you're dating is."

"Really?" I couldn't help grinning.

"You don't need to sound so happy about it," she grumbled. "I'll lose my mind if I have to stay with her and Dad."

I grinned harder.

"So can I stay with you or not?"

"Okay," I agreed graciously. She was my sister, after all. Oh, I was going to enjoy this.

"Thanks."

I chose to ignore the fact that she didn't sound especially thankful. "When do you arrive?"

"Tonight."

"*What?*"

"Tonight," she repeated calmly. "I'm on the evening flight from San Francisco. I should be at your house by ten or so."

"Tonight?" I squeaked. "Isn't that awfully sudden?"

"No."

What could I say to that? "What if I have plans? It's Friday night, after all."

There was a shrug in her voice. "I'll just use my key to get in."

Oh, yeah. I forgot I gave her a key in a moment of weakness when I first moved in. Floundering, I grasped the last straw I could. "How did you get the time off?"

She hesitated. "I'm on sabbatical."

Sabbatical. There was more to this than she was letting on.

But before I could grill her, she said, "I have a few things to take care of. See you tonight," and hung up.

I held the phone out and stared at it.

I didn't come clean with Mom about Barry, and Daphne was coming to stay with me. I groaned and let my head fall onto my desk with a thunk.

"You okay, Mena?"

I lifted my head to see Lewis standing in front of me, his forehead wrinkled with worry and a brown paper bag clutched against his chest.

I held my hand out. "Drugs. Now."

He plunked the bag down on my desk. "I couldn't remember if you wanted Advil or Excedrin, which has caffeine so it might help you more, so I got you both."

I watched as he pulled everything out of the bag and set it in front of me. One box of Advil, one bottle of Coke, one box of Excedrin, and a fourth item. I picked it up. "What's this?"

"Oh." He flushed crimson. "I got you some Midol. Just in case."

I narrowed my eyes at him.

He shrugged with an apologetic grin. "Just covering my bases."

I grunted and reached for the Coke.

"Anything else I can do for you? File some papers? Get you some food? Wash your car?"

I pointed away from me. "Go."

"Right." He turned and fled. Ten feet away, he turned around and called out, "Don't forget to take the Midol."

I felt my cheeks burn as the programmers who worked around me stared. Instead of trying to explain, I sighed and took a swig of Coke.

As optimistic as I was, I didn't think I was going to find my soulmate, or even a workable temporary boyfriend, by next week. It was clear I needed to rethink my options.

But MacGyver had it right: Any problem can be solved with a little ingenuity. And that was one thing I had in spades.

Chapter Seven

Lessons Learned from MacGyver
#7
Desperation makes one kind of flexible.

"Let me get this straight, Doc. Daphne's on her way to Portland and she's going to stay with you."

I frowned at Matt. "What could I say? 'No, you can't sleep here?' I can't say there's no room. There's an extra bed in my office."

He wiped his hands on a crumpled paper napkin—I don't know why, since he reached for another slice of pizza. "How is that going to go for you?"

"Grr."

He grinned. "That's what I thought."

I scowled. I would have said something rude, but I was at his apartment and that would have been impolite. Tempting, though.

Matt lives on the third floor of an old apartment building. It's a little cave-like if you ask me—the ceilings aren't especially high and it's facing the wrong way to get much light, but it has lots of funky charm.

Kind of like me.

Anyway, one of the features I hold in morbid fascination is the wall of mirrors in his bedroom. If the mirrors were in anyone else's room, I would have had a field day with them. Smirks abound.

Not so in Matt's. Thinking of him and the mirrors was like thinking about my parents having sex. Gag. Not a visual I needed in my head. So I avoided going anywhere near his bedroom.

I nabbed another wedge of pizza before he ate the whole thing. "I didn't know she was coming tonight. When she asked, I thought she meant she was coming a day or two before the party, not for two weeks. Two weeks!"

Matt chuckled. "Maybe it won't be so bad."

I stared at him.

"Or maybe it will." He sprinkled red pepper flakes from a to-go packet on his slice. "One good thing's come out of Daphne arriving early."

"What?"

"You came over with pizza and beer."

Trust Matt to think of his stomach. I handed him a fresh napkin.

He wiped his mouth. "How are things going on the man front?"

I snorted.

"That good, huh?"

"I'm running out of time and I have no prospects." I picked off a green bell pepper and tossed it into the pizza box lid.

Matt swallowed his bite before he replied. "None? There's got to be some fool out there who'll go out with you. Aside from the fact that you suck in bed. No pun intended."

"Watch it or I'll break a couple of your fingers the next time we work out."

"You're so violent. No wonder you can't get a man." He studied me as he took a swig of beer.

It took two minutes of silent scrutiny to get to me. I threw down my napkin. "*What* already?"

He shook his head. "Just tell your mom you broke up with Barrington. She'll understand. He may have been a nice guy, but he wasn't for you."

"Why not?" I asked indignantly.

"You're kidding, right?"

I pouted.

He froze midbite. "You aren't kidding. Don't you remember why you broke up with him? The lack of spontaneity? The boring routine? The slug-like kisses?"

I lowered my eyes to the piece of pizza I was picking apart. "Maybe he can change."

"I can't believe it." He tossed his napkin into the pizza box lid. "What are you saying?"

"That maybe Mom was right. Maybe Barry was the best choice for me."

Matt showed off his gutter vocabulary. (I always found it amusing that a nice guy like Matt would have a mouth like that on him.)

Once he finished venting, I said, "I've been rethinking my plan."

"Aw, hell."

"I think maybe I should ask Barry if he wants to get together again."

Matt leaned back in his chair and gaped at me.

I took that look to mean he was amazed at my ability to forgive Barry for saying I was boring in bed. "Like you said, Barry's a great guy. He makes an excellent living and he's handsome. If I make Barry more like MacGyver . . ."

"Stop with this MacGyver fetish already." He gazed at me like I was an escapee from the state mental hospital. "A mullet-sporting loner is not the epitome of manhood."

"But what he could do with a Swiss Army knife!" Shiver. Then I thought about Rio's hands and shivered again.

"Doc, you are seriously disturbed."

I needed to get him to focus on the important issue here. "MacGyver aside, Barry's the only shot I have to be in the limelight." I gasped as something occurred to me. "What if I can get Barry to propose before the party? Can you imagine the attention having a honking diamond on my finger will get?"

He pushed away from the table. "I need another beer."

"Get me one too, okay?"

He mumbled something but I ignored it. Instead I dreamed about Barry slipping a ring on my finger. Maybe I could get him to do it *at* the party.

"Doc, you're forgetting one thing," Matt said when he came back and set a beer bottle in front of me.

"What?"

"You broke up with Barrington. Badly." He sat down and drank from his bottle. "He's never going to want you back."

Smiling like the siren I am, I shook my finger at him. "Don't underestimate the power of my feminine wiles."

"I'm telling you, no guy will go back to a woman who said she thought of other men while she had sex with him."

"We'll see." I smiled enigmatically (I hoped).

"You're better off calling Jeremy," he muttered as he began to clean up our dinner mess. The look on my face must have given something away because he closed his eyes and groaned. "You called him, didn't you?"

"What do you take me for? I'm not *that* desperate." I rubbed the tip of my nose. "I emailed him."

He groaned again.

"But you were right. Jeremy isn't for me."

"Turned you down, huh?"

I crossed my eyes and stuck my tongue out at him.

"I don't know why you can't find a man. You're so charming." He picked up our trash and headed for the kitchen.

I followed him, hopped onto the counter, and sipped beer while he rinsed out our empty bottles.

If we were at my place, I would have left the pizza debris on the table overnight. Maybe longer.

Unlike me, Matt's tidy. Not anally immaculate like Daphne (alphabetizing your kitchen utensils is just plain freakish), but his bed is always made, his office is always orderly, and his bathroom is clean.

I waited for him to say something. And I waited. Then I waited some more.

But it became apparent by the care he was taking in wiping the sink down that he wasn't going to volunteer anything. So I stepped into the fray. "You've got no comments?"

He glanced at me before resuming his scrubbing. "Would you listen to anything I said?"

I pursed my lips. "Depends on what you say."

"You already know how I feel."

I nodded. He'd made that abundantly clear, but I still thought making up with Barry was the most logical course of action given my timeframe.

But Matt was my best friend, and I didn't want him to be angry at me. I put my hand on his arm and squeezed. "I promise I'll stop this scheming and actually look for my soulmate."

He blinked in surprise.

"After the party."

He shook his head. "You're impossible, Doc."

"But you still love me."

"Kind of like an old shoe I can't bring myself to throw away because it's so comfortable." He tugged me off the counter and smacked my butt. "Get going. Your sister's due to arrive at any time."

I pretended to gag.

He grinned, put his arm around my shoulders, and propelled me toward the door. "You know what Dwight says?"

"To always wear a cup?"

"No. That you reap what you sow." He stopped in front

of the door and faced me. "Be careful what you do because it'll come back and bite you in the ass."

I smiled at him and patted his cheek. "That's sweet, but you don't have to worry. I'm not going to do anything crazy."

He snorted as he opened the door and pushed me out.

I resisted as a token gesture of displeasure. "I'm not."

"No. You crossed the line from crazy to downright insane a week ago."

I stuck my tongue out at him as he closed the door in my face, his laughter seeping through the crack.

As I walked to my car, I considered what Matt said. Only a little, though. I didn't take it too seriously because he never made his lack of fondness for Barry a secret. Aside from calling him Barrington (which *was* his real name, even if no one called him that), Matt never overtly said anything disparaging. But I could tell how he felt anyway.

I didn't mind his warnings. Matt loved me; of course he was going to look out for me. I did the same for him. Not that he'd dated anyone in forever.

I frowned as I let myself into my car. I should ask him what was up with that.

On the ten-minute ride home, I weighed everything: my desire for a soulmate, being the apple of my parents' eyes, what Matt said, being the apple of my parents' eyes, the other guys I'd met, being the apple of my parents' eyes, and Barry's kisses.

Maybe I was placing too much importance on being my parents' pride and joy instead of Daphne. Maybe Matt was right; it wasn't that important.

I parked in front of my house and stared out the windshield. Instead of seeing the bumper of the car in front of me, the other houses, or even darkness, I flashed on the day in the sixth grade when I got my period for the first time. I wasn't scared or anything—I knew what was going on. I'd seen the sex ed movies. And I'd caught it soon enough that it didn't leak and embarrass me in front of my classmates (God, what a horror that would have been).

In fact, I was kind of excited. I remembered how Mom and Daphne had a special women's tea to mark Daphne's passing into womanhood, and I couldn't wait for Mom to pick me up and take me out to celebrate. I thought we could get a banana split with extra cherries.

So I sat in the nurse's office and watched the clock over the doorway click each minute by, and still my mom wasn't there to get me. Every fifteen minutes, I bugged the nurse, asking if she was sure she talked to my mom when she called our house. The answer was always yes with a barely disguised eye roll.

I found out later that afternoon when I got home that my mom forgot, because right after the nurse called her, she got a call from my sister's principal saying Daphne was chosen to attend some special summer program for kids at Lawrence Livermore Labs in California. She'd be the youngest teenager to ever attend.

How could getting your period compare with that?

I shook my head to clear the memory and got out of the car with renewed determination. Matt didn't understand—how could he?

There was nothing to consider. I needed Barry back.

The porch light was on. I hadn't been home since that morning, so it meant Daphne had arrived.

I ran up the steps to my front door and made a face as I unlocked the door. Then I made another face just to get it out of my system before I confronted my nemesis.

Pasting a smile on, I entered, closed the door behind me without locking it, and skipped up the steps to my living area. "Daph! You here?"

"Don't call me Daph."

I grinned. I loved yanking her chain.

She came out of the front room, aka my office, as I hit

the landing in the living room. It was dark everywhere but for a light in the hallway (leading to the bathroom and my room at the back of the house) and the blaze of illumination behind Daphne from my office.

All the light coming from the office was the first thing I noticed. I only had one desk lamp in there. I frowned. Where did the rest of it come from?

The second thing that caught my eye was how the light made a halo around Daphne. Like she was a living angel.

I'd forgotten just how angelic she looked. Her hair was perfect—gold and gleaming—and her clothes were immaculate even at the end of the day.

I glanced down at myself and picked at a strand of cheese stuck to my T-shirt.

"Aren't you being loud? What about your tenant downstairs?"

Hello to you, too. "Magda's out of town."

"Oh." Her forehead crinkled, like the idea of being out of town was a foreign concept. "Did you have a good time out? You're back so late."

A deaf person would have heard her faintly disapproving tone. Grr. She was so passive-aggressive. She herself said it was okay if I was out.

Instead of showing my irritation, I smiled and said, "Yeah. I had a great time. Matt says hi."

Her forehead unfurrowed a touch. "Oh, how is Matt? I didn't realize you still saw him."

This time I did frown. "Why wouldn't I see Matt? He's my best friend."

She shrugged. "Things change. People change."

Whatever that meant.

"Besides," she said as she went back into my office, "isn't your boyfriend jealous of him? And vice versa?"

"No." Scowling, I followed her. "Matt and I have a relationship that transcends all other relationships."

She glanced at me briefly before dragging one of her suitcases onto the bed and unzipping it.

Suitcases? I gawked at them. "Don't believe in traveling light, huh?"

"You never know what you might need," she replied, her face averted.

I studied her. Something was *not* right. "What's going on?"

"I'm unpacking."

"No, I mean, what's going on, really?"

"I said I'm unpacking." Cool and composed, she pulled out a stack of shirts.

Overly composed if you asked me. But damn it, I wasn't going to hang around and make an effort if she wasn't going to cooperate. "I'm going to bed then. Maybe we can have breakfast."

"Sure. Did you lock the door?"

"Of course." Evil, I know, since I purposefully didn't. But her obsessive need for security drove me mad.

"Goodnight, then."

I crossed my eyes at her rigid back and left.

After a quick stop in the bathroom to brush my teeth and wash my face, I turned the hall light off and shut myself in my bedroom.

I love my room. When I bought this house I turned the attached deck into an enclosed sitting area with windows all around it. I had an oversized lounging chaise in there and at night I liked to lie on it and stare at the stars.

It was the perfect way to unwind tonight, so I stripped down to my underwear and flopped onto it. The stars weren't visible since the weather had turned again, but it was still peaceful.

I briefly considered calling Matt and asking him to play his violin for me, but the solitude was just what I needed.

I had to plot.

Grabbing a pen and pad of paper I kept on the table next to the lounge (along with the latest Kung Fu magazine), I wrote:

How to Wiggle My Way Back into Barry's Heart

All lists should have titles. How successful the list is depends on the title. Tapping the pen against my lips, I considered the (fairly ugly) situation and pondered where to start. Tough decision. So I listed my choices randomly.

1) Invite him to Hurley's and profess my never-ending regret
2) Call him pretending to be a psychic from Dionne's network and tell him he had to get back together with Mena, otherwise his life would go to shit
3) Tell him I was briefly possessed, but the exorcism was a success
4) Check his blog to see where he was going to be in the near future and make sure I ended up there too
5) Tell him I had a month to live and my last wish was to get back together with him

"Hmm." The last one had merit.

Seriously though, the idea of showing up where he was going had potential. Barry often publicized his social schedule on his blog. Once, I'd asked him why; he said it was so his mom could find him if she needed to. I wanted to ask why she couldn't just harass him over the phone like my mom, but he distracted me with a fish kiss.

Enough said.

I automatically started to go to my computer to look at his blog, but then I remembered Daphne was in my office.

"Damn." I dropped my list on the floor and dangled my arms and shoulders off the edge of the chaise. "Tomorrow," I promised myself.

Tomorrow I'd find out what he was up to and then I'd make my move. Barry was as good as mine.

Chapter Eight

Lessons Learned from MacGyver
#21
A little research can go a long way.

Buzzzzzzz.

With my head buried under my comforter, I reached an arm out and smacked my alarm clock.

Buzzzzzzz.

Damn thing. I hit it again, which sent it skittering off the nightstand. I took satisfaction in the metallic plink of something breaking off, even if it meant I had to put it back together. That would teach it to go off.

Buzzzzzzz.

Lifting my head out of the covers, I glared at it. Why wouldn't it stop?

Buzzzzzzz.

"Shut up!" I yelled.

What time was it, anyway? I leaned over, dangling off the edge of the bed. The clock was lying face-down, so I couldn't see the time. Then I saw the cord lying unplugged, probably from when it went flying.

Buzzzzzzz.

Wait a minute. It was still broken. I hadn't gotten around to fixing it. It couldn't be ringing.

Buzzzzzzz.

I realized the annoying sound was coming from down the hall toward the front of the house.

Daphne.

"Damn it!" I shoved the covers aside and stumbled out of my room. As I trudged toward my office (yes, the obnoxious noise was still going on), it came to me that it was Saturday. "Hell." I walked up to the closed door and banged on it. "Daphne! Turn the frickin' alarm OFF."

Silence. Then a faint, groggy "Sorry."

Grr. I mashed my lips together to keep myself from spewing more obscenities at her. By all rights, I was justified. She woke me up *by alarm* on a Saturday. God help her if it was . . .

But I knew it was before I even went into the kitchen and looked at the time. Six-thirty. In the morning.

She chose that moment to come out of my office. Bad move on her part. She never did have great timing where I was concerned.

"What the hell were you thinking?" I growled.

"I don't understand what you mean." Without so much as a blink, she sat down at the kitchen table and began lacing up her running shoes.

I crossed my arms and glared. "The alarm clock. It's frickin' Saturday."

"Stop swearing."

My teeth ground so hard I could feel the enamel wearing down.

"And I set my alarm because I wanted to go running this morning."

"Excellent reason." The bite of my words was sharp. "Good thing you set it so loud because I think there's someone in the next county that wanted to get up butt early too."

She glanced at me as she rose and stretched. "I said I was sorry."

I shook my head and went to the cupboard to get my coffee supplies out. No way was I going to be able to fall back asleep with my blood boiling. I had to reach on my toes to get the bag of beans because they'd somehow gotten pushed back.

"Do you need a hand?" Daphne asked helpfully.

I glared at her over my shoulder. If looks could kill, she should have been day old roadkill.

"Fine." She threw her hands in the air. "Be difficult. I'm going for a run. See you later."

It took me three cups of coffee before I felt human, and even then it was debatable. There's nothing like starting your morning on the wrong foot. Especially your Saturday morning.

When Daphne came back an hour-and-a-half later, I was sitting on the living room couch with my feet propped on the table. Out of the corner of my eye I saw her start to say something (probably to tell me to get my feet off), but she wisely closed her mouth and went to the kitchen instead.

Seconds later she joined me, a glass of orange juice in her hand. She sat down in the loveseat perpendicular to me.

I made an effort to be civil. "How was your run?"

"Fine."

I waited for her to elaborate. She didn't. I shrugged and concentrated on the last bit of coffee in my cup. The first sip is the best, but there's almost as much satisfaction in the last swallow.

"You know coffee depletes your body of nutrients, don't you?"

The look I gave her must have clearly communicated what I thought, because her lips tightened into a thin, pale line.

At least it shut her up.

And I had two weeks of this to look forward to. I wondered if Matt would let me sleep on his couch.

"Want me to make breakfast?" she asked after a long stretch of silence.

"I thought we'd go to Mom and Dad's. They probably want to see you." Since you're their favorite.

She ducked her head, suddenly very concerned about a loose string at the waistband of her shorts.

I frowned. Something was up. "What is it?"

"Well—" She bit her cupid's-bow lips that were a perfect shade of raspberry without lipstick.

I waited. When she said nothing, I barked impatiently. "What?"

She mumbled something, her chin tucked against her chest.

"What?"

"They don't know I'm here."

At least I could hear her, but I was confused. "Where do they think you're staying? Mom wouldn't let you stay in a hotel."

"No, Mena, they don't know I'm *here.*"

I nodded. I got that, but I still didn't understand where they thought she was staying. It's not like Daphne has any friends.

"*Here,*" she repeated. "In Portland."

"In Portland?" Then it dawned on me. "They don't know you're here?"

Even her scowl was enchanting. "That's what I said."

"Where do they think you are?"

"At home in Palo Alto." She narrowed her deep ocean eyes at me. "And I don't want them to know."

Whoa. A threat from the perfect one. I couldn't help grinning malevolently. "What'll you give me to keep quiet?"

"I won't tell Mom it was you who broke that antique lamp in the living room."

Damn. I studied my sister with new appreciation. That was a good one. I didn't know she had it in her. But I couldn't let her know about my admiration, so I said, "Mom won't care. That was twenty years ago."

"Yes, she will, and you know it."

True. Mom tended to cling to transgressions.

Still, I couldn't help needling Daphne more. I shook my head and tried to look concerned. "I don't know. That means I have to lie to them. I don't feel right about that."

She gave me an annoyed look. "You've never had qualms before."

Also true, but I wasn't going to admit it. "It's going to be hard. Real hard."

"I'm sure your conscience will find a way to deal with it. I'm going to take a shower." She got up and went to my office, closing the door firmly behind her.

I stretched my arms out on the couch behind me and grinned. Teasing her was one of life's greatest pleasures.

But I sobered as I wondered why she wouldn't want our parents to know she was here. Something was going on, and it didn't seem good.

I stared at her bedroom door. Should I go ask her?

Nope. I shook my head. Our relationship wasn't exactly close, and she'd rejected my concerned overtures before. She was SuperDaphne anyway—she probably had it all under control. What did she need help from me for?

I don't know why I felt compelled to hang out at home to see if Daphne wanted to do anything, but I spent a couple of hours waiting for her to come out of her room. It became apparent that she wasn't intending on emerging any time soon (I put my ear to the door to make sure she hadn't fallen over in there and knocked herself unconscious).

I had no problem with her being reclusive. Fine with me if she wanted to lock herself in there the whole time she was here. The problem was my computer was in there with her, and I needed to go online to check out Barry's blog. I only had two weeks to get him back—plenty of time, really, but I didn't want to leave it to the last minute.

I sat at my kitchen table, tapping my fingers against the wood. I stared at my office door and tried to guess how long she would be holed up in there. I mean, I thought she'd have to use the bathroom eventually, but I had doubts she was really human, so maybe not.

I would have called Matt; he'd let me use his computer any time. But I knew how he felt about Barry and my plan.

Leaving work or the public library.

Work would be convenient, but the library would be anonymous. The Web logs wouldn't trace anything back to me. Not that Barry checked his Web logs but you could never be too careful.

So I grabbed a jacket (it was drizzly today), hopped in my car, and headed to the downtown branch. All the terminals were occupied when I got there, so I killed time browsing their record section. (Yeah, I was surprised they still had records too. The scary part: They had more vinyl than they did CDs.)

Finally a computer opened up. I dove into the seat, cutting off an elderly woman. I smiled at her and said, "I'll just be a minute."

"Bitch." She flipped me off and tottered away.

Oo-kay.

I shook my head and typed in the URL for Barry's site. Then I waited for it to come up (you'd think the library would have a better connection). It seemed like forever, but it was probably only ten seconds before his site appeared on the screen.

"Ah." About time. I rubbed my hands together and got to it.

"Blah, blah, blah." Barry liked to go on and on sometimes. I scrolled down, trying to find his weekend itinerary. It had to be here somewhere.

"Got it," I muttered a moment later. He was so predictable. I skimmed through it.

Then I froze.

Aw, hell.

Couldn't be. I rubbed my eyes and reread the paragraph. Unfortunately, the words didn't change—it was exactly as I read it the first time.

Barry had a girlfriend. The bastard. What nerve. It'd barely been over a week since we'd broken up.

"Shit shit *shit*." I could feel the woman next to me staring at me, so I turned to her with a contrite smile and said, "Sorry."

This was a rebound fling, I reassured myself. I took a few deep breaths, trying to calm my rapidly beating heart.

When the danger of fainting from hyperventilation had passed, I slowly read his Web page again.

If what he'd written was true (and I had no reason to doubt it—he was the most honest man I knew, next to Matt), he'd met her the day after we broke up. He said they "clicked."

"Clicked!" I exclaimed to the woman next to me. "*We* used to click."

Her eyes were so round, I thought they were going to pop out of her head. What? She'd never seen a woman scorned before?

I ignored how she scooted her chair away from me and read on. Barry described his new flame in great detail, but if that weren't enough, he also had a small picture of them together.

"Can you believe it?" I asked the woman. "They've only been dating a week and already they have a picture together."

The woman must have decided I was a harmless freak because she leaned closer to take a look. "She's kind of pretty."

I scowled. "She has no chin."

The lady pursed her lips. "But her eyes are so beautiful, you don't notice her lack of chin much."

"Hmmph."

"And look at her hair." She pointed. "How it looks so silky and how it's all in place."

I turned to glare at her. "Whose side are you on anyway?"

"I'm just saying." She shrugged, her nose in the air. With a pointed look at my hair, she gathered her things and walked away.

My hand flew to my ponytail. My hair could look like that, if I really wanted it to. Maybe.

I frowned at the picture. Barry's rebound looked familiar. Something around the blond hair, the way she smiled for the camera . . . She looked, I don't know, angelic.

I stiffened. Angelic. I leaned toward the computer until my nose was inches from the screen.

Holy shit—she looked just like Daphne. She looked more like Daphne's sister than I did.

Barry was dating a Daphne look-alike. In essence, he cast me aside for Daphne.

"Bastard." I glared at him, standing so happy with his arm around her.

Yes, the little voice inside was adamantly pointing out that I was the one who cast Barry aside. Still. He wasn't supposed to go out the next day and replace me with someone who looked just like my nemesis.

Pout.

Maybe my mom was right—maybe Barry *was* a great catch. If he got a girl like Daphne just one day after I (erroneously) dumped him, he couldn't be so bad after all, right? How could I have missed his greatness?

Aside from the obvious, this development was disastrous. It threw a wrench in my plans. Barry was supposed to be pining for me, not panting after her. We had history. I was going to go to him, grovel, and get back in his good graces. And he was supposed to accept me back after a sufficient number of kisses (blech—I didn't want to think about that).

Then he'd take me to Daphne's party, propose to me with a honking rock, and then after a suitable amount of time I'd tell him we should break up. Or, better yet, I'd do something that would cause him to break up with me. That way, he'd save face.

Never call me ungenerous.

"This is not a problem," I told myself firmly. There had to be something I could do. This was a salvageable situation. Why? Because it had to be.

I leaned back in the chair and dangled my head backward. I noticed the line of people waiting to use the computers, all of whom were giving me dirty looks.

I crossed my eyes at them and got up. I needed to move anyway. Moving would help me come up with a solution.

I walked around downtown, past Pioneer Square, up to Nordstrom. I walked down Broadway. Because I happened to pass by the Teuscher store (I didn't plan it, I swear) I stopped in and bought a couple of champagne truffles—a couple as in four or five. I ate them on the way back to my car. The sugar rush gave me the boost I needed to figure out what to do.

I had to break up Barry and his new girlfriend.

Chapter Nine

Lessons Learned from MacGyver
#114
The decisions we make shape our lives.

Deciding to break Barry and his girlfriend up was one thing; actual execution was another.

I spent the entire weekend thinking about this. I turned off my cell phone and meditated on the problem (Dwight would have been so proud of me). I holed up in my room and plotted. I schemed. I made lists, threw them away, and recompiled them. I sketched out my war plan until every possible scenario was covered. MacGyver couldn't have done better.

I was ready.

Daphne holed up all weekend too. In fact, she was so inconspicuous, I forgot she was there.

Until Monday morning. I stumbled out of my bedroom, moaning, my eyes half-shut. Somehow I made it into the kitchen and set a pot of water on to boil. I opened the cabinet where I kept my coffee paraphernalia. I got the beans, the grinder, and the press pot down.

As I was plugging in the grinder, I noticed something amiss. Something wrong. I scowled and picked it up.

A jar of Folgers Crystals.

I shrieked. *Sacrilege.*

Then Daphne hurried out of her room with a coffee mug. She paused when she saw me, then joined me in the kitchen. "I thought you'd be at work by now."

I glanced at the clock. "Only nine."

"I know." She frowned. "Won't your boss be upset if you're late?"

"Not late."

She stared at me. "What's wrong with you?"

"Nothing." Except you. But I didn't say that. Honestly, I thought I was doing really well for not yet having my coffee. I was making words, after all. I could have been grunting.

I ground my coffee, caressed it into the press pot, and poured boiling water over it. I slumped against the counter and watched Daphne make herself another cup of that—that— Shudder. I couldn't even think of anything horrible enough to compare Folgers to. I had to turn away as she drank it. Disgusting.

I mixed sugar into my cup and took it into the living room. Daphne followed, making ridiculously happy noises as she drank her shit. "I love this stuff," she said as she sighed and settled onto one side of the couch.

I narrowed my eyes at her. Death wish. Is that what this was? But I made special dispensations because she was, technically, my sister.

However, I couldn't help but say, "I thought coffee robbed your body of nutrients." That earned me a frown and several minutes of silence.

Too good to last though.

"So." She smiled at me in that fake happy way she did sometimes. "What's on the agenda for today?"

"Grr." I glared at her as I growled. That's what I had on my agenda.

"Hmm." She raised her eyebrows, her lips thinning in disapproval. "I know you have work. Right? But do you have anything planned afterward?"

If I had a pillow, I would have hidden under it. Better yet, I would have smothered her with it.

"Because I was thinking maybe we could go out." She tried smiling. "You could show me the hot spots. I've been gone for so long I don't know what's hot anymore."

Clarification: Daphne had never known what was hot. She'd stayed home and studied on weekends before she went off to college at fourteen.

"I thought we could go dancing." She shrugged, gazing at me steadily.

"You couldn't wait until I'd had at least another cup of coffee, could you?"

"Excuse me?"

Like I was going to buy that innocence act. "You're trying to confuse me."

Her frown was instant. "I don't know what you're talk—"

"Admit it." I pointed a finger at her, eyes narrowed in suspicion. "You're trying to throw me for a loop. You've planting cameras around my house and are just waiting to capture for posterity the moment I fall into your trap."

"What trap?" She scrunched her nose. "I just wanted to know whether you were busy tonight or not."

"Yes."

"Yes, what?"

"Yes, I'm busy."

She stared at me for a beat, shook her head like she was trying to clear it, and rose from the couch. "You're insane."

Then I had a thought. Conveniently, she was already walking out of the room so I didn't have to bother to hide my grin. "Hey, the hottest bar in Portland is a strip club. Wanna go? Monday nights women get in free."

"You're sick," she called over her shoulder.

I couldn't help it if I took perverse satisfaction in teasing her. I'm sure it was genetic—probably nothing I could do about it.

And I didn't lie about the strip club. It *was* the hottest bar in town. There were more strip clubs in Portland than regular bars. Hell, there were more strip clubs per capita than anywhere else in the country.

Feeling better now that my morning had turned around, I showered, dressed, threw away the Folgers, and took off for work. Instead of taking the bus, I opted to drive (I had a stop to make after work).

Which reminded me: I needed to call Matt.

Because I hated making calls while I was driving, I waited till I got to my cube. Matt went to work way before I even woke up, so I knew to call his office.

He answered on the fourth ring. "Yeah?"

I grinned and wondered if he realized how distracted he sounded. He was probably too distracted to realize. "Hey. It's me."

"Hmm?"

"Philomena Donovan. Your best friend."

"Uh-huh."

I took out a whistle I kept in my drawer for occasions just like this and blew. Loud and piercing.

The few programmers who were in early (because ten o'clock is early for most programmers, unless they hadn't gone to sleep yet from working all night) yelped in surprise. One fell off his chair onto the pile of candy wrappers under his desk.

Matt fumbled with the phone before he yelled at me. "Jesus Christ, Doc! What the hell?"

It always worked. I put the whistle back, ignored his

sputtering indignation, and said, "I'm not going to be in class tonight."

"That's all this assault was about? That you're not going to be in class? I think you could have spared my hearing and just sent me an email."

Matt was always touchy when his work was disrupted. "I thought this was more personable. Besides, I haven't talked to you all weekend."

"Whose fault is that? *My* phone wasn't turned off so my friends couldn't reach me."

He knew me so well, sometimes it was irritating.

"So what's such a big deal that you're missing class? Dwight's not going to be happy."

I couldn't very well tell him I was launching stage one in my assault on Barry—I doubted it'd go over well. So I resorted to the most logical course of action: evasion. "Daphne wants to see some hot spots."

Silence. Then he said, "I can't believe you'd lie to me."

"I'm not lying," I protested. I wasn't. Daphne really did want to go out. I just didn't say we weren't doing that tonight. "She really does."

More silence. "If you don't want to tell me what you're doing, just say so. Don't make things up. Have a little more respect for me than that."

"I'm telling you, she really does want to see the night life."

"Since when?" There was still a trace of suspicion in his voice.

"Since this morning. Listen, I have to go. I'll call you later."

"Be careful, whatever you're up to."

I crossed my eyes at the receiver.

"And don't make faces at me," he said before he hung up.

Good thing I loved him.

I set the phone down and looked up at the disgruntled programmers who were milling around shooting daggers at me from behind their Coke-bottle glasses. I smiled sweetly at one of them. "Hey, Darby. You have a Snickers wrapper stuck to your butt."

Muttering, he flushed red and twisted left and right to look behind him. I tried not to laugh, but he looked like a dog chasing his tail.

I ducked my head so he wouldn't see me, well, snickering. Then I turned on my computer and got on with my day. The first thing I did was check my email.

Mistake. Big mistake.

To: pdonovan@congo.com
From: jmorgan@congo.com
Subject: Thinking of you . . .

When are you free this week? I need to kiss you.

Eew. I almost gagged. What a way to start off the morning.

And what was he doing sending personal stuff like this through company email? I quickly tapped out my reply.

To: jmorgan@congo.com
From: pdonovan@congo.com
Subject: Re: Thinking of you . . .

you shouldn't send out personal email from your work account. the company has everything you send archived. and you never know who may read it.

I hit send without addressing his obviously delusional desire to kiss me (blech). Or telling him as sys admin I had access to every email everyone in the company sent out. (No, I didn't exercise that power—not usually, anyway.)

His response arrived seconds later.

To: pdonovan@congo.com
From: jmorgan@congo.com
Subject: Come on, Mena

You're driving me insane. Tell me you'll see me this weekend.

I sighed. Damn, it was hard being a femme fatale.

To: jmorgan@congo.com
From: pdonovan@congo.com
Subject: Re: Come on, Mena

need to check my schedule. i'll let you know.

Fortunately, he didn't email me back. Maybe the Japanese investors were visiting today and he was busy. Maybe he'd be busy all week.

Hey, a girl can hope.

After about a dozen nagging phone calls from people having trouble logging in to various servers and Web sites, hours of Lewis fawning over me, and a meeting that seemed to last until the end of time, I was ready to call it a day. More than ready. I'd been champing at the bit to make my first move in getting Barry back.

His blog, for once, made no mention of what his plans were for the coming week, but that was no problem— we'd dated for a year, after all. Sure, off and on, but I had basic knowledge of his habits. Like, for instance, on Mondays he had private boxing lessons at the gym with Rio.

It was brilliant, really. Men always wanted what they

couldn't have. Especially if it belonged to a friend. And Barry was more competitive than most. If I dated Rio, Barry would remember how much he wanted me and dump his Daphne-impersonating girlfriend and beg me to take him back. I'd appear desirable simply because he couldn't have me.

Guilt niggled at me. Then I remembered the expression on Rio's face as he told me about his girlfriend using him, and the guilt increased.

But I stifled it. I had no choice. I had to play dirty to win. Besides, Rio *had* invited me to drop by. And it wasn't like I was lying to Rio, or even using him. I was just asking him out for a drink.

I hopped into my Prius and drove to Barry's gym. It was northeast of downtown Portland, about a fifteen-minute drive on a good day. The gym itself wasn't anything to write home about—it was a renovated factory with a few separate rooms for their various classes. No frills. It surprised me that Barry would be a member there; his family is old Portland money, and his lifestyle is ritzy despite his philanthropic bent. The gym wasn't even convenient; it was in the opposite direction of his house.

When I got there, there was a guy manning the desk. He gave me a sweet smile that was at odds with his tough, muscle-bound exterior. "Can I help you?"

There was something in his voice that made me automatically smile back. "I'm here to meet Rio."

"He's in Studio Three." He looked at his wristwatch. "His lesson should be over in about ten minutes."

"Can I wait for him outside the room?" I batted my eyes and tried to look innocent. "I promise not to interrupt. I just don't want to miss him."

The guy's eyes narrowed (I suppose innocent was a stretch for me), but he nodded and said, "Sure. It's down the hall and to the right. There're windows so you can watch Rio teach from outside."

I looked where he pointed and then beamed at him. "Thanks."

"Sure thing, sweetheart."

Men were so easy.

I followed his directions to the room, but there was only one man there, and even from the back I could tell it was Rio.

God, he looked good.

I put my hands up to the glass and stared in, checking out the room to make sure Barry was in there for my grand entrance. No such luck. I glanced into all the studios, looking for him. A yoga class and a couple of guys fencing, but no Barry.

Damn. Had I missed him? I went back to Studio Three, just to make sure I hadn't missed him, but he wasn't there. I rubbed the tip of my nose and wondered what to do.

Before I could decide, Rio turned around. His smile started at his eyes and slowly stretched to his lips. Lips that I had the urge to know intimately.

Reminding myself that it was Barry I wanted, I opened the door and walked in. "Hi."

"Hi." His blue eyes seemed especially bright, like he was happy to see me.

I tried to remember the last time someone looked at me like that. Blank. "Um, I'm stopping by."

"I can see that."

"You asked me to, remember?"

A corner of his mouth twitched. "I remember."

I mentally groaned. How much more inane could I get? It was his fault; he wore another loose tank top and I could see his nipple from the side. Had he no shame?

I cleared my throat. "So I'm here."

"Yes, I can see." He crossed his arms and leaned against a large cupboard.

My mouth went dry at the way his biceps bulged. Not obscenely like a hardcore bodybuilder, or the guy at the reception desk, but lean with intricately woven ropes of muscles.

"Did you come to check out the gym?" He asked it like he knew the gym wasn't what I had interest in checking out.

"No. Actually, I came to see you."

His smile bloomed again.

God, I wished I had a bottle of water. "But it's a nice gym."

"Thank you."

"Um, you're welcome." I pretended to look around the room, but really, I was trying not to fidget under his amused gaze. "So how did you get into boxing?"

"My dad. He loves boxing." He unwrapped one of the wrist wraps wound around his hand and began meticulously rolling it. "And then I continued in the Navy."

"You were in the Navy?" Mental wince. No way would my parents *ever* condone a military guy. All the other strikes against Rio were incidental compared to this one. Not that it mattered. I was here for Barry. Really.

"Yeah. Only four years active." He shrugged. "I liked it, but it wasn't what I wanted to spend my life doing."

"What do you want to spend your life doing?"

"I want to make a difference. Who doesn't?" he asked with a self-deprecating smile. "That's why I started—"

"Mena? What are you doing here?" Barry walked into the room, a frown wrinkling his brow. "Are you here to see me?"

"You?" I tried to smile coquettishly, even though I was jumping up and down inside because my plan was back in action. "No. I came to see Rio."

"Rio?" His frown turned to a scowl as he looked back and forth between me and his friend.

Yes. It was working.

"Are you thinking of taking up boxing?" he asked disbelievingly.

"God, no." I'd suck at boxing, only because it had rules like no hitting below the belt. What was the point if you couldn't hit wherever you wanted to? "Actually, I came to see if he wanted to go out for a beer."

"*Rio?*"

I batted my lashes and hoped I looked innocent. "You don't mind, do you?"

He stared at me suspiciously.

Okay, maybe I'd gone a little overboard. I backpedaled. "You know, because if you mind—"

"No." But his scowl remained. "I don't mind."

"Great." Only I could tell he did. I didn't have to fake my pleased smile. I turned back to Rio. "Are you free tonight? I know it's short notice."

"I had some paperwork to get done." He gazed at Barry, looking for God knows what. But whatever it was, he seemed to find it, because he faced me and said, "But beer with you beats going over the books. Give me a couple of minutes and I'm all yours."

There was a world of meaning underneath his casually spoken words, and I just about dissolved into a warm puddle at his feet. But I valiantly kept it together, telling myself to remember the plan, and flashed him what I hoped was a modest Mona Lisa smile.

Barry cleared his throat. "Listen, I have to go."

I shrugged like I didn't care. Inside I was jumping up and down like an excited child. He sounded pissed. It was working. As I watched him leave, I wanted to clap my hands in delight. In a week he'd be mine again, no doubt about it.

Chapter Ten

"This man's idea of black tie is a dirty shoelace. Definitely not into formality."
— Bannister (on MacGyver),
"The Enemy Within" Episode #15

I turned to Rio and smiled wide and happy. "Hi."

He chuckled. "Give me a second to change."

"Sure."

He flashed me another brilliant smile and strode out of the room, his bag in hand, toward what I supposed was the locker rooms.

Things couldn't have turned out more perfectly. Barry was probably clutching his steering wheel, seething, right now.

Okay, I admit it, it didn't hurt that Rio was hot. Scorching if you wanted to get specific. It wasn't a hardship to go out with him.

Wincing, I dropped a mat on the floor and sat down. That didn't sound nice. I wouldn't like it if someone used me like a piece of meat; why would I expect Rio to be any different? Though he had playboy written all over him. He was probably using me as much as I was using him.

Too bad he wasn't the kind of guy I could take home to my parents. Despite his clean-cut hair, he looked wild and barely tamed. Not the respectable, socially conscious son-in-law they wanted. But if I was looking to take home some-one who looked like he'd pin me to a wall and devour me (shiver), this man was the one. Although I doubted my parents would appreciate that quality like I did.

Besides, sexual attraction did not make a soulmate. And I doubted we'd be compatible beyond in bed. A guy like Rio couldn't possibly keep me interested, because after the sex wore out, what would we have to talk about?

"Hey."

I looked up to find him leaning in the doorway, watch-ing me with an amused glint in his eyes. "Are you medi-tating?"

"Every chance I get," I said as I got up and put the mat back.

He stepped aside to let me pass. I sniffed apprecia-tively. Nice. Real nice. So nice I wished I'd paid attention to what he smelled like before he took a shower. How a guy smells when he's sweaty is important. You wouldn't want a guy with stinky sweat grunting over you in bed. At least, I wouldn't.

He walked me down the hall to the reception area, close but respectful of my space. I kind of wished he would have put his hand on the small of my back, but he didn't.

Pout.

The hulk manning the reception desk smiled at us. "You out of here, Rio?"

"Yeah. Are you okay to close up tonight?"

"No problem." He glanced at me inquisitively before returning his gaze to Rio. "Have fun."

Rio nodded and held the door open for me.

Surprising. Somehow I didn't expect him to be gentle-manly. "Thanks."

"There's a quiet bar close by. Do you want to follow me or would you like to drive over together?"

"I'll follow you." Not because I was scared he'd try something, but because it seemed more convenient when it was time to go home. He didn't know it, but despite his obvious strength I could break him like a twig if I wanted to.

Another reason I wanted to follow him was I needed a few minutes alone to figure out my strategy. Being with Rio was distracting. I seemed to be losing focus of my goals. So I needed to firm them in my mind. Once I was safely alone in my car, I made a quick mental list:

1) Find out when Rio hangs out with Barry
2) Get myself invited
3) Find out location (in case #2 doesn't happen)

Piece of cake.

I idled, waiting for him to drive around. When I saw his car, I gasped. I would have jumped out and swarmed it right then and there, but he was already crawling toward the intersection so I put my car into gear and followed. He wasn't kidding; it seemed like two minutes had passed before we were parking.

The second I pulled into the space, I unlatched my seatbelt and hopped out of the car.

"You have a Shelby Mustang!" I exclaimed, circling the beauty that was his vehicle. "'67 GT 500?"

"Yeah." He climbed out, grinning. "You like cars?"

"Are you kidding?" I shot him a quick, incredulous glance before returning my gaze to the vision in front of me.

It *was* a vision. Gleaming silver with thick black racing stripes down the middle, it looked like a predator on wheels. I'd never seen one this pristine outside of a movie. Maybe he'd let me ride in it one day. Asking to drive it was too forward, even for me.

"This has to be one of the most beautiful cars ever made," I said reverently. The Mustang I'd resuscitated back when I was in high school was a '69 coupe, but in no way did it compare to Rio's.

"You can touch it if you want."

I blinked at him. "Really?"

He chuckled, leaning against the driver side door. "I don't think she'll mind."

I shook my head. If it were my car, no one would be allowed near it. Ever. But since he said it was okay, I touched the left front fender. With one finger.

Warm under my fingertip, like it was flesh and blood. Emboldened, I laid my palm on it and caressed the passenger side. "What kind of engine?"

"A Ford 427."

"Beautiful," I murmured. I felt his stare on me and I looked up to find him studying me. The ever present amusement was in his eyes but there was something else too—something deep and complicated and searching. And I wasn't comfortable with the surge of feeling it aroused in me.

I flushed, ducked my head, and dropped my hand. "It's a nice car."

"Thanks." He tipped his head. "Ready to go?"

"Yeah." I fell into step beside him. After a moment of silence, I asked, "Do you know what would happen if Microsoft manufactured cars?"

Rio glanced at me sideways. "What would happen?"

"Your car would crash twice a day for no reason."

He laughed. "And the airbags would ask 'are you sure?' before deploying."

I blinked. Did he just not only get my joke but laugh at it? *And* make an excellent comeback?

Weirded out, I didn't realize where we'd arrived until

he stopped and motioned to a dimly lit doorway. "It's right here."

I stared at the black door. "Are you sure?"

"Come on." He took my elbow and my heart stopped.

It was the barest pressure, but I felt it spread up my arm, down my spine to my toes and back. Twice. Hell, my nipples stood at attention. That was talent.

As soon as I got over that sensation (why couldn't Barry's touch affect my nipples this way?), I noticed the interior of the bar.

I blinked. The floor was shiny (not sticky at all), it didn't reek of stale beer, and the upholstery was leather, not new but definitely not ratty. Nice.

Instead of taking me over to one of the booths in the back, he escorted me to the well-lit bar.

I admit it, I was a bit taken aback. Why didn't I rate a dark booth? As I hopped onto a bar stool, I wondered if guys just didn't see me as that type of woman. I was beginning to have major doubts about myself. I knew I wasn't angelic like Daphne, but I didn't think I was that bad either.

Maybe I was. Look at Ian—he brought two of his friends so he wouldn't have to be alone with me. Jeremy wouldn't come closer to me than an Internet connection. And Johnny only wanted to get me in bed but, if Barry was right, he'd be way disappointed.

I gazed at Rio. Had I misread him? Was this a friendly thing? It had to be. Otherwise he would have sat next to me in the dark booth in the back and tried to feel me up.

I looked down at my boobs. Not that I had much in that department; Daphne got it all. Greedy, I tell you.

It got me to thinking: Why did he want to see me again? I doubted he had a shortage of women to go out with. Why me? I only wanted to know because I needed to make sure he asked me out again.

That was my story, anyway, and I was sticking to it.

So I decided to subtly weasel the answer out of him. I could be sly. He'd never know what I was after.

I turned in my seat to face him and said, "Why did you want me to stop by the gym?"

I know—the subtlety of a brick.

Rio apparently wasn't one for beating around the bush either. He ran his fingers over his super-short crew cut, already dry from his shower, and said, "I felt like I had to secure a way to see you again or I'd never see you. And that seemed—" he frowned "—unbearable."

He looked as puzzled as I felt. I waited for my intuition to scream *creep*, but there was just placid silence. In fact, except for the discomfort of the acute sexual attraction, I felt supremely at ease with him. Not to mention that if not seeing me was unbearable, he'd be sure to ask me out again. That thought caused a ripple of excitement. Directly related to getting Barry back, I told myself.

"Hmm." What else could I say? That's great? I feel the same way? Let's go rent a hotel room?

Focus. I was here to get back together with Barry. Rio was just a means.

I gave him a sidelong glance. If only I could clean him up and take him to the party. But even if I could disguise his sexuality (ha!), there was the fact that he worked as a boxing instructor at a gym. My parents wouldn't see him as living up to his potential. And he drove a gas-guzzler. Granted, it was a gas-guzzler that showed great taste and class (even Dad would drool over it). Still.

Pout. It would have been fun. But Barry was the only feasible option.

I sighed, deep and long.

"That was quite a sigh." Rio signaled the bartender.

"It's been a long day."

"Want to tell me about it?"

Tempting, but I didn't think he'd take well to my plans. At the moment, I wasn't sure how I felt about my plans myself. So I said, "It's nothing that a beer won't cure," realizing too late how I sounded like a lush.

He didn't notice. Or he was too kind to comment. "What would you like?"

"A pale ale, please."

Rio ordered my beer and a Hefeweisen for himself. The bartender poured them while we watched in silence.

I picked up my glass as soon as he set it in front of me. Sipping slowly, I tried to center myself, but it was hard since guilt was starting to settle in. Maybe Matt was right and I *was* temporarily insane. I should have come up with an excuse to bale out on this date.

Hell, I didn't even know if it was a date. What made a date? Food and drink? Food and kissing?

I glanced at his lips. What would they feel like? Not like mushy triceps, that's for sure.

"Is your beer okay?"

I looked up to find Rio watching me, concern wrinkling his forehead. I tried to smile reassuringly. "It's great." Then I realized I hadn't had a sip lately, so I took one quickly.

The corner of his mouth kicked up. "Good."

"Is your beer okay?" I asked, just to be equitable.

"I'm sure it's fine."

I winced. "I'm being a moron, aren't I?"

"Not at all. I think it's cute."

I groaned. "Bunnies are cute."

"Then what are you?"

"Fierce," I said without thought. Then I thought of MacGyver and added, "And resourceful."

He held up his pint. "To using everything at your disposal."

I blinked and then clinked my glass against his. "That's a fighter's principle."

"What is?" he asked as he took a sip.

I waved my hand toward him. "Using everything at your disposal. You aren't a fighter."

"I'm a boxer," he said with a small frown.

"Yeah, but that's not really fighting." The second it came out, I knew I'd put my foot in my mouth. I didn't even need to see the way his forehead furrowed. "Wait. That's not what I meant. I know you're a boxer, but boxing has rules. You can't even knee the groin in boxing."

He winced. "Damn good thing too."

"So you can't very well use everything around you."

"Sure you can."

"No, you can't."

He sighed. "I don't deny there are rules in boxing, but that doesn't mean you don't use everything you can to your advantage. Boxing is as much strategy as it is brute strength."

I snorted before I could help myself.

His eyes narrowed. "How much do you know about fighting?"

"A little." Slight understatement. I was a fighting goddess.

"How much is a little?" he asked suspiciously.

Enjoying myself, I shrugged and took a casual sip of my beer. "I've studied Kung Fu here and there."

He leaned close and said, "Fight me."

I blinked. "Excuse me?"

"Fight me," he repeated. "Come by the gym sometime and work out with me."

I watched him drink his beer, his eyes on mine over the rim of his glass. *Fight him.* The thought made something in the pit of my stomach quiver. In a good way.

Rio set his beer down. "Chicken?"

I shook my head. "Calling me a chicken isn't going to work."

"Why not?"

"Because I've used that tactic on my sister all my life."

"You have a sister?"

"Yeah." Props to me for not gagging as I admitted it.

He gazed at me steadily, waiting. I knew he was waiting for me to elaborate, but I didn't want to talk about Daphne. She wasn't relevant.

Fine. Okay, I admit it. I didn't want to tell him about her because I was afraid he'd want to go out with her instead. Hey, I had precedence. Every guy I brought home while Daphne was home visiting lost interest in me the second they saw her.

Hell, I bet that was why my mom wanted to have Barry at the party, so he could meet Daphne and fall in love. That made me frown.

"You have the most expressive face."

"Huh?" I asked articulately, facing him.

Rio trailed a finger down my hairline. "I can almost see your thoughts pass over your features."

I grimaced. I hoped not. My thoughts weren't very pretty lately.

Get a grip. I pulled up the mental list I composed on the way over and decided to ask him how well he knew Barry. "So Rio—" I frowned. "What kind of name is Rio anyway?"

"What kind of name is Philomena?"

Touché. "Greek. My mom was going through a mythical phase when she had my sister and me."

"Let me guess. Your sister's name is Persephone."

"No." I scowled into my beer. "She got a normal name. Daphne."

"I like Philomena better."

I studied him. He had to be kidding me. "You do?"

He nodded. "It's more interesting. Complicated but beautiful in its simplicity. Sexy."

Now I knew he was kidding. "You never said what kind of name Rio is."

"It's short for Riordan. I suppose we've never officially met." He stuck his hand out. "Riordan McKenna."

"Philomena Donovan." As I slipped my hand into his,

goose bumps crawled up and down my arms. The shivery kind that triggers a pool of warmth between your thighs.

Then I frowned as his words registered. "That sounds like an Irish name."

"I'm Irish."

I leaned back and gave him an exaggerated once-over. "Yeah, I see how you could be Irish," I deadpanned. It was his mocha skin—not.

"My dad's Irish but Mom's Puerto Rican. I get my coloring from her. My eyes and my name come from my dad." He grinned. "Mom says my eyes were wasted on me, but she's just jealous."

I looked into said eyes. Definitely not a waste.

"Mom always wanted a daughter too. She complains that the family is too full of testosterone."

"Do you have any brothers?"

"No. Just me and my dad."

I nodded. If Rio's dad were anything like him, I could believe it.

"Go out with me again."

I blinked. "Excuse me?"

"Go out with me." He rubbed my knuckles and smiled in an adorably boyish way that seemed like it should be at odds with his manly exterior. "Please."

Staring into his eyes, I realized I'd forgotten all about Barry, Daphne's party, and my parents breathing down my back. At this moment, all that mattered was the touch of his MacGyver hands on me and his earnest look that showed just how much he wanted to see me again.

But everything came back with a crash, weighing on me so heavily I could barely breathe. I wanted to shove it all away and go back to enjoying Rio's company.

Only I had an objective to reach. So I tried to smile. "I'd like that."

And as much as I meant it, I still felt guilty.

Chapter Eleven

"You can learn a lot about someone by the things he keeps on his desk—provided you can get to his desk."
— MacGyver, "The Eraser" Episode #24

By the next morning the plan was back on with renewed force.

I hadn't meant to go back to it. Not really. The night before had made me question my motives. How important was this scheme anyway? I was going to all this trouble to win Barry back just to please my parents, and spending time with Rio made me seriously question my logic in wanting Barry back. I admit, my hormones may have had something to do with how I felt about Rio, but they were tingly with excitement and hard to ignore.

Until my dad called.

I don't know why I didn't let the call forward to my voicemail. Guess I was in a good mood and thought nothing could bring me down.

I should have known better.

I picked up the receiver on the second ring. "Mena speaking."

"Hello, Mena."

"Hey, Dad. What's up?" Unusual for him to call me,

much less call me at work, but in my upbeat frame of mind I didn't think twice about it.

"Your mother and I have been trying to reach Daphne for a couple of days now but keep getting her answering machine. Have you heard from her?"

My spirits drooped a little. Daphne again. "Uh, I spoke to her last night."

It wasn't a lie. I did speak to her. I just didn't tell him it was face to face.

"Hmm." I could hear him rolling that tidbit of information over in his brain. "This is unlike her."

I heard the faint worry in his voice; I felt bad for contributing to it, but I'd promised Daphne. As a concession, I said, "Want me to pass her a message when I talk to her next?"

"Yes." His relief made me feel like I made the right decision. "Tell her to call her mother or me. And tell her I'm going on a nature walk the Sunday after her party and wanted to know if she wants to come along. It's Sheep Moth mating season, you know."

I waited for him to ask me if I wanted to come along too. Each second that ticked by made me realize how silly I was for expecting that. He wanted to spend time with Daphne, his favorite daughter.

"I better let you get back to work. You should come to dinner soon, Mena."

"Yeah, Dad. Sure." I mumbled my goodbyes and hung up, my chest heavy. Would it have been so terrible for him to ask me if I wanted to watch Sheep Moths mate too?

The thoughts churned over and over in my head for the next hour until I'd decided I had to go ahead with my plan. My parents needed to see that I was as worthy as Daphne. Even if that took Barry. Hey, I'd do what I had to do.

As if my morning hadn't been absolute crap (at least after my dad called and burst my bubble), I looked up to see Johnny heading down the hall straight for me.

Shit. And I'd been doing such a great job avoiding him since his email barrage.

I glanced under my desk, knowing it was too late to duck. If I saw him, he saw me. So I sighed and gathered my courage.

By the time he got to me, I had a mild smile pasted on my face. "Hey, Johnny."

"There she is. Just the woman I wanted."

I flushed. At least he could have tempered it with a "to see" at the end. But he did it deliberately (his cocked eyebrow was a good indication).

Please, God, don't let anyone else have heard. I did a quick scan of my work area. Several of the other programmers had popped their heads over their cubicles and were smirking at me.

Guess I wasn't that lucky.

He sat on the edge of my desk (which creaked so ominously I thought it was going to collapse—it's only made of plywood, after all) and leaned toward me. "Pucker up, Donovan."

"Johnny!" I pushed him back and he fell off his perch.

So I pushed him a little too hard. I didn't feel bad about it in the least, mostly because he was making a spectacle of me in front of my peers. All the other programmers were watching with interest and whispering now.

"Come on, Donovan." Johnny got to his knees, rubbing his butt, and crawled toward me. "Just one kiss. I'm dying here."

I stuck out my booted foot to stop him from advancing. It hit his chest and, thank God, he halted. "You know I'm not that kind of girl," I hissed through my teeth, conscious of all the interested stares we were getting.

He grabbed my ankle and pulled, which made my chair roll toward him. "Come on. Just one." His eyes lit with an unholy gleam. "Unless you want to go back to your electronics closet."

"It's called a server room." At least he could get his ter-
minology right. I used my other leg to push away from him.
"And I'm not going anywhere with you. Let go of my leg."

He tugged me closer. "Then promise you'll go out
with me."

"No." No way was I going to be intimidated into a date
I didn't want.

"I won't leave until you agree." His fingers started to slide
up the leather of my boot, slipping under my pant leg.

I yelped when I felt him brush my skin. "Fine! Okay.
I'll go out with you. Call me tonight."

"No."

I blinked.

He smiled knowingly. "You never answer your phone.
We're setting a date now."

Sigh. "When?"

"Friday."

"I can't. My sister's in town."

His smile grew. "Bring her along."

That was actually a great idea. I could pass Daphne off
to him. I beamed. "That's great. Friday. Meet me at Kells.
Nine o'clock."

He narrowed his eyes suspiciously. "Is your sister a
dog?"

"Hell, no. She's beautiful."

I guess my answer was firm enough that it appeased
him. "Kells on Friday." He gave me a look that had promise oozing out of it. "I can't wait."

As soon as his back was to me, I crossed my eyes. I
watched him walk away, mostly to make sure he wouldn't
jump out and attack me when I wasn't looking.

"Hey, Donovan. What are you? Human catnip?"

I looked up to see the guys all grinning at me. The blue
glow of their monitors made them all look demented
(it didn't take much). I did the only thing I could do: I
stuck my tongue out at them.

"Oh, yeah, baby. More," one of them groaned, and they all laughed.

I made a rude gesture with my middle finger and tried to ignore them the rest of the afternoon.

By six, I was so ready to go home. If I had to endure one more joke, I wouldn't be responsible for what would happen to the engineering team (two words: semiautomatic rifle). I grabbed my stuff and took off for the bus stop.

The bus was late. I stood outside in the drizzle for fifty-three minutes before one showed up. By the time I got home I was pissy and looking forward to a soothing, quiet bath. But then I remembered Daphne was here.

"Shit," I muttered under my breath. I was so not into dealing with her tonight. But I had to, because I needed my computer and it was in the room she'd commandeered.

Maybe I'd get lucky and she'd be out.

Heading back down the stairs, I quickly unlocked the door in the off chance she'd notice and then took the stairs two at a time. "Daph! You home?"

"Don't call me Daph," came the faint reply.

When I got to the top of the stairs I looked left and right. Where the hell was she?

I strode down the hall to the bathroom. As I reached for the door, it swung open.

We both shrieked (mine was more of a surprised gasp). Daphne jumped back until she was pressed against the counter, her hand on her heart.

"Oh my God, Mena! Can't you make a little noise?"

"I did. And you replied." My sister's intelligence was overrated at times if you asked me.

"That's not what I meant."

Frankly, I didn't care what she meant. I needed out of my damp clothes. I strode to my room, closed the door, and stripped. Wrapping myself in my terrycloth robe, I thought about how I could get closer to Barry. Seeing me with Rio seemed to work really well. He'd practically been frothing, he was so disgruntled at the gym. I needed to engineer more of that.

I needed to get him to run into Rio and me.

But to do that, I needed to know his every move. Which meant I needed my computer.

After I bunched my hair into a ponytail and took several calming breaths, I left the bedroom. "Daph!"

"Don't call me Daph."

The placid reply came from the living room, so that's where I headed. She sat on the couch, the TV on, watching some sort of science program.

I cleared my throat. "I need to use my computer for awhile."

She gave me a sidelong glance. "Are you asking my permission?"

"It's in my office, which you've commandeered."

"Oh. Yes. Go ahead. I'm thinking of going out for dinner anyway."

By herself? What was I saying—it wasn't like she had friends. I almost felt bad enough to suggest going with her. Almost. I came to my senses as soon as I opened my mouth. I couldn't imagine anything more excruciating than spending an hour with her one-on-one.

Before I could get myself into trouble, I hustled into my office and closed the door.

Then I screamed.

Daphne burst through the door. "What?"

The door whacked my butt and set me sailing onto the bed.

"What is it?" Daphne brandished the remote control. "Is there someone in here with you?"

"Someone's broken in and robbed me!" I wailed. "My furniture's all wrong."

"Oh, is that all?" She dropped her arm. "I rearranged a few things."

"My furniture?" I scowled at her. "Where's the crate that had all my old *Wired* magazines?"

She shrugged. "I recycled them for you when I was cleaning up the room."

"Cleaning up my room?" I looked around. *Shit.* She'd messed up my entire office. I rushed to my computer. "What happened to my desk?"

"I cleared the top and wiped it down."

"But all my papers . . . My notes . . . My *stuff* . . ." I looked around for them, but all I saw was my keyboard and trackball neatly centered on the desktop. I bet if I pulled out a ruler, they'd be perfectly centered on the monitor.

"I went through all the papers and filed them," Daphne said proudly.

I goggled at her. Was I supposed to be happy about that? "They were already filed and in order."

She frowned. "They were all over your desk."

"They were in order all over my desk. How am I going to find anything now?" I put a hand to my forehead and willed myself to calm down. This wasn't important. I needed to concentrate on Barry.

Then I saw them. Blank walls.

I gasped. "Where are my posters?"

"Oh, I took those down."

I clenched my fists so I wouldn't wrap them around her neck. "They were vintage MacGyver posters. Originals. You can't find posters like that anymore." I took a deep breath. "Tell me you didn't throw them away."

"They were scruffy," she said defensively.

"Tell me you didn't throw them away."

"Fine." She huffed. "I rolled them up and put them under the bed."

I dropped to my knees and looked under the bed. Wilting in relief when I found them, I cradled them in my arms and got to my feet. "I can't believe you took down MacGyver."

She waved the remote at my bundle. "I can't believe you're still into that. You should have outgrown it by now."

I narrowed my eyes and shifted so she couldn't touch my posters. She'd better not disparage MacGyver.

Then it registered that she was wielding a remote control. "What were you going to do with that? Turn the burglar off?"

She looked down at it and blushed. "I thought you were in trouble. Obviously I shouldn't have bothered." She turned on her heels and marched out.

"Yeah, you shouldn't have," I called after her, talking more about cleaning my office than her coming to my rescue. Though that was pretty ludicrous in itself.

I set down the posters on the floor next to my desk and wiggled the trackball until my computer came to life.

Before I began doing anything, I took a moment to center myself (Daphne's maid service really upset me). I did a mental breakdown of what I needed to do and why.

Primary objective: I needed to know where Barry was going to be to bump into him while I was with Rio.

I tapped a finger against my lips. What was the best way to do that? I opened a browser and pulled up his Web site, but there wasn't any info on what he'd be doing the next few days.

Emails. He and his new girlfriend probably emailed at least some of their plans. It was the only way he ever communicated with me. His cell phone was purely for business. And his mother.

I shook my head. Reading other people's emails wasn't right. Not to mention that willfully trespassing into someone else's server was a touch illegal.

Okay, can we say felony?

But I was only going to look at a couple of Barry's emails. Not even look, just glance. I wasn't going to tamper, and they wouldn't be able to trace it back to me (I was that good). It wouldn't do any harm.

"I shouldn't do this," I said finally.

And then I opened a terminal emulator and started the relatively simple process of hacking into the email server.

The security on his company's mail server was a joke, and I got in way too easily. It almost negated my guilt, because if you're going to make it that easy, you deserve to have your server messed with.

I made quick work of Barry's recent emails, skimming through until I found one dated this morning.

Rubbing the tip of my nose, I quashed another wave of guilt and opened it.

To: bwallace@wallacecorp.net
From: sunshine_happy@yahoo.com
Subject: Hi honey!

I had a great time last night. Dinner was so great—I LOVE Hurley's. Maybe next time we go I can ask the chef how to make that mousse thing with the cheese.

But do you know the best part about last night? When you kissed me goodnight at my door. It was *SOOO* romantic! I thought I was going to ooze out from my toes.

I've got to get back to work. I'll miss you tonight! I'll think about you every second we're apart. Will you call me when you get home?

X O X O X
Cindy

Blech. Ooze out her toes? I was tempted to email her myself and recommend a doctor for that.

And she was delusional if she thought Barry was going to call her tonight. He was abysmal on the phone unless it had to do with work, and then he could be on it for hours. Maybe she'd get fed up with him and dump him.

"It'd make my life easier," I murmured. One thing was certain: If he kissed her at the door, they weren't having sex. Another plus. It meant a) they weren't that close yet and b) Barry hadn't had sex in weeks. That'd make him susceptible.

I pursed my lips thoughtfully as I opened his reply.

To: sunshine_happy@yahoo.com
From: bwallace@wallacecorp.net
Subject: Hi back.

Sweet Blossom,

I'm glad you like Hurley's so much. It's my favorite restaurant. Would you like to have dinner at my place tomorrow night? I can get take-out from Hurley's.

I can't wait to kiss you again. And your toes. Did I mention how adorable they are? Like little candies. I could just eat them up.

I have meetings all day into the evening. Call you when I get home around ten-thirty tonight, Sweets.

Love,
Barry

Sweet Blossom? He never called me any endearments. Pout. He obviously liked her a lot. He signed his email with "love." I'd been lucky if he took the time to type his name. And the whole thing with the toes was just plain unsanitary.

But at least now I knew that they were having dinner at his place tomorrow. It was a start.

One question: What excuse did I use for going over to his house?

Chapter Twelve

Lessons Learned from MacGyver
#92
*A party can be an invitation for someone to hack into your
    computer.*

I finally came up with the perfect reason to go to see
Barry: I'd return something he left at my house. Guys
always wanted their stuff back after a breakup, right?

Picking out what to wear on my mission to Barry's
proved to be a challenge. There was a balance I had to
strike: sexy without being obvious, desirable without
being blatant.

Hard, but certainly not impossible. I settled on a
denim miniskirt and a lacy sleeveless top in leopard print
(to remind Barry what an animal I was—or could be if
he wanted to give it another try).

Rio called me as I finished dressing. "Go out with me
tomorrow."

The pit of my stomach shivered at his low command.
I grinned even though I gave him trouble (I couldn't
help it—it's in my nature). "You have nerve, ordering
me instead of asking."

"If I asked, you might say no."

Oh, he was good. "But you didn't say please."

"Somehow I don't think you care much about manners."

I shrugged and went with a different argument. "Tomorrow's Friday. What makes you think I'm free?"

"It's not a matter of you being free. It's a matter of how much you want to see me again."

"You're awfully cocky," I said, grinning.

"You like cocky."

There were a thousand nuances in his voice, and all of them were speaking directly to my womanly parts.

Then I winced, remembering I'd told Johnny to meet me and Daphne at Kells. Damn. "Actually, Rio, I'm supposed to meet up with a friend and my sister."

"Oh."

I must be perverse because his disappointment made me jubilant. "If you don't mind, you could meet me there."

Rio perked up right away. "You don't mind? I'd hate to intrude."

"You won't be intruding. I'd love it if you came. I'd love to see you."

Okay, truthfully, maybe a small part of me wanted him to come along because it gave me a date to boast to Barry about. But I *was* looking forward to seeing Rio. Actually, I was kind of surprised at how happy I felt that he was going to be there.

Only I didn't have the right to feel that way. And, since I was going for this truth crap, there was also a layer of something that felt an awful lot like self-disgust.

But I shoved all of that aside. I had things to do. I told Rio the details of where and when, hung up, and went to find Daphne. "Daph!"

"Don't call me that," came from my office/her bedroom.

I pushed open the door, which was ajar, and leaned in the doorway. I tried not to notice the room itself; it still raised my blood pressure to see how she'd messed with my stuff. "Hey."

She looked up from where she was propped on the bed reading. "What is it?"

I tried to see what she was reading, but she angled the book so I couldn't see it. Probably some scientific text about the characteristics of the twenty-third chromosome, or something equally fascinating. My sister really knew how to cut loose and have fun. (Yes, that was sarcastic.)

I shook my head and got back to the reason why I was there. "Are you doing anything tomorrow night?" Ha! As if. But I thought I should be polite since I needed her to come along.

She stared at me with her cool gaze. "Why do you ask?"

I tried to look nonchalant. "I'm going out and I thought you might like to go."

"You did." It wasn't a question as much as an incredulous statement.

"Well, sure. You wanted to go out and experience some nightlife, didn't you?"

She eyes narrowed suspiciously. "Yes . . ."

"I thought this would be a good opportunity." I smiled winningly. Mental note: Check in front of mirror to make sure smile is actually winning and not sickly.

"Hmm."

I tried to decipher what that "hmm" meant, but with Daphne, anything was possible. She didn't exactly emote.

So I tried another tack. "I invited this guy I think you'll like."

"You did?" Her brow furrowed like I'd uttered the most profound riddle.

That hurt. I wasn't *that* bad a sister. I hoped not, anyway. I pushed aside the pout that was coming on and concentrated on my goal. "Of course. I think you'll like him. He's successful, smart, and handsome."

"All right." She smiled. Her version of a smile, which was more of a bare tilt of her lips.

"Good." Relieved, I turned to leave. "I'm going out now, but I'll be back soon."

"Lock the door on your way out."

"Right."

"I mean it. I know you're leaving it unlocked to bother me."

"I'm truly hurt you think that." I waved over my shoulder. "Later!"

"Mena, I mean it."

"I know." That's why I left it unlocked again.

Evil grin. Being the younger sister had to have *some* perks.

I hopped into my car and drove to Barry's. I had to concentrate to remember exactly where it was. In the year we'd dated I'd been there only a few times. Barry usually came to my place for sex. It was that unwritten rule we had about keeping our lives separate, I supposed. But now that his blossom was having dinner at his place, I was beginning to think that maybe he didn't like me enough to share his space. Pout. I was as likable as the next girl. At least I thought so.

I frowned and parked in front of his home. It was a fancy pseudo-colonial I think he'd told me his mother picked out. I remembered thinking how fussy it was, on the outside as well as the inside. Didn't seem to suit him, but what did I know?

"Now or never." I took a deep breath, hopped out of the car, and stalked up the walkway to the front door. Hand raised, I hesitated there for a second, wondering what I was doing. The answer was immediate: Showing my parents I was as good as Daphne. I couldn't back down from this.

I knocked firmly, waited two seconds, and then rang the doorbell for good measure. As the door swung open, I pasted a smile on my face. "Hi, Barry."

He stared down at me and blinked several times. "Mena?"

Didn't he recognize me anymore? "Yeah. I was just driving by—"

"You were?"

Okay, so maybe that was a little hard to believe, because he didn't live close to anywhere I might want to go. But that was beside the point. "Yeah. I had an, um, errand."

"Oh." His frown deepened. "Mena, this isn't a good time."

"No problem. I understand." I nodded, wondering how I was going to get into his foyer with the way he was guarding the door. "I just wanted to—"

"Barry?" A sticky-sweet voice drifted from the living room. "Is everything okay?" Barry's blossom stepped into the entryway, a tentative smile on her lips.

In person, she was more like Daphne than on the Web. Except for her eyes, which were a warm, approachable brown rather than an icy, stay-away-from-me blue. I tried to find something wrong with her—a big wart on her chin or bad fashion sense—but Barry's blossom was nothing short of perfection. Long, shiny blond hair, big brown eyes, and creamy skin (lots of it—her dress was tiny). Even the expression in her eyes held no hint of malice or anything but friendly inquisitiveness.

Did I mention her dress was really little?

Barry cleared his throat. "Uh . . . Um . . ."

Glancing at him, I saw he was torn between complete adoration and horror. I guessed the adoration was for his sweet blossom and the horror was for me. (I'm intuitive that way.)

His blossom took the initiative. She stepped forward with her bright smile and stretched her hand out. "I'm Cindy. Are you a friend of Barry's?"

I snapped out of my stupor quickly enough to realize this might have been the opportunity I was looking for. I accepted her shake. "Yes. I'm Mena. I'm sorry if I'm interrupting anything."

"Oh! I'm so happy to meet you." She squeezed my

hand between both of hers. "Barry's told me so much about you."

I flashed on Cameron Diaz in *My Best Friend's Wedding* telling Julia Roberts something very similar right before she tried to kill Julia with her driving. No way was I getting anywhere near a car with Cindy.

Barry cleared his throat again. "Was there a reason you stopped by?"

"Barry, don't be rude," Cindy chided as if she had the right. "Invite her in."

Before I could open my mouth, Cindy jerked me inside. "We have enough for dinner, right?"

"Oh, no. I wouldn't want to impose," I said politely. I really didn't; I'd probably choke if I tried to eat anything.

"Then a drink." She smiled warmly at me and led me into the living room. "Close the door, Barry, and get Mena a drink."

Barry looked as shell-shocked as I felt, but I noticed he quickly hopped to do Cindy's bidding. I pouted. He was never that obedient with me, the bastard.

Cindy sat down on a fancy, uncomfortable couch and pulled me down next to her. "You'll have to tell me all about Barry."

"Um. Yeah." I smiled, hoping I didn't look like I was going to throw up. I certainly felt like that though.

Barry returned quickly. I'm not sure I'd ever seen him move that fast. I had the impression he didn't want to leave me alone with Cindy. I wondered why.

"You didn't tell me why you're here," Barry said as he handed us our drinks.

Champagne. I wrinkled my nose and pretended to take a sip before setting it on the table in front of me. "I was going through some stuff and I found this." I riffled through my purse and pulled out the CD. "I thought you might want it back."

Barry frowned as he took it. "Sounds of the Forest?"

"The rainforest," I corrected.

He studied the cover before he finally said, "This isn't mine."

I blinked. "It isn't?"

Of course, I knew it wasn't. I'd bought it once when I was having trouble sleeping. I thought the soothing sounds would lull me to sleep. Mostly it just served to improve my tropical bird call.

My idea of returning something to Barry was brilliant. The only flaw was Barry had never left anything at my place. So I had to improvise.

I pursed my lips because I thought it'd make me look puzzled. "Are you sure it's not yours?"

"Positive." He handed it back to me.

"Huh." I stared at it for a second and slipped it back into my purse. "I could have sworn it was."

Cindy patted my hand. "Now that you're here, Mena, tell me about you."

I didn't want to tell her anything about me, except maybe that I'd had a parent-pleasing boyfriend whom I wanted back. How would she take that? But I shrugged and said, "I study martial arts," so she'd know she shouldn't mess with me.

She perked up. "For real?"

"Yeah."

"You aren't kidding me?"

"Nope."

"Wow."

Scintillating conversation. But my feathers were somewhat smoothed by her impressed gawking. I thought of telling her I was a third degree black belt and that I could break her with just a look, but I thought that might be overkill so I kept quiet.

I did, however, have the presence of mind to bring Rio into the conversation. "That's why Rio and I get along so great. Because we're both fighters." I fluttered my eyelashes and glanced at Barry to see if he took the bait.

Bingo. At the mention of Rio's name, Barry stiffened and set his champagne flute down. "Rio?"

Then I had another brilliant idea: I'd ask for Barry's permission to date his friend.

Well, not his permission per se, but asking him if he minded was a great way to highlight that I was dating Rio. It'd give him a chance to feel jealous again too.

So I fluttered my lashes some more. "You don't mind if I date him, do you, Barry? You guys being friends and all."

Cindy answered for him. "Of course he doesn't mind. Do you, Pookie?"

"No." He scowled. "No, I don't."

Woo-hah. I hid my grin behind my glass and pretended to take another swig of the wretched champagne.

"I like Rio *sooo* much," Cindy chirped in her saccharine voice.

"You do?" She'd only been dating Barry for a week and she'd already met Rio? I'd gone out with him for a year and I'd barely met any of his friends. I frowned at Barry.

He downed the rest of his drink.

Oblivious, Cindy nodded. "We should all go out sometime. Like a double date or something."

"Right," I said sarcastically. Then I blinked and smiled wide. "*Right.* That'd be super."

"Totally." Cindy smiled delightedly, not knowing how easily she was falling into my plans.

"Maybe even tomorrow." I spoke quickly, aware Barry was beginning to stir. I needed Cindy to agree to my suggestion before he could veto it. "We're going to Kells and it'd be great if you could stop by."

"Oh!" She clapped her hands together. "That'd be fab. Is that the new champagne lounge?"

"Uh, no." Kells? I resisted the urge to guffaw. "It's an Irish pub."

"I don't think you'd like it, sweetie," Barry said quickly. "They serve beer."

She shrugged flippantly. "I've always wanted to try beer. It'll be fun."

She'd never had beer? What alternate universe had she been sequestered in?

Before he could offer any other objections, I said, "Great. Nine o'clock."

She clapped her hands together again, once. "I have to go shopping for the perfect outfit."

I raised my brows at Barry. What planet did he find this woman on anyway?

He cleared his throat. "Sweetie, dinner's getting cold . . ."

That was my cue to leave, but the perverse part of me settled back like I didn't understand I was being subtly encouraged to move along.

His sweet blossom didn't play along either, though I'm not certain she got it. She grasped my hand and said, "You should stay for dinner." She smiled at Barry. "We have enough food, don't we, Pookie?"

"Uh . . ." His will visibly shriveled under her sweet imploring gaze. "Well, I guess."

I shook my head. Pathetic. I was tempted to stay, but I wanted to be more subtle than that. "I need to get home. But thanks for the invite." I disengaged myself from Cindy's eager grip and edged toward the foyer. "But you guys should go ahead and eat. I'll show myself out."

Barry pulled Cindy to her feet and practically dragged her toward the archway that led to the dining room and kitchen. "You don't mind?"

I recognized the question for what it was: his proper upbringing requiring him to be polite. "Go ahead and enjoy yourselves, kids. I'll see you tomorrow."

I smiled and waved as I walked out of the room before Cindy could follow me. In my haste, I bumped into the table in the foyer where Barry dumped the crap in his pockets when he came home.

The table rocked and his cell phone jumped off and onto the floor. Wincing, I reached down to pick it up.

Knowing how much he loved his phone, I flipped it open to make sure it wasn't damaged. I didn't want to be accused of foul play later.

I shook my head. The idiot left Bluetooth on. It was such a security risk—I don't know how many times I'd warned him. Anyone who had a Bluetooth device within a certain range could get access to everything stored on his cell.

Shrugging, I flipped it shut. And I froze when it really hit me. The Bluetooth functionality on Barry's cell phone was on. *On.*

This was opportunity slapping me upside the head. If MacGyver were here, he'd—well, he'd rig the phone as a detonation device and blow up Barry's house.

But I didn't need to go that far. If I turned on Bluetooth on my phone, I could download all his calendar information—his dates and appointments, all his contact info . . . I'd know where he was and when.

It'd be accidental, of course. Though this wasn't a felony like trespassing on a server. At least I didn't think so.

I rubbed the tip of my nose. It wasn't like I had to use the info, but it'd be a comfort to have. Just in case.

I pulled my phone out, clicked Bluetooth on, and synced the devices. *Come on, come on.* I waved at Barry's phone, which I'm sure made it transfer everything faster. Once it finished, I flipped the phone shut, put it back on the table, and turned to leave.

Then I stopped.

"Hell." I turned around, intending to grab Barry's phone again, but I walked into the table again, only this time hard enough to send a lacquered dish skittering to the floor.

"Mena? You still here?" Barry called from the kitchen.

Oh, shit. "Just tying my shoe." My fingers fumbled over buttons as I accessed his calendar and deleted a couple of entries marked *Cindy.*

When I heard the clicking of Barry's dress loafers on

the parquet floor of the hall from the kitchen, I flipped the phone shut and put it back.

"See you tomorrow," I called out as I ran out the door. I hurried to my car before Barry noticed I was wearing slip-on shoes.

Heart pounding, I drove off. I was about a block away when I realized his Bluetooth was still on. I screeched to a stop and rubbed my nose.

MacGyver would go for it.

"I shouldn't do this," I told myself. I didn't even know if it'd work; I only read about it online. It would be like an experiment. To test the boundaries of technology.

"I *really* shouldn't do this," I repeated. But I didn't listen. Instead I turned around, drove back, and parked several blocks away. I hopped out of the car and softly shut the door. Dropping into a crouch, I hobbled through the neighbors' yards, over the short fence, and into Barry's—right in a rose bush.

"Shit," I mouthed, conscious of the lit kitchen windows fifty feet away. Thank God there were curtains, otherwise I'm sure Barry and Cindy would have seen me.

Biting my lip as thorns prodded my skin, I tried to gently untangle myself. I mouthed another curse.

Finally I got myself loose, if worse for wear, and snuck around the side of the house to the front. Fortunately there was a bush on either side of his door that provided adequate coverage for me to hide. I ducked behind the one on the right and flipped open my cell.

A minute later it was done: I'd planted several calls from other women onto Barry's call log.

"Who knew?" I whispered, shaking my head in wonder. I closed my phone, scurried back to my car, and took off. All the way home I swore that I was never going to do anything like that again. And I wasn't going to use the info I'd stolen. I'd get rid of it.

Later.

Really, I would.

Chapter Thirteen

Lessons Learned from MacGyver
#48
Sometimes even your worst enemy needs your help.

Friday night. My goal: get Barry back.

It wasn't going to be easy. Cindy had managed to get her hooks into him solidly for only having known him for so short a time period.

But Rio was going to drive Barry into a jealous frenzy *and* I had home court advantage. Kells was my turf. Hell, she'd never even had a beer. And I'd have Rio to make me look desirable.

"Not to mention I look damn good," I said to my reflection. I opted for jeans tonight because I thought a skirt would be out of place. Plus my favorite pair of Diesel's fit like perfection and made my butt look grabbable. My spaghetti-strap camisole could have doubled for silky lingerie and left my belly bare. I decided to go braless with it, and when I bent over—well, suffice it to say one could get a peek at my charms if one wanted to.

I was going to make sure Rio wanted to catch glimpses, and that he actually did catch them.

I winced. Barry. I meant Barry.

Though the thought of Rio sliding the strap off my shoulder with his callused hands got my juices flowing (if you know what I mean).

"Enough." I shook my head and took a deep breath to center myself. I couldn't be distracted with Rio; I had more important matters at hand.

I left my hair down, loose and flowing past my shoulders, lined my eyes to make them stand out, and swiped some gloss on my lips. Sticking my driver's license, a credit card, and some cash in my pocket, I went to see if Daphne was ready. "Daph!"

"Stop calling me that."

It came from the office. Because I didn't need the aggravation of seeing how she'd messed with the room, I sat down in the living room to wait. Tapping my fingers on the armrest, I called upon every ounce of patience in my body. Five seconds later I yelled again. "Daphne! Come on, we have to go."

"Okay," she said. At least, that's what I think she said— her voice was so muffled it could have been anything, I supposed.

She tentatively emerged from the room, a frown wrinkling her delicate forehead. "Am I dressed appropriately?"

I rolled my eyes. She was always worried about being proper, always had been. I was about to give her a flippant answer (what did it matter what you wore to a pub, even a nice one like Kells), but then I noticed what she was wearing: wool pants, flats, and a long-sleeved blouse that she'd buttoned all the way up to her chin. As if the uptight librarian outfit wasn't bad enough, her hair was twisted so tight her eyes looked almond-shaped and there wasn't a hint of color on her face.

But I wanted to get to Kells so I could have a drink before anyone arrived (to calm my nerves). And Johnny wasn't going to mind Daphne's nun-like appearance;

knowing him, he'd be turned on by it. So I said, "You're fine. Let's go."

I was at the top of the stairs going down to the front door before I noticed she wasn't behind me. I turned around with a frown. "What?"

She looked down at her clothes. "You look more casual than I do."

"I always look more casual than you do."

"But you look—" her mouth worked for several seconds before she could mutter her thought "—sexy."

I grinned. If my sister thought I was sexy, Rio was going to die.

I mentally smacked my forehead. *Barry.* Barry was going to die.

"I don't look sexy." She worriedly smoothed the front of her silk shirt.

Sigh. A sister's job is never done. "You look fine. Sexiness is a state of mind."

Daphne frowned at me like she couldn't process that tidbit of information.

I sighed again and waved her over. "Come on. Would I steer you wrong?"

I immediately knew I'd said the wrong thing. I didn't need to see the suspicion crop up in her eyes.

When in doubt, appeal to her sense of propriety. "Look. You don't want to keep Johnny waiting, do you?" I asked, fully aware Johnny would probably arrive late.

"All right," she said hesitantly. She slung her hefty purse over her shoulder and reluctantly shuffled toward me.

I opened my mouth to tell her she needed only some money and her ID, but I decided to avoid that debate. I doubted she'd do anything where she'd be hindered by her bag. Like dancing. Daphne, dance? Ha!

We walked down together and I locked the door under her eagle eye. I noticed Magda was back by the light illuminating the window in her door.

"Your tenant is so quiet," Daphne whispered.

I shrugged and held out my keys. "Will you put these in your purse?"

She gave me a look I didn't bother to decipher, but did as I asked. I skipped down the steps and headed left to the corner.

My sister caught up quickly (damn her long legs). "Where are you going? Your car is the other direction."

"To catch a cab." I wasn't planning on drinking much but better to be prepared. Maybe Rio could bring me home.

Shit—I meant Barry. *Barry* could bring me home.

I walked briskly the couple of blocks to NW 23rd. The neighborhood had received a facelift some years ago, and now it was a yuppie paradise of trendy little shops and coffeehouses. Great street for catching cabs.

Daphne strode beside me, bumping me with her luggage of a purse. "Why are we taking a cab? Is something wrong with your car?"

Was she for real? Oh, yeah—she never went out. "In case we drink." I gave her a severe look. "It's not good to drink and drive."

She glanced at me in exasperation before looking down again to watch her step. "Do you drink a lot?"

For a moment, I was tempted to tell her my plans. She was my sister and it seemed like the kind of thing to share. But then I woke out of that delirium. This was Daphne, not some cool older sister who'd help me plot. If I told her, she'd chastise me ceaselessly. "Nope. I usually don't drink much. I don't like to take chances though."

She nodded solemnly and managed to stay quiet for all of two seconds before she asked, "What does your tenant do?"

I stood on the corner and waved at a passing taxi, who didn't bother to slow down. "She's a hooker."

"Excuse me?"

My lips quirked of their own volition. "She's a hooker. High-priced though. Rent isn't cheap."

Daphne looked like a guppy, the way her mouth was opening and closing. It was hard not bursting out in laughter. Somehow I resisted. But I couldn't help adding, "Don't worry. She makes house calls. She never brings her johns home."

"Mena! I can't believe you'd rent out space in your house to a—a—"

I frowned and signaled another cab. "Hooker's not a dirty word."

She grabbed my arm and jerked me to face her. "Do Mom and Dad know?"

The taxi that screeched to a stop next to us saved me from having to reply. "Oh, look. Our ride." I broke her grip by rotating my arm in a counterclockwise circle, opened the door, and hopped in. Daphne climbed in as I told our driver where we were going.

My sister managed to stay silent for five seconds before she leaned toward the driver and said, "Wouldn't it be more expedient to take Everett?"

The driver and I exchanged looks in the rearview mirror. "Daph, I think he knows where he's going."

"My name is Daphne, and if he took Everett instead, he'd avoid downtown traffic, thereby arriving sooner."

Save me from anal sisters.

"There are so many stops on Burnside. I'm sure it's simply to delay our ride and charge us more." She narrowed her eyes at him suspiciously.

"Daphne, let the man drive." I yanked her back and gave the driver an apologetic look. He just shrugged as if to say it was his fate to be questioned on his routes.

We got to Kells pretty quickly for a Friday night. I paid our cabbie, including a big tip (he deserved combat pay for dealing with Daphne) and led her to the door.

"Hey, pretty lady." The bouncer checking IDs smiled at me.

I smiled back. I didn't know his name but I went often enough that I recognized him. "How's it hanging?"

"Long and low." He grinned. "And I'm primed for action."

I grinned back and handed him my driver's license. He gave it the requisite stare before returning it, stamped my wrist, and gestured toward the door. "Don't get into too much trouble tonight."

I laughed. "What fun would that be?" Then I turned to wait for Daphne, who was watching the interchange with wide eyes. She startled when she realized the bouncer and I were both gazing at her and clumsily dug in her purse for her license.

"She with you?" the door guy asked as he gave Daphne one of those slow head-to-toe-and-back perusals guys were so good at. Only I had the feeling it wasn't because he thought she was hot.

I felt a stirring of protectiveness in my gut. Unusual and I couldn't explain it, so I ignored the feeling. Maybe I ate some bad food. But I *did* frown at the bouncer and say, "She's my sister."

Which caused him to bestow one of those slow all-over looks on me before he gave Daphne another one. He shook his head and stamped her wrist without really looking at her license. "Enjoy yourselves, ladies."

I frowned at him and dragged Daphne through the door. "Jerk."

"I thought you were friends."

I glanced at her. "What makes you say that?"

"The way you talked to him." She hiked her purse more securely on her shoulder as she blinked to adjust to the dim lighting.

"Nope. I don't make it a habit of being friends with assholes like that."

I think she mumbled, "I thought he was a perfectly decent man," but it was under her breath so I couldn't be sure.

I looked around to see if anyone from our party was here. No one. Excellent. Dragging Daphne to the bar, I leaned across so the bartenders (all male) would notice my cleavage. I didn't have much, but what I had I knew how to use.

Sure enough, one came over right away, ignoring all the people waiting before me. "What can I get you?"

Men were so predictable. "I'd like a Guinness and she wants—" I didn't know what Daphne wanted. Seemed like I should, but I didn't think I'd ever seen her drink before. I turned to her and asked, "What would you like?"

She stared wide-eyed at all the liquor bottles glittering like jewels behind the bar. "I don't know," she replied in hushed wonder.

I frowned. "What do you like? Beer? Vodka? Gin?"

"I don't know," she said again with the beginnings of panic.

She was almost thirty—she had to have had some kind of drink at some point, right? Why couldn't she just pick one?

But I must have had an out-of-body experience because instead of saying that, I patted her arm and said, "I'll take care of it."

The relief on her face was embarrassing. I turned to the bartender so I wouldn't have to face it. "What kind of mixed drink is your favorite to make?"

"I know just the thing." His devilish grin should have tipped me off, but I was still unsettled by Daphne's uncertainty. "A Sexual Trance."

He set my pint and the frou-frou drink in front of me and rattled off an absurd total. Daphne's drink must have contained liquid gold, because Guinness wasn't that expensive. Not that I cared, really, as long as she loosened up.

Daphne accepted her beverage when I handed it to her, holding it up and examining it like an unknown compound in a beaker. "What's in it?"

"Don't know. He called it a Sexual Trance."

She pepped right up. "I like that."

I watched her as she took a tentative sip. Her face lit up like she'd discovered the cure for cancer. "You like it?"

"It's delicious," she replied fervently.

I frowned at the way she started chugging it down. "Careful there. Those drinks are strong."

"Nonsense. This is all fruit juice. I don't taste any alcohol." She tipped her head back and downed the rest. Setting the empty glass on bar, she smiled. "I want another one."

I was so taken aback by her smile—the first one that didn't have a trace of the usual tightness in her face—that I didn't notice she motioned the bartender over.

"Excuse me, could I have another one of these? Uh, a Sexual Trance?" She pushed the glass toward him.

He grinned at her. "You liked it, huh? Killer, wasn't it?"

"Yes."

I rolled my eyes. Did she even know what killer meant?

He set down a fresh drink in front of her. She rummaged in her enormous purse for her wallet. It took her so long, he took care of two other customers before she was ready.

She picked up her drink and tried it. "This one tastes even better."

The way she was guzzling her drink worried me. I'm sure it was because I'd have to hold her hair back while she purged it all later and not because this behavior was totally unlike her. "Take it easy on this one, okay?"

She ignored me and studied the room. "It's busy here, isn't it?"

"It gets busier." I took her arm and tugged. "Come on. Let's grab that booth before someone takes it."

We weaved our way through the tables and claimed the booth. It was in the middle, far enough from the bandstand to offer privacy and close enough to the door so everyone joining us should see us right away.

Daphne slid in across from me, her head bobbing. "This music's pretty good. Is it Celtic?"

It was the Beastie Boys. "It's got Celtic roots."

"I thought so." She surveyed everything around her in that way she had when she was dissecting and evaluating. I could feel her foot tapping along to the beat of "You've Got to Fight for Your Right to Party."

I was facing the front, so I immediately saw Rio when he stepped in. If I hadn't seen him, I would've known he was in the house at the collective sigh from all the women.

I couldn't blame them. He looked *good*. Yeah, it was all well and good that I could see his muscles rippling under his tight T-shirt and that his jeans hugged his package lovingly (yes, I looked) and that his eyes lit up when he saw me. But what really turned me on was the way he stalked toward me so confidently. With single-minded purpose. I bet he approached everything with that kind of concentration.

Yum.

I remembered how he said *fight me* and felt my nipples harden. I was practically panting by the time he reached our table.

He smiled. "Hi."

I felt overwhelmed by the intensity of his gaze, like I was the only person in the room with him. I had to clear my throat a couple of times before I could say "Hi" back.

Daphne scooted closer to the edge of the booth. "Who are you? Mena's boyfriend? I'm her sister Daphne." She held her hand out and toppled over.

Rio caught her by the elbow. "Careful. You okay?"

"Peachy, thanks." She smiled unsteadily. "Mena got me a date too, did you know that?"

"She's pretty generous." Rio guided her back into the security of the corner of the booth.

"Mostly she's always been a spoiled brat. Did you know she blew up my favorite Barbie?"

He glanced at me.

I shrugged. "It melted more than it blew up."

"She was a brat," Daphne declared. "But she's okay now. Sometimes. Except for when she throws my coffee in the garbage."

Hell, Daphne, air out all our dirty laundry right in front of the hottest man in the room. I held my hands up helplessly. "She's not used to drinking."

Rio's smile was understanding. "I'm going to get myself a beer. You need another?"

I glanced down at the Guinness I'd barely touched despite my earlier plans. "I'm good."

"I could use another one of these drinks." Daphne peered down into her glass. "They disappear so fast."

"No, she couldn't," I told Rio quickly.

"Be right back." He flashed me his sexy smile again.

I watched him walk toward the bar. I swear I'd never been one for men's asses, but for him I could make an exception.

"He's almost as yummy as my drink," Daphne said, her eyes following him too. "But I'm relieved he's not my date."

I faced her and frowned. "Why?"

"He's too overwhelming." She shuddered. "I wouldn't know what to do with him."

I would. My entire body flushed as my imagination took flight. I fanned myself with my hand, hoping it was dark enough to hide my burning cheeks.

"It *is* rather warm in here, isn't it?" My sister waved

herself too. Then she unbuttoned her two top buttons. Only she must have still been warm because she undid another button.

"Much better." She smiled at me and downed the rest of her drink.

I thought about telling her you could see her underwear, but she wore a white chemise on top of her bra so it wasn't like she was flashing anyone. I figured I'd let her be. Getting her to drink water was going to be hard enough.

"No wonder Mom was raving about your boyfriend."

I frowned. "What do you mean?"

She pointed at Rio. "I'd rave about him too. He's testosterone personified. Mom probably sees all the potential grandchildren in his loins—"

"Daphne!"

"—and Dad sees a guy he can bond with in football season." She frowned. "The name Barry doesn't quite suit him though, does it?"

How was I going to handle her when the real Barry showed up with his new girlfriend? I couldn't have her telling our parents Barry and I split.

I looked longingly at Rio. It would have been perfect if I could have taken him to the party but, contrary to what my tipsy sister thought, our parents weren't going to like him.

Daphne pouted when Rio came back with only a pint of beer. "Where's my Sexual Trance?"

He and I exchanged a look and I slid out of the booth. "I'll get her a glass of water. Be right back."

At the bar, I looked back at the table to see Daphne talking to Rio with more animation than I'd ever seen, except when she was talking about childhood diseases. Panic and jealousy rose in me. I almost ran back to the table, but then I saw that Rio's body language wasn't like someone interested, so I calmed down.

Still, I returned as fast as possible. I set a big glass of water in front of Daphne and slid in next to Rio. "Everything okay?" I asked him.

He smiled. "Great."

Daphne scowled at the water. "This doesn't look like a Sexual Trance."

"It's H_2O." I thought maybe if I told her the chemical compound she might understand what it was, since plain English wasn't working.

She pushed it across the table. "I want a Sexual Trance."

"Don't we all, but you're going to drink this." I slid the glass back at her.

"Make me." She crossed her arms and glared at me.

I rolled my eyes. "Oh, really mature, Daph."

"Don't call me Daph."

I looked beseechingly at Rio.

He put his arm around me and whispered in my ear. "I can't really blame her for wanting a sexual trance."

His breath stirred every cell in my body to life. I froze, aware of the exact proximity of his lips to my neck, of the way his fingers toyed with the spaghetti strap of my top, of his thigh pressing against mine.

He was going to kiss me, I just knew it. I lowered my eyelids, ready, willing, and more than able—

Someone cleared his throat at the foot of the booth. Rio and I looked up simultaneously to find Barry and Cindy holding hands (he'd *never* held my hand when we went out) with Johnny lurking behind them. Cindy watched us with bubbly curiosity. Barry gaped as if he couldn't believe his eyes. Johnny frowned at Rio's hand on my shoulder.

I smiled even as I groaned mentally. "Hey, guys. You all know each other except for Johnny." I pointed to him and everyone looked at him. "He's Daphne's date."

"I am?" The confusion on Johnny's face was comical.

"He is?" Daphne leaned around Cindy to get a better look at him.

His expression cleared up when he got a better look at her. "Mena was right. You're hot."

Hot? My sister? I looked at her. With her buttons undone and leaning over like that, he had an eyeful. And she had a lot to ogle. Frankly, I could support anything that got Johnny's attention off me.

Daphne's face lit up, emphasizing her angelicness. "You think I'm hot?"

"You're totally hot. Can I buy you a drink?"

She jumped out of the booth eagerly. Impressive—she barely stumbled. "I want a Sexual Trance."

An unholy grin grew across his face. "And I'm the man to give it to you."

He was plastered to her side as they went to the bar. A match made in heaven.

"Is she going to be okay?" Rio said in my ear.

"Yeah. Johnny's okay."

"I was more worried about her having another drink."

"She's the most responsible person I know. I'm sure she'll stop after this last drink." I hoped. I was more focused on him whispering in my ear. Barry and my objective slipped to the back of my mind. All I wanted to concentrate on was the goose bumps from Rio's breath on my skin.

The thing was, I didn't really want him to stop. In fact, I wanted to feel his breath on other parts of my body. But I dragged myself from my prurient thoughts and smiled at Cindy and Barry. "I'm glad you could make it."

"I'm so excited to be here," Cindy gushed as she bounced onto the bench where Daphne had been sitting. "I've never been to a bar like this before."

Barry squeezed her shoulder. "What would you like to drink, sweets?"

She beamed up at him. "A glass of chardonnay, please."

Chardonnay? In a pub? I don't know why I was surprised. Her clothes were just as out of place. She had on another fancy little dress that was more appropriate for an upscale jazz bar.

But Barry didn't notice how out of place she was. He only nodded and went to do her bidding.

No biggie. He was already disconcerted by the way Rio was touching me. By the end of the night I was sure Barry would realize how much he wanted me back.

Rio tugged a lock of my hair. I looked up at him with a frown. He had a half-smile on his face as he said, "Where did you go?"

"Excuse me?"

"Cindy asked you a question."

"She did?" I looked at Cindy, who watched me with tolerant amusement.

"It's okay. I can totally understand why Mena's off in space." She gave Rio a sidelong look and giggled. "You two are *sooo* cute together."

"Um. Thanks." I just couldn't bring myself to give her and Barry the same kind of comment. Even if they did look compatible. Grr.

She leaned across the table. "When did you guys know?"

I frowned. "Know what?"

"Know. You know—*know*." She gasped in exasperation at my probably blank look. "Like, I knew Barry was The One when I saw him across the room at South Park Seafood. I was having lunch with my daddy and Barry came over after dessert to introduce himself to my daddy and ask him if he could take me out. It was so romantic." She heaved a princess sigh. Then she snapped back to business. "When did you and Rio know you were it for each other?"

I turned to Rio and beseeched him for help.

To his credit, he didn't smirk. "I knew as soon as she insulted my fighting ability."

Cindy's eyes widened. "You didn't, Mena!"

"No, I didn't." I elbowed him in the sternum. "I just said boxing wasn't fighting."

She smiled sweetly at the two of us. "You're just *sooo* cute! I'm *sooo* happy you found each other."

Barry came back at that moment, so I snuggled into Rio's side and said, "We are too."

Barry frowned at me (yay!) and slid in next to Cindy. "Here you go, sweetie." He handed her the glass of white wine.

"Thank you, Pookie." She pecked his cheek and hugged his arm. "You're so good to me."

Gag. I downed some beer to keep myself from vomiting

Daphne returned with Johnny in tow. He held a couple of drinks too, including another one of those drinks Daphne was hooked on. I scowled at him. He shrugged as if to say, "I couldn't deny her, could I?" He set the drinks on our table, snagged a couple of chairs, and seated Daphne before taking his seat. Very close to her.

She didn't notice anything amiss. She flashed him a loopy smile and took a swig of her drink. When she set it down on the table, it sloshed over the sides. "This is so cozy."

"Isn't it?" Cindy gushed. She leaned over Barry to get at Daphne. "You're Mena's sister? Ohmigod, you're so beautiful. Are you a model?"

Daphne's brow wrinkled. "A model what?"

I perked up. Maybe alcohol was the way to lower her IQ, to make her less perfect.

"You know. A model," Cindy explained precisely. "Like photographers take pictures of."

Daphne tapped her lips thoughtfully. "Well, they did take my picture for *BioPharm International.*"

"I knew it!" Cindy beamed at Barry. "Didn't I guess that, Barry?"

"You sure did, sweets," he replied fondly.

I frowned at him. I could see a certain naïve sweetness to Cindy that could, maybe, for some people, be attractive, but Barry hated sugar.

"Wait a minute," Daphne interjected suddenly. She swayed toward the table so Johnny had to dive to save their drinks from being knocked over. "I thought he—" she pointed at Rio "—was Barry."

"Um, no." Wow, was I thirsty. I lifted my beer and hid behind the glass.

"I knew it!" Daphne exclaimed, pointing at Rio. "You don't look like a Barry. A Barry seems more uptight, like someone my parents would approve of."

I grabbed Rio's chin and pulled his face to mine. "Want to dance?"

"Let's go." He took my hand and led me to the dance floor.

Such as it was. Mostly it was a clear area around the bandstand where people stood during live concerts. Later, it'd be packed by the sheer volume of bodies trying to cram into the bar. For now, though, there was plenty of space for me and Rio to get down to Christina Aguilera.

I started winding myself up to shake some serious booty when Rio spun me into his body. Staring into my eyes, he let go of my hand, put his on my hips, and led me into the salsa.

Only one word for it: delicious. He moved me in a way that would have been illegal in some states. It felt so right that I didn't want to think about it. So instead I focused on how sexy Rio was and how close his lips were to mine. It wouldn't take very much to reach up and kiss him.

God knows I was dying to. Just one kiss, so I could prove once and for all that he wasn't the sex-god he appeared to be.

A flash of pink caught my eye. I turned to look and

stumbled over my feet when I saw Barry whirling Cindy to our right.

"You okay?" Rio murmured in my ear.

I nodded, even though I was totally blown away. Barry never danced and here he was, shaking his groove with Cindy. He was no Patrick Swayze, but he looked like he was having fun. I didn't know whether to applaud Cindy or pout because the one time I went dancing with him he'd just stood to one side, bored, watching me dance.

Loud cheering from the bar area pulled my attention. I looked to check out what was going on, expecting to see people doing shots.

Rio stopped abruptly. "Isn't that your sister?"

I blinked, positive I was seeing things. It couldn't be Daphne. Daphne wouldn't do a striptease on top of a bar. Her hair wouldn't fly around her head—it'd be subdued in a tight knot. And she definitely wouldn't take off her shirt in front of a bunch of cheering strangers and swing it around her head.

My beer must have been spiked. I had to be hallucinating.

Then the woman looked up and gave me a loopy smile. "Mena! Look, I'm dancing. I'm getting D-O-W-N!"

Okay, I wasn't hallucinating.

"Come on." I took Rio's hand and pushed my way to the bar, dragging him behind me. Shoving a couple overzealous boys aside, I wiggled up to the bar. "Daphne, what are you doing?"

"Dancing." She giggled and shook her ass in my face.

Johnny wedged his way next to me. "She's great, Mena," he said loudly to be heard over the commotion. "Thanks a lot."

"Yeah." Not.

"She's not frigid like you. Were you adopted?"

I glared at him, but he was too busy raptly gazing at

Daphne's bare belly to notice. I felt Rio's chuckle on my neck, so I turned around to glare at him too.

"Was she a stripper?" Johnny did a white man's bop with his head. "She's got moves."

"Daphne," I called, aware of the desperation creeping into my voice. I held my hand out to encourage her off the bar. "Why don't we go to the dance floor? There's more room there."

"I wanna dance here." She whirled her shirt one more time and let go. It landed on my right arm.

"Need some help?" Rio asked from behind me.

"I got it." I crumpled the blouse and tossed it to him.

"Take it off, baby!" one of the guys at the other end yelled. A cheer went up from everyone watching her.

Daphne paused. I could see the cogs turning in her head and I groaned. Before I could do anything, she whipped her chemise over her head and sent it flying. Then she did a shimmy in her bra that would have made J.Lo green with envy.

A whooping cheer went up through the bar, but what caught my eye was the trio of bouncers cutting through the crowd to get to her.

Shit. Try explaining to our parents why their perfect daughter spent the night in jail. Guess who'd get the blame?

I grabbed my sister's leg. "Come down *now*."

"Stop it. I'm sick of dancing all by myself. Tonight I'm gonna dance with someone else."

Great. Now she was quoting Madonna. I tugged. "You can dance with someone else on the dance floor."

She shook me off, lost her balance, and stumbled off the bar. Fortunately, her fans caught her. Unfortunately, they turned the moment into an impromptu mosh pit and passed her overhead.

I tried to catch her as she went by, but the crowd carried her away from me. Rio caught hold of her, pulled her down, and propped her between us. Which would have been a relief, except apparently some industrious onlooker had unhooked her bra, so when she stood up, it slipped off her shoulders and hung in the crook of her elbows.

Daphne giggled. "Oops."

I lifted it back up in place and reached around to hook it again.

"No." She slapped my hands away. "I wanna be free."

I scowled. "That's going to be really hard in prison."

"Let me." Rio took the ends of the bra and fastened them in two seconds flat. He must have noted my look because he shrugged. "A skill I learned in back of the bus in seventh grade."

"Hooking bras up?" I asked, my brows raised.

He grinned rakishly and draped Daphne's shirt around her. "I had to hook them back up in order to practice unhooking them again."

Of course. Silly me. "Let's get her out of here."

"I'll take her home," Johnny piped up.

I'd forgotten about him. As if I would let my sister go home with a guy who encouraged her to strip in public. "No thanks. We got it."

He latched onto Daphne's arm. "She's my date."

She gave him her wobbly smile. "You're my date too."

I yanked Daphne back. Her head snapped forward and her hair covered her face like she was doing an impression of Cousin Itt. She went heavy and dangled from our arms; I knew she had passed out. "We'll take her home."

As Rio and I edged away, Johnny grabbed my hand. "Will you at least give her my number? I have to see her again."

Rolling my eyes, I huffed in exasperation. "Fine."

He didn't let go. "Promise."

God, he was relentless. No wonder he was so successful in biz dev. "I promise. Now let go before we get thrown out of here."

The bouncers arrived at our side, their arms crossed, shooting us that intimidating glare they must practice in front of a mirror.

I tried to smile at them. "We're leaving."

"Yes, you are," one of them replied flatly.

I glanced at Rio and we dragged Daphne's dead weight out the bar and to his car. We propped her against the door so Rio could get his keys out of his pocket.

"Maybe we should put her in the trunk."

Rio slipped the key in the lock and glanced at me as he popped it open. "Excuse me?"

"I'd hate it if she threw up in there." His Mustang was so beautiful.

He picked Daphne up like she was a doll instead of an Amazon and set her in the front seat. "Does she usually throw up when she's drunk?"

I shrugged. "I'm not sure she's ever been drunk before."

"I think we can take our chances," he said with a smile as he closed the door.

I knew he was doing me a favor, but I couldn't help taking advantage of the situation. "Maybe I should drive since I know how to get to my house." I batted my eyes for good measure.

Chuckling, he reached for my hand and pulled me flush against him.

Was he going to kiss me now? He was, I just knew it. I licked my lips, hoping they were sufficiently soft and supple and not like sandpaper.

He dropped the keys in my hand, closed my fist, and pressed a kiss to my knuckles. "You can drive."

Must have heard wrong. I shook my head to clear it. "Excuse me? I thought you just said I could drive your baby?"

"I did."

I gasped. Then I shot out of his arms and climbed in before he changed his mind. Of course, I had to get back out to let him in the back seat, but then we were settled.

I took a deep breath and grinned into the rearview mirror. "I'll try to keep it under a hundred."

He smiled indulgently. "Thanks."

And we were off.

I had a sexual experience driving that car. Good thing my house wasn't far because another five minutes driving it and I would've had an orgasm right there.

I double-parked in front of my house, hopped out, and waited for Rio to emerge. He'd just closed the door when I jumped him. Literally. My arms went around his neck and my legs gripped his waist. His hands automatically went to support me under my butt.

I laughed triumphantly, throwing my head back. "That was the best ride I've ever had!"

I felt his grip tighten on me. Still laughing, I brought my gaze to his. And immediately sobered.

The way he watched me made me conscious of how my parts fit against his. And that, judging by their firmness, his parts were interested in getting to know mine better. And in his eyes I could see him offering me a better ride.

Gulp.

As nervous as I felt about that (yeah, part of me still stung from Barry saying I was boring in bed), I realized I wanted it. I wanted him, more than I'd ever wanted anyone. Ever.

And, damn it, I was sick of waiting for him to kiss me. This was the twenty-first century. Hell if I was going to wait docilely till he was ready. *I* was ready, and if he didn't want me he wouldn't be bursting through his jeans like he was right now.

So I lifted a hand to his neck and pulled his head down until my lips were a breath away. His gaze intensified, alternating between my lips and my eyes.

Any other man would have rushed forward to take what I offered. It took me a second to realize why Rio wasn't. Not that he didn't want me, but to draw out the anticipation between us. He didn't kiss me because he wanted me so much. The evidence was right before me.

Triumph surged. I smiled, just a little. He was mine.

I wanted to taste him so badly, but I stayed where I was, hovering in front of his mouth. When I spoke, my voice was sex-kitten husky. "I really like—" I licked my lips "—your car."

His fingers bit reflexively into my haunches and his eyes flared with need. "I can tell."

I tightened my legs around his hips. "I wouldn't mind driving it again."

"That can be arranged."

"Good." I released my legs and slid down his body as slowly as I possibly could (I'm a wicked girl and proud of it). I almost groaned as I passed over his erection. It made me want to climb back up and do it all over again.

Clearing my throat, I stepped back, though he stopped me by tangling his hand in my hair. "Phil."

I could only swallow as a reply.

His hand loosened from my hair, his fingers grazing my collarbone before drifting, light as feathers, to the spaghetti strap on my left shoulder. He traced the thin strap down to the lace edging the satin covering the outside of my breast. His fingertips slipped under the lace, brushing lightly against the outside swell of my breast.

Couldn't help it—I gasped.

His lips curved but there wasn't any humor in them. "I can play dirty too."

"I love dirty," I managed to say. "The dirtier the better."

"I like that about you." His nail scraped dangerously close to my nipple.

If I shifted just a little he'd brush it. I wanted that

almost as much as I wanted him to strip me and take me on the hood of his car. Though it'd leave a dent, which was sacrilege. I glanced at the sidewalk. It didn't look *too* hard.

But Rio eased his finger out of my top and said, "We should get your sister inside."

I frowned. Sister? Oh yeah, Daphne. I peered in the car, guilty that I'd forgotten about her, but she was still passed out so I doubted she'd care.

While Rio dragged her limp carcass out of the car, I ran ahead to open the front door.

Rio's steps sounded heavy on the porch steps. Turning, I saw he had Daphne cradled in his arms. I looked at the stairs leading up to my home and winced. "Do you need help carrying her upstairs?"

"No," he said, slightly breathlessly. "Lead the way."

I took the steps two at a time, rushing through the living room to her bedroom.

"Phil?"

"In here," I called out as I turned down the sheets.

He walked in and I helped him get her on the bed. Silently we took Daphne's shoes off and untangled her from her shirt. The rest of her clothes we left on. Covering her, I turned the light off and we walked out.

Rio slipped his arm around my waist. "She's going to be hurting in the morning."

"I know." I didn't even feel gleeful about it. See, I can grow. I can change.

He faced me, and his other arm snaked around me so he cradled me loosely in front of him. "Do you have plans tomorrow?"

I grinned. "I do now."

He grinned back. "I've got morning classes but I can pick you up at one."

"In the afternoon?"

"Is that a problem?"

I shook my head. "Of course not, but what are we going to do at one in the afternoon?"

He lowered his head and nuzzled my neck with his nose. "The same thing we'd do any other time."

I tilted my head a little, just in case it hadn't occurred to him to kiss my neck.

But he let go with a slight caress of my hips. "I should go."

"You should?"

He smiled and pushed back my hair. "It's probably best. No telling what may happen if I stay."

"I'm willing to find out."

Chuckling, he swung an arm around my shoulder. "Walk me out."

Pout.

When we got to the bottom of the stairs, I put my hand on the doorknob and leaned on it, blocking the doorway with my body. If I were six years old, I would've told him he had to pay the toll. But I was twenty-eight, almost twenty-nine, so instead I said, "What're you going to give me to get out?"

Rio must have known exactly what I wanted because he leaned in and pressed his hips into mine. "Goodnight, Phil."

His lips were right *there*. This time he was going to kiss me, I just knew it. For real. I half-closed my eyes as his hands gripped my shoulders.

He whirled me around, opened the door, and let himself out before I knew what happened.

"Hey!" I stared incredulously at the closed door. I heard the rumble of his engine and the slow purr as the car pulled away from the curb.

He tricked me.

I started to laugh, delighted that he outmaneuvered me like that. He'd left me wanting him. More than I thought was ever possible.

Chapter Fourteen

Reasons to date Rio:
1) His MacGyver hands
2) Laughs at my jokes
3) Likes me better—period
4) His car

Reasons to date Barry:
1) Um . . .

I got up bright and early the next morning at ten o'clock. It was a perfect morning. No alarm clocks going off, no rabid sister making a racket in the kitchen.

Hopping out of bed, I took a luxuriously hot shower and got dressed in what I thought was an outfit that would fit anything Rio had planned for today: jeans, a sporty tank top, and my funky red tennis shoes. I tossed a sweatshirt on the bed so I'd be ready to go and went to the kitchen to make some coffee. Yeah, I did all that before I had coffee. Amazing what you can do when you're motivated.

I expected to find Daphne mixing her vile beverage, but there wasn't any sign of her in the kitchen, not even a washed cup. Odd. I looked toward her room. The door was still closed. Maybe she hadn't gotten up yet? Was that possible? She was always up at dawn.

I shrugged and set a pot on the stove to heat for coffee. I'd measured the beans and started grinding them when the office door slammed open.

"What are you *doing*?"

I whirled around, relaxing when I saw it was just Daphne.

A demonic looking Daphne. Her hair was matted to one side of her head but stuck up in a messy clump on the other. She still had on her plain white bra and wool pants, wrinkled beyond acceptable Daphne standards. But it was the crazy look in her bloodshot eyes that really inspired fear.

She looked a little too unstable to trust her at my back, so I kept an eye on her. "How's it going?"

She growled—really. I almost dropped the grinder I was so shocked. I'd never heard her make a sound like that. Ever.

My good mood must have made me sympathetic because I said, "Hungover, huh? I'm making coffee."

She growled again, stomped into the kitchen, and pulled out a new container of instant coffee, all the while glaring at me.

I shrugged. Hey, I tried. I readied my press pot, poured in the water, and leaned against the counter to watch my sister fix the crap she called coffee. I didn't grin, though I wanted to. Especially when she opened every cabinet looking for the mugs and still couldn't find them.

Finally, I couldn't help myself. I pointed to the cupboard to the right of the sink. "In there."

She scowled daggers at me and pulled the cabinet door so forcefully it banged open and instantly shut again. She muttered something—Daphne never cursed so I'm sure she didn't say what I thought she did—and opened it again, this time managing to actually get the mug out.

I watched in morbid fascination as she made her coffee, wondering how someone so smart could drink Folgers. Shudder. "You have any plans today?"

She barely glanced at me before she stalked into the living room and huddled on the couch.

I followed and plopped down on the other side of the couch. "I take it you feel less than optimal this morning."

"Philomena," she barked.

I raised my brows.

"Shut. Up."

I pursed my lips and considered her. "Are you saying you don't feel like the attention? Because last night you sure wanted some."

She narrowed her usually lovely eyes that, this morning, looked rusted over.

"Don't expect me to feel sorry for you. It's not like anyone poured those Sexual Trances down your throat."

She moaned softly and buried her face in a pillow.

Oh, bother. With a huff, I got up and went to the medicine cabinet in the bathroom. I poured four Advil onto my palm and went back to Daphne, who hadn't moved an inch. "Here."

When she didn't look up, I shook my hand in front of her. At the rattling, she peeked. I held out my open palm and, when it registered what I offered, she pounced.

I sat down again, sipping my coffee and studying her. Her head was still lowered, but the expression on her face was more one of waiting, like she was counting the seconds till the ibuprofen kicked in.

I shook my head. "You'd think you would have learned in college."

"When?" She tilted her head enough to scowl at me. "When I was sixteen and a senior in college? Because I know the other seniors really wanted to hang out with a teenager. Or when I was studying twenty hours a day?"

She had a point. I'd never thought of it that way. "Is that what this is all about?"

Daphne moaned. "Mena, just leave me alone."

"Something's wrong with you. You come here and don't want to tell Mom and Dad. You want to go out. You drink exotic drinks. *You dance on a bar.*" I frowned. "Are you terminal?"

"SHUT UP."

I opened my mouth to ask her more questions, but she got up (slowly, probably because of her head), threw the pillow at me (it missed—she has abysmal aim), and stormed off to her room (closing the door softly, once again probably in deference of her head).

Interesting.

I scrounged around till I found my cell phone and called Matt.

"Hello?" he asked on the fourth ring.

"Do you think Daphne's dying?"

"Why do you ask?"

"Because she's acting weird."

"If that were the precursor to death, I could argue that you're a breath away."

"Ha, ha. You're so funny."

"Want to come over today? I was thinking of rebuilding a server I got from work. You can bring over a couple of Philly cheesesteaks."

Of course this was about his stomach. "Sorry. I've got plans."

"What kind of plans?"

"The kind that are none of your business." I didn't want him to know I was going out with Rio. Matt didn't like the guys I went out with. Plus I really had no clue what we were doing. Rio was very mysterious about it.

He audibly bristled. "What the hell do you mean, it's none of my business?"

I hummed. It's unholy, the pleasure I get from harassing my loved ones.

"If you don't want me to know your plans, you either don't know what you're doing—"

Matt knew me so well.

"—or you're afraid I'm going to disapprove." He paused. "Do I need to be close to a phone in case they only allow you one call?"

I laughed. "I'm not doing anything illegal. At least, not that I know of, though the day is young and you never know."

"Do your plans have to do with Barrington?"

I rubbed my nose, thinking. Originally, going out with Rio would have had a lot to do with Barry. But this time Barry wasn't aware we were going out, and Barry wouldn't be there to see Rio and me interacting.

Also, there was the matter of how Rio played me like a violin last night. He'd had every atom in my body quivering for a kiss, his kiss. And they were still reverberating. I hadn't thought of Barry once since Rio put his hands on me.

So I concluded, "No. It doesn't have anything to do with Barry." It didn't. It had everything to do with dying to know if Rio tasted as scrumptious as I thought.

"I'm not sure I believe you."

I frowned. "It's not like I can lie to you."

"Yeah, but you aren't being entirely truthful."

"Fine." I huffed. "If you must know, I'm going out with Rio."

A pause. "Who's Rio?"

"A guy I met."

"And this has nothing to do with Barrington?"

I hesitated. "No."

"You're lying."

"No, I'm not."

Disbelieving silence.

"Okay, maybe in the beginning seeing Rio had a little to do with Barry—"

"Who is Rio?"

"A boxing instructor."

"A boxing instructor," Matt repeated. "How did you meet a boxing instructor?"

I made a face.

"Because, correct me if I'm wrong, but the only person you know who takes boxing is Barrington."

"Fine! God. Interrogate me, why don't you?" Scotland Yard needed to recruit him. "He's Barry's instructor, but I'm not going out with him because of Barry."

Matt snorted.

"I'm not."

"You're lying again, Doc."

I growled. "Okay, maybe I started seeing him because of Barry, but that's not why I'm going out with him now."

"You have absolutely no ulterior motives?"

"Um. No."

He said nothing.

"All right already! There's his car, but that's only secondary." Mostly.

"What kind of car does he have?"

"A '67 Shelby Mustang." I heaved a lusty sigh. "It's absolutely beautiful."

"You're so pathetic." But there was a smile in his voice. "Will you have time for me tomorrow?"

"Want to do pizza and a movie tomorrow night?"

"Yeah. About seven? You rent the movie, I'll bring the pizza."

"You're coming here?"

"Sure," he replied. "Is that okay?"

"Um—" Daphne was here. My first impulse was to say I'd meet him at his house. But I didn't want to leave her alone. She'd been acting so strange. "Yeah, come over here."

"Watch yourself today."

I stuck my tongue out. He was such a big brother.

He chuckled. "Save that for your date, he'll appreciate it more. Later, Doc."

Matt thought he was such a comedian.

I still had a lot of time before Rio was due but I didn't know what to do with myself, so I decided to take the latest *Wired* magazine and the phone (in case Rio called) down to the stoop to look it over as I sat in the sun and waited.

On my way out the door, I noticed Daphne's jar of Sanka on the kitchen counter. I walked over, picked it up, opened the trash—

Sigh. I dropped the lid shut, opened the cupboard, and put the jar back where Daphne had hidden it. Smiling faintly, I went downstairs to wait for my date.

I was reading about the latest in wireless gadgets when the side door opened and Magda emerged from the basement.

She cocked her brow when she saw me on the porch. "Enjoying the weather?"

I smiled, eyeing her ever-present bag. Was it my imagination or did it have a monster-sized dildo bulge on the side? "Yeah. Thought I'd wait for my ride out here since it's so nice for a change."

She set her bag down and turned to lock the door. "Big plans?"

"Just getting together with a friend. You got anything fun on the agenda for today?" I blinked innocently as if it were a casual question.

She hefted her bag onto her shoulder. "Just work." She smiled, but it didn't quite reach her eyes. "Take it easy."

"Yeah," I said, scooting over so she could ease past me down the steps. "You too."

I watched her long-legged confident stride go down the block and disappear around the corner. I grabbed the cell phone and dialed Matt.

"Hello?"

"Why do you think Magda parks around the corner?"

Pause. "Does she always?"

"Whenever *I* see her."

"Hm. Maybe she's afraid one of her johns will follow her home. Or that he'll randomly drive by and see where she lives."

I nodded. "Yeah, I hate taking my work home too."

"Exactly."

"Okay. Thanks." I heard Rio's car come around the corner before I saw it. "Gotta go."

"Behave yourself," Matt said, hanging up before I could make a retort.

I closed the phone as I hopped down the steps. Rio pulled up as I reached the sidewalk. Before I got in, I stopped at the mailbox to deposit my magazine in there (no need for Rio to know how much of a geek I was—that's the kind of thing that needs to be eased into).

He got out and came around the car as I reached it.

My heart rate kicked up and my gut tingled in an ohmigod-this-is-it kind of way. Like the intellectual I am, I said, "Hey."

He smiled and stopped inches in front of me. I could smell his just-showered scent and was suddenly overwhelmed by this need to burrow into him and sniff his body.

"What's wrong?" he asked, watching me intently.

He always watched me intently. Like he wanted to peel away my layers and discover what was underneath. Unnerving, yes. Arousing, oh God, yes. I'd never had anyone look at me like that, like I was all the mysteries of the world rolled into one package he wanted to unravel.

His brow furrowed and he reached out to push back a strand of my hair that got loose from my ponytail. "Phil? You okay?"

I smiled and leaned into his touch. "I'm perfect."

The corners of his lips turned up just a little, but his eyes were serious as he said, "Yes, you are."

I smiled brilliantly—I couldn't help it. "I'm glad we're going out today."

"I am too. Are you ready?"

I had the feeling he was talking about more than getting in the car and going, but I pretended it was a simple question and nodded. He was reaching to open the door for me when I asked, "No chance I can drive, is there?"

He glanced at me. "You know where we're going?"

Pout. "No."

He grinned as I climbed into the passenger seat. "Maybe you'll get a turn later."

Yes! I grinned at him as he closed the door and fastened my seatbelt like the good girl that I am.

I am. For real. Underneath it all.

I watched him settle into the driver seat and start the car. Masterful was the only word for the way he took command. It made me shiver in anticipation.

I never thought I'd be the kind of woman who'd want a guy to dominate her. It wouldn't work, but something inside me was dying for Rio to try.

"What are you thinking?"

I started, turning to face him. "Excuse me?"

His glance was brief so he could keep his eyes on the road. "You were miles away. I wondered what you were thinking."

"My mind was just wandering." I blushed, wondering what he'd say if he knew.

He knew. I could tell by the look he gave me. In his eyes, I could see him struggling to trap my hands above my head and me writhing against him to stop it.

Whew. I fanned myself.

He grinned, but I noticed his knuckles were white from gripping the steering wheel so hard.

"So," I said brightly. "Where are we going?"

"To the coast."

"I love the coast. What are we going to do?"

"Not what you want to do."

Pout again. "Why not?"

He glanced at me. "We haven't kissed yet and you want to go there?"

I faced forward, my arms crossed. Did it matter what we did first? "Are you the type of person who'd take exception to me ordering dessert first? Because I'll tell you right now sometimes I want pie before dinner."

"Thank you for letting me know."

Were his lips twitching? "I'm serious."

"So am I." He glanced at me. "Thank you for telling me. I like knowing about you."

"You do?" I asked suspiciously.

"Of course."

"So you should know I like kisses," I said, like a princess.

He briefly looked over at me again. "Good to know."

"I *love* kisses." I glanced at him to make sure he was paying attention. "I'd do *anything* for kisses."

"Also good to know. What else do I need to know about you?"

"That my family is insane and my best friend is a guy." I'd never mentioned Matt before. I figured he should know up front. Guys were weird about stuff like that, and no way was I changing my relationship with Matt. No way in hell.

"How long have you been best friends?"

"A loo-ng time," I stressed with a meaningful look. "Since we were fourteen."

Rio nodded. He appeared to understand what I was saying, but I knew for certain when he asked, "Will he approve of me?"

I pretended to size him up. "Depends on how you treat me."

"And how well kissed you are?"

I smiled. "Exactly."

We spent the next half hour in silence; Rio drove and I watched the scenery go by. A couple of times I tried to get where we were going out of him to no avail. Though we were headed toward the coast, so I don't know why he wouldn't tell me. But I just went with it. Dwight would have been so proud of me.

We passed a winery I recognized because Barry favored their sparkling wines. Sparkling wine was the same as champagne, and I hated them both. Barry always foisted them on me, as if the next time I'd realize how much I loved them. I never did.

I shifted in my seat so my left leg was bent under me and I faced my date. "Rio."

"Yes?"

"I don't like champagne."

He remained silent for a long time, like he was processing what I told him. I could tell he realized the importance of this statement even if it baffled him. Finally he said, "I won't buy you champagne then."

"Thank you." I relaxed and settled back to enjoy the rest of the drive. While I watched the scenery, I plotted. (Hey, it's what I'm good at.)

If Rio was going to insist on refraining from kissing me, more power to him. It was honorable. Stupid, but honorable.

But I wasn't going to make it easy on him.

I saw a reflection of my grin in the window and it was

pure evil. I couldn't help it. I was down with his reasoning—
excellent intentions. That didn't mean I had to play along.
Not that I was going to take him down and pillage his
mouth. No, I was going to respect his wishes. I just wasn't
going to make it easy on him.

Sometime while I was plotting his downfall, Rio
turned off the two lane highway that led to the coast. I
sat up and took a look around. "Where are we going?"

"We're almost there."

"That didn't answer my question."

"Do you always have to be in control?"

"Not always." What a lie.

He glanced at me, brow raised.

Hmmph. "Is that such a bad thing anyway?"

He chuckled. "No, but don't you think it could be re-
freshing to surrender every now and then?"

The first thought that popped into my head was Rio
in pirate garb and me in a flowy peasant dress, open to
the waist, tied to his bed.

"What is it?" he asked.

I squirmed in my seat. "Do you own an eye patch?"

"No."

"A whip?"

"Uh . . . no."

Shoot. Oh, well. Christmas wasn't far off. I sat up. "Is
that a carnival?"

"Yes."

"I love carnivals," I murmured, staring at the moving
rides. It'd been so long since I'd gone to one.

"I know."

I frowned at him. "How do you know?"

A faint smile curled his lips. "I asked your sister last
night when you went to get her a glass of water."

"Oh." I didn't know what to make of it, that Rio did
something so thoughtful as well as Daphne remembering such a detail. "The last time I went to a carnival, it

was on the waterfront and Matt, my best friend—" I
glanced at Rio to see how he'd react to my mentioning
Matt. Nothing but interest. "Well, Matt challenged me to
a cotton candy-eating contest."

"And you won." He didn't sound surprised.

"Of course." I grimaced. "I still can't stand the sight of
cotton candy though."

He laughed. "No champagne, no cotton candy. Got it."

We had to walk through the dirt parking lot for quite
a while, but with each step I got more excited about the
carnival. "Are we going to ride the Ferris wheel?"

"If you'd like to ride it."

"Yes!" I jumped up and down only once. No, I didn't
clap too (my left hand was busy burrowing into his jeans'
back pocket). "And the merry-go-round."

"Sure."

"I want a corndog too."

"Okay."

"And—"

Laughing, Rio stopped and squeezed me to him. "You
can have anything you want."

"Really." I glanced at his lips. "Anything?"

His gaze fell to my mouth. "I'll get in trouble with that
kind of promise, won't I?"

His voice was low and husky and touched something
deep inside me. Low inside, like in the vicinity of my private red-light area.

My mom didn't raise a dummy (Daphne excluded), so
I plastered myself against him, reached up, and ran a
finger over his lower lip. It felt soft and firm and perfect.
"Do you want to get into trouble?"

He leaned down until his lips hovered over the most
sensitive spot on my neck. "You're playing a dangerous
game."

"I'm not playing," I whispered in his ear.

With a finger, he lifted my chin and gazed into my eyes. "I'm not either."

"Aren't you tempted to kiss me at all?"

The barest smile touched his lips. "I'm dying to kiss you."

I wrinkled my nose. "Then why don't you?"

"It's not time yet."

As far as I was concerned, it was way past time. "Are you sure?"

"Positive."

I sighed and pulled back. "The next time I try to entice you to kiss me, play along and act like I'm irresistible, okay?"

"You are irresistible."

Ha. So said Iron Man. But I let him pull me along to the carnival.

True to his word, we did it all, without reserve. We rode rides, played games, and ate corndogs (just two, because I didn't want to throw up in his beautiful car on the way home). I won him a pretty big purple panda and he won me a tiara, which I immediately put on my head and refused to take off. Amazingly, he ran circles around me at the bumper cars, but I beat his pants off at the arcade games. Not literally, unfortunately.

I got so caught up in the moment and the fun we were having, I forgot to taunt him to see if I could wear down his willpower. I didn't even remember my plan until nighttime when we were leaving, and even then the seduction began innocently (I swear).

We were walking to the car, holding hands, when impulsively I turned to him. "I feel great."

He grinned. "I'm glad."

"No, I mean really great." I threw my arm out as if to hug the world. "I haven't felt so light and carefree in weeks. Maybe months. It's like all this weight I was carrying on my shoulders is gone."

"Did you have a lot of weight on your shoulders?"

"You wouldn't believe how much. But look at me now." I bounced on my toes as I walked to show him how light I felt.

He stopped and drew me to him. He held the panda in one arm and was holding my hand with his other, so he bent down and rubbed his nose to mine. It was a simple gesture, but it stopped my heart with its tenderness.

"God, I love—" he paused "—being with you."

I felt curiously deflated. I didn't know what I thought he was going to say. We'd only known each other for a week, after all. So I just smiled.

"You don't know how happy I am you walked into my gym," he murmured in my ear.

I shivered and opened my mouth to reply. But I felt the butterfly brush of his mouth against my jaw and I was lost. His face rasped faintly against my cheek and I shivered again, wondering how his five o'clock shadow would feel on other parts of my body.

He let go of my hand and, gazing into my eyes, held the back of my neck. His fingers slowly speared through my loosened ponytail, using it to tilt my head back so we gazed into each other's eyes.

Oh, God, he was going to kiss me.

My mouth fell open, partly in preparation and partly because I couldn't believe the moment was finally here. I lifted my hand to his shoulder for more balance (in case kissing turned to groping).

His thumb caressed the corner of my jaw in slow deliberate strokes. I wanted to tell him to do that lower but I didn't think I could form the words. Breathing was challenging at the moment.

He brought his head down until I could feel his lips hovering over mine. All I had to do was crane my head forward a tiny, *tiny* bit and we'd touch.

Only I didn't want to be the one to initiate it. As much as I was dying for it, I wanted him to initiate it first, this time. It seemed paramount.

Next time, he was mine.

So I swallowed and waited, trying not to sway forward. His fingers tightened in my hair; oddly, it made my nipples tighten too.

Kiss me, damn it.

He dropped his forehead to mine, briefly, and stepped back.

No.

But I managed to control myself from shrieking in frustration, even when he let go of my hair. I cleared the passion that had lodged itself in my throat, smiled like the siren I am, and asked, "Can I drive home?"

He studied me like he was considering pinning me to the ground and ripping my clothes off. I tried to convey with my gaze that I wouldn't be averse to that idea. But then he smiled and handed me the keys. "Go for it."

We made it back in record time, even though I took the long way just so I could savor the Mustang. Reluctantly I pulled in front of my house. It was dark except for the porch light and a light inside Magda's apartment.

"Is your sister home?" Rio asked, also looking up at my home.

I shrugged. "She was in bad shape this morning. I have no idea what her plans were for today."

He nodded and turned to face me.

The dark emphasized how masculine he was and the sharp planes of his face. I gave in to my longing to run my hand over his short hair (who knew it'd be so soft?), finally letting it rest on the nape of his neck. His eyes looked fathomless and I thought I could drown in them.

"It's late. I should escort you in."

I nodded, even though all I wanted to do was climb

onto his lap and rub myself all over him. But I managed to control myself and got out of the car.

We walked up to my porch. I unlocked the door and then turned around to face Rio. "Today was one of the best days ever."

"For me too." He trailed a finger down my cheek and then picked up my hand, massaging my knuckles. "What are you doing tomorrow?"

"I have plans tomorrow night but I'm free during the day."

He nodded. "I'll pick you up at eleven."

I grinned. "Are you always so bossy?"

"I prefer to call it singleness of purpose." He caressed my hand one last time before he let go. "I'll wait till you're inside."

I rolled my eyes, but I didn't actually tell him I was a third degree. With a smile and a wave, I went in and locked the door (so Daphne wouldn't have a fit in the morning).

Running up the stairs, I rushed to the living room window. Grinning, I watched him drive away.

I couldn't wait till tomorrow. As I went to my bedroom, I wondered what he had planned. Not that I cared. Though if he really wanted to please me, it'd be some activity we could do naked with a can of whipped cream.

Chapter Fifteen

"I learned something a long time ago: never laugh at what you don't know."
— MacGyver, *"Silent World" Episode #31*

The night before I'd been all gung-ho about launching Operation: Irresistible. The objective: Make Rio kiss me.

But I woke in the morning as groggy as usual. To achieve the mental sharpness I needed to pull this off, I had to have some coffee. Immediately.

I stumbled into the kitchen, eyes closed, and fumbled for my coffee fixings. The eyes-closed part was a real mistake, because I walked into a cabinet and stubbed my toe.

When Daphne jogged up the stairs a minute later, I was still hopping around on one foot, clutching the other and cussing a storm.

She looked at me, her delicate brow wrinkling. "Is that a new Jazzercise routine?"

I glared at her. Die, Daphne, die.

She shook her head and pushed me aside. "Go sit down. I'll make your coffee."

"You don't know how to make coffee."

"I've watched you." And to prove it, she put the kettle on and got out the grinder.

"Lucky guess," I mumbled.

"Go sit down." She slanted me a devious look so unlike her, I wondered if I was in the right house with the right sister. "I won't slip you any of my instant."

Yikes! I hadn't even considered that.

"Calm down, Mena. You get so worked up. Just go sit down."

Fine. I ignored that she took down a jar of Taster's Choice and went into the living room.

Eight minutes later (I timed her with the DVD clock) she came out with a steaming mug. "Here."

I gave her a suspicious glare and took the cup. I sniffed it to make sure she hadn't done anything weird to it and then took a tentative taste.

"Hey." I perked up. "This is good."

"You don't have to sound so surprised."

"I'm not."

She leveled a look at me as she sat down.

"Okay, I am." I shrugged. "Can you blame me? Have you ever made real coffee before?"

"Not for a snob." She reclined and stretched her legs in front of her. In running shorts, her legs looked miles long.

I looked down at my legs and wondered what they looked like. Then I wondered what Rio thought they looked like.

"That's new," Daphne said, breaking into my thoughts.

"What?"

She shrugged one shoulder. "I called you a snob and you didn't jump down my throat."

I frowned. "I don't always jump down your throat."

Her silence said more than any number of protests could have.

"I don't."

She raised her mug to her lips and sipped noisily.

I crossed my eyes at her and concentrated on my coffee.

One minute later (who knew the DVD clock would come in so handy?), she said, "Aren't you up early? Do you know it's Sunday?"

I nodded. "I have a date this morning."

She practically fell out of the chair. "You agreed to a date in the *morning*?"

I didn't dignify that with a response.

"Because you aren't a morning person," she went on, "so you must like this guy a lot. It's Barry, isn't it?"

Barry? I wrinkled my nose. "God, no."

"No?" Her forehead creased. "But on Friday you looked like you got along really well."

We did? He hung all over Cindy most of the time, but maybe Daphne was confused. Or in a trance, as it were.

"When you were dancing, it looked so sexy."

Oh. *Oh.* Rio. Right. She thought Rio was Barry. "Right. Yeah, I'm going out with B-b—" I just couldn't say it "—him again."

Her eyes got dreamy. "He looked like he wanted to tear your clothes off and just take you."

I frowned. "Take me where?"

"You're impossible." She shook her head. "Is that where you were all day yesterday?"

"You noticed I was gone."

"Yes. There was less stomping up and down the house. I don't know how your tenant lives with it."

"I don't stomp. I walk with purpose." I decided to change the subject. "Hey, Matt's coming over later for dinner and a movie, okay?"

Her expression didn't change, not really, but somehow suddenly she looked very sad. "Sure. What time do you want me to leave?"

"Leave?" What kind of crack was she smoking? "Who said you had to leave? I'm just telling you so you don't ruin your dinner."

Her cup smacked onto the coffee table. "You're inviting *me*?"

"Isn't that what I just said?" Hope her medical plan covered hearing loss. I enunciated the next sentence to make sure she got it. "If you make sure you are home at six, you can go with me to get the movie."

"Okay." The way her face lit up was embarrassing. And made me feel bad for not including her in my plans more often.

I cleared my throat, murmured that I was going to take a shower, and escaped. I didn't think I could handle messy emotions this morning. If I was going to make Rio sit up and beg, I had to get moving.

I refreshed my coffee on the way to the bathroom. Deciding to take a bath instead, I turned the faucet on and sat on the toilet, sipping my astonishingly good coffee, while the tub filled. I dumped some lavender bath salts in and eased myself into the hot water.

Heaven. The only way life could be better was if Rio were in the tub with me.

Of course, after soaking for twenty minutes, I had to turn the drain, wash my hair, and rinse. I washed my hair the day before, yes, but I thought I should wash it again. Just in case.

I paused mid-rinse. Maybe I should shave my legs too.

"Better safe than sorry," I told myself, picking up the razor.

Half an hour later I was fresh, smooth, lubed, and ready to get dressed. Wrapped in my robe, I contemplated my wardrobe. I didn't want to wear jeans again, and I wasn't sure a skirt was appropriate for whatever we were doing.

I had a pair of red bell-bottom capris in my hand when Daphne walked in. "What are you doing on your date?"

"I don't know," I answered absentmindedly. If the capris, then which shoes?

"Why don't you wear this dress?" She reached into the closet and pulled out a summer dress.

"What, *you're* giving *me* fashion advice?" Still, it actually

was a great dress—a white-and-black halter top with a
billowy skirt that ended above my knee. Demure, yet not.

"You probably look great in it," she said with a tinge of
what I swore was jealousy.

"Yeah, but what if we do something active?"

She shrugged and leaned against the wall. "He should
have told you what the appropriate dress was then."

True. I studied the dress again. It *would* make an impression. "I bet he'd have a hard time keeping his mouth
off me if I wore this."

Daphne got a curdled look on her face. "Please spare
me the details."

"I'll wear it," I decided. And I'd wear a pair of white flip-
flops with it, just in case we did a lot of walking. And I'd
put my hair up. I read in some girly magazine once that
men liked to see the long expanses of women's necks.

I'd just finished getting ready when I heard the
doorbell.

"I'll get it," Daphne called from the living room.

"Oka—*no*." That was all I needed, for her to chat with
Rio and call him Barry. I rushed out of my room, barely
passing her before she reached the lower landing. I
placed my hand on the doorknob a fraction of a second
before she got to it.

I looked up at her and smiled sweetly. "I got it."

The doorbell rang again, and her forehead wrinkled.
"Aren't you going to open it?"

"Yeah." Why was she rushing me? I twisted the knob.

Even though I knew it was Rio—I was expecting him,
after all—I felt a hiccup of startled delight. I grinned,
probably like a fool, and said, "Hi."

"Hi." He took in my appearance as if he were catalogu-
ing every stretch of bare skin showing, right down to
my toes.

I felt a nervous urge to smooth my dress down, which
I restrained with great difficulty. "Is it okay? Tell me now
so I can change. I wasn't sure what we were doing—"

"It's perfect." He tucked a loose strand of hair behind my ear, brushing my neck with the backs of his fingers. "You look . . ."

He stalled, like he was searching for the right word. I wanted to supply him a couple that I thought fit the blank, but instead I waved my hand in encouragement.

"Kissable," he said finally.

I smiled wide. Operation: Irresistible was a success.

Daphne cleared her throat. Loudly.

I crowded Rio out the door. As I closed it behind me, I called out, "See you later, Daph."

A muffled "My name is Daphne" sounded behind the thick wood of the door. But I barely paid attention to her because I was with Rio. I didn't even roll my eyes when she clicked the lock on the door.

I'd already decided I was going to play it cool and let him take me wherever it was he had planned. So about two seconds after Rio took my hand and started leading me down the porch steps, I asked, "What's on the agenda for today?"

He grinned at me and squeezed my hand. "Eager, huh?"

So what if I was? "Just curious. Can I guess?"

"You won't, but go ahead."

Ah, a challenge. I stared at him thoughtfully and tapped my pursed lips. "Well, we did bumper cars yesterday. Paddle boats?"

"No."

I waited until he got into the driver's side to query him again. "Rollerblading?"

"No." He turned the ignition.

I faced him and tried to discern clues from his face. Impossible. "You're excellent at poker, aren't you?"

He glanced at me as he pulled out into the street. "How did you know?"

"Lucky, I guess," I mumbled. But I wasn't going to be so easily defeated. "Sailing?"

"You already said that," he pointed out.

"No, I didn't."

"You guessed paddle boats."

I frowned. "That's not sailing."

"What is it, then?"

My frown deepened at the amusement in his voice. "Not sailing."

He chuckled. "Any more guesses? Or are you going to give up?"

I shot him a narrow gaze. "Wineries?"

"No."

"Skateboarding?"

"No."

"Bungee jumping?"

He cocked a brow at me.

"Hmmph." I sat back, arms crossed, and frowned at him.

"Are you giving up?" he asked, his lips quirking.

"Never," I declared.

He laughed as he merged onto the highway. "I love that about you."

"Don't think you're going to divert me with sweet compliments."

"Never." He took my hand, set it on his thigh, and covered it with his own. It was high on his thigh, and I had to fight the desire to walk my fingers up to the holy land.

I eyed him suspiciously but didn't say anything because I was afraid I'd have to move my hand, and that thought was simply not pleasant. So we drove on in silence, Rio rubbing his thumb in the grooves between my knuckles and me trying not to hop up and straddle him while he was driving. Amazingly, it required all my concentration, and I didn't realize we were downtown until we parked.

Frowning, I got out of the car and tried to think of what we could possibly do downtown on a Sunday. "Are we going shopping?"

"Would you like to go shopping?"

"No." Frankly, I didn't care as long as it was with him, but I didn't want to give him a fat head. I waited for him to come around the car and slipped my hand in his.

He touched my lips with a finger. "You look cute when you pout."

"I'm not pouting."

He raised a brow.

"I'm not." I resisted the urge to stamp a foot when he grinned.

"Come on." He tugged my hand to cajole me into walking. He didn't have to try very hard—I would have followed him anywhere to find out what he'd cooked up for today.

I quizzed him about our destination while we walked, but he wouldn't even give me a clue, except that we were almost there. Then we stopped in front of a set of stairs up to a classic-looking building.

My jaw must have dropped all the way to the sidewalk, I was so shocked. "The Pioneer Art Museum?"

He grinned. "Told you that you wouldn't guess."

"The Pioneer Art Museum?" I asked again, inanely. I turned to gawk at him. What did a boxer know about art?

It was like he read my mind. "My mom is an artist. I was practically raised inside museums." He started up the steps.

I followed his wordlessly, still in shock. Over the art and that he could read me so well. "An art museum?"

"They have an exhibit I wanted to see. Chagall." He glanced at me. "I wanted to share it with you."

I wasn't sure I knew who or what Chagall was. "I don't really know much about art."

"You don't have to know anything to appreciate it." I must have looked disbelieving, because he slipped his arm around my waist and guided me up the stairs. "It'll be fun. I promise."

That I didn't doubt; I just didn't want him to think I

was lacking in any way. I remembered all those times my mom harassed me to go with her and Daphne to the museum, telling me one day I'd regret not going with them, and mentally cursed. I hated when Mom was right.

Rio paid our admission and snagged a map. He opened it and studied it like it led to hidden treasure. "Let's look at the permanent collection first."

"If the Chagall exhibit is the highlight, then maybe we should hit it first."

He grinned. "Sometimes it's better to have dessert last."

Pursing my lips, I pretended to think about it. "Nope. Can't think of one occasion where that would be true."

Laughing, he led me off on our museum adventure. Mostly, the paintings didn't look any different than the paint-by-number pictures I used to do when I was a little girl, but I tried to pay attention to each and every one so Rio wouldn't think I was bored out of my mind. Which I was. He wasn't even holding my hand anymore, so I couldn't even claim that pleasure. Instead, he walked ahead of me, stopping every now and than in front of a canvas.

I concentrated so hard that by the second room I'd developed an enormous headache. I guess it was obvious something was amiss by the way I was rubbing my temples, because the next thing I knew Rio walked up behind me, snaked his hands around my waist, and hugged me to him. "This isn't going over as well as the carnival, is it?"

"Well—" I frowned at the painting in front of me "—I just don't get why a picture of a bowl of fruit with a bird perched over it is so great."

"It's not."

"It isn't?"

"No."

I tried to turn around to confront him, but his arms were like bands of steel holding me in place, so I settled for glaring at him over my shoulder. "Then why the hell are we here?"

"You're approaching this all wrong." He nodded toward the painting. "Art is subjective. Not everyone would find this painting intriguing."

"I know. Only fruitflies and dogs with avian fetishes."

He chuckled against my neck. "What you need to do is walk around until you find a painting that strikes a chord with you. That arouses your passions. Come walk with me."

I would have rather had him arouse my passions, but I decided to humor him and try what he suggested. With his arm still around my waist, he led me through several rooms until we were in a different wing.

The paintings here were different; more naked women and less fruit.

"Don't study all the paintings. You'll go insane that way," he cautioned. "Pick one that intrigues you."

He let go of me and wandered off, drawn by a picture of a particularly robust nude woman. I hoped that wasn't what he was attracted to, because compared to her I was a stick.

Instead of looking at more art, I studied Rio. Forget the paintings—the look on his face was absolutely mesmerizing. Like he was staring at an Alienware ALX computer with four NVIDIA GPUs and a liquid cooling system. He gazed at the blob of paint like it was the most amazing thing he'd ever seen.

I didn't know whether to be jealous or in awe of such feeling. Feeling overwhelmed and needing breathing room, I headed off into an adjacent room.

"A lot of naked women," I murmured, looking around at the other museum goers. You'd think more men would hang out here; it was a whole lot more tasteful than subscribing to Playboy. No articles though.

In the center of the room, there was a large painting of a young woman reclining on a white sheet, a bird settling on her hand. Something about her expression attracted me.

"Gustave Courbet was known for his nudes."

I turned and looked at Rio, who had once again plastered himself behind me. This time I relaxed into his embrace as I faced the painting again.

"A couple of his paintings were banned for a long time because they were considered scandalous."

I wrinkled my nose. "I could see that, I guess. She looks kind of—" I shrugged "—thoroughly debauched. Like he ravaged her before he painted."

"She does look happy," he agreed.

I wanted to be her. Limp, on a bed, with perky nipples. "There's still a damn bird in it, though."

He grinned. "Let's go look at some modern stuff."

Rio took my hand and we casually strolled through the galleries, stopping occasionally when he wanted to point out a famous painting he thought I might recognize or if he thought something would please me. He even told me interesting facts about the artists and how his mother educated him.

I watched him as he talked about his mom. His love for her shined through his eyes. "She sounds pretty great."

"She is," he agreed with a bright smile. "Talented too. She's an accomplished painter herself." He brushed my cheek with the back on his hand. "She'd love you. She'd say you're the daughter she always wanted. She'd like your spirit."

I cleared the lump that formed in my throat at that admission. "My mom tried to take me to museums too. But I stayed home to play with my computer. Daphne went, though."

At the time, I didn't think my mom and Daphne really wanted me there with them. Now I remembered Mom imploring me to go along with them. At least for a little while; after a while she didn't bother asking anymore.

Hmm.

Rio led me to a series of paintings that were obviously from one artist.

"Oh, my God," I exclaimed. "Talk about scandalous."

He laughed and squeezed my hand. "These are by Georgia O'Keeffe. She's known for her florals."

"Um, Rio?"

"Yes?"

"These are *not* flowers."

He grinned. "Sure they are."

I blinked a few times and then let my eyes go unfocused, like those 3-D pictures where dolphins and boats pop out if you stare at them just right. After a minute, I shook my head. "Nope, I only see womanly parts." I narrowed my eyes at him. "That's why you like art, isn't it? Because of its pornographic qualities."

He laughed. "These *are* erotic."

I raised my brows hopefully. "Do they give you ideas?"

He closed the distance between us, his hands gripping my hips. "You give me ideas."

I tipped my head back and flirted with danger. "What kind of ideas?"

"Of the floral variety."

I pictured myself spread open for him like the flowers in the paintings, bared to his touch. I grabbed the museum floor plan out of his hand and fanned myself.

His grin was dark and knowing, like he had a line straight into my mind. "Let's go see the Chagalls."

I nodded, but remained in a sexual fantasyland. I didn't snap out of it until we stood in front of a painting that took my breath away.

It was love personified, sexy and innocent at the same time. The man sat on a chair with the woman sitting on his lap, their figures entwined, his hands suggestively and protectively on her. At first glance you knew the couple in the painting were soulmates.

There was a depth of emotion in this one that I didn't

see in the other works of art. It was exactly what I wanted, and it brought tears to my eyes.

"This one," Rio said, holding me tight against him. "This one attracts me. Because of how deeply it's making you feel."

I rested my head on his shoulder and stared at the painting until it was time to go.

The trip home was silent. You could have heard a pin drop (except for the purr of the engine). I was still dazed by the last painting.

Thrilled, disturbed, and confused, I glanced at Rio. He specifically wanted to show me that painting. What was he saying?

I turned, folded my left leg under me, and stared at his profile. I tried to will myself to see beneath the surface, but all I saw were the beautiful sharp planes of his face. It was a face I could see waking up next to for, oh, the next sixty years or so.

He threw me a quick glance before returning his eyes to the road. "You okay?"

"Yeah." No. I sighed. I wasn't sure. I opened my mouth to ask him what our excursion meant to him. Then I wondered if I really wanted to know, because once you have knowledge, there's no going back.

And what would it mean? Say Rio admitted he believed he was my soulmate. After I got over the jumping up and down screaming phase, what then? Take him home to my parents? Right. I could just see it. *Hi, Mom and Dad— I dumped my well-off, successful boyfriend and hooked up with a boxer who was in the military, but he gets me even if he isn't socially conscious and has little means.*

Like I said, right.

I was better off not knowing what showing me Chagall meant to him.

To hell with it—I wanted to know. "Why did we go to the museum?"

Rio pulled over to the side of the road, turned the car off, and faced me. "Why do you think we went?"

"I asked you first."

His lips quirked a little but he refrained from smiling. "Don't you already know?"

"No."

He raised a brow.

"Okay, maybe I do know." I rubbed the tip of my nose. "But I want to hear it from you."

"I'm not entirely sure you're ready to hear it," he said as he took my hand.

"Oh, I'm ready," I reassured him.

He studied me as if he were probing beneath the layers of my psyche. I opened my eyes wide so he could look inside me easier and see I meant it. Only I held my eyes open like that for so long, they dried and I had to blink furiously.

Rio laughed softly and cupped my face with his free hand. "God, I love you, Philomena Donovan."

I stopped blinking, thankful I was sitting down because I would have toppled over at the admission. As it was, I almost slid off the seat onto the floor.

His smile turned wry. "See? I didn't think you were ready."

"No! No." I shook my head. Then I nodded. "I'm ready. Really."

He didn't look like he believed me.

"Well—" I frowned in confusion "—how do you know? We'd barely talked until a couple of days ago."

"Phil, I knew the first time I met you. I've just been waiting for you to realize Barry wasn't the one for you."

"Really?" I tried to stay logical, but the excited girly part of me inside wouldn't sit still. "From the first time?"

He tipped his head, his gaze direct and revealing. "Didn't you?"

I pursed my lips. "I'm not sure."

His eyes called me a liar.

Okay, so if I really thought about it, yeah, there was something there from the beginning. I'd thought it was just sex. Guess I was wrong.

I scrunched my face. "But we haven't even kissed yet."

"No. We haven't." His thumb was a slow drawl on my lips. "I should get you home."

The nerves in my lips had never felt so alive. If a finger could do that, imagine what his lips could do. I bet they were really talented. I bet they could perform any number of tricks. I stared at them and imagined.

"Now I know I should get you home." He dropped his hand but I could tell he didn't want to by the sex-laden tone of his voice.

Without thought, I lowered my gaze to his lap.

Gulp. Talk about sex-laden.

He put both his hands on the steering wheel, took a deep breath, and restarted the car. We got to my house too quickly, and I was still at a loss as to what to do when we got there.

Rio came around the car and opened my door for me. I stepped out and he plastered himself against me, his gaze full of longing and want. He pressed forward and lowered his head.

This was it. This was when I'd finally find out how he kissed, how he tasted. This was the time for action. I wanted to lean into him, grab him, and hold him close.

But I couldn't. Barry and my parents and Daphne's party loomed over me. Not to mention the little four-letter word Rio had bandied about earlier. Which was huge. Exciting, but in a life-flashing-before-my-eyes kind of way.

So right as his mouth hovered over mine, I pushed him back. "I need time to think."

He studied me, like he was going to say something, but changed his mind and just nodded. He took a reluctant step back, and then another until he was back in the car.

"Well, damn," I said as he drove away.

Chapter Sixteen

Lessons Learned from MacGyver
#143
The best partners are the ones you always seem to fight
  with.

Sitting on the mat, I tried not to fidget as Dwight lectured us, but it was hard. Let me count the ways.

1) We'd just finished working out and I was sweaty. My underwear stuck to me uncomfortably. As if that wasn't bad enough, it had shifted so it straddled the dividing line, if you know what I mean. And I couldn't dig it out because of my cup (yeah, I wear one just like the guys—it's not fun getting hit in the cootchie).

2) I couldn't stop thinking about what Rio said to me yesterday. His words went around and around in my head until I was crazy dizzy and even more confused than I was at the museum.

3) I'd drunk a lot of water during my workout and I needed to pee.

"Philomena."

"Yes, sir." I snapped to attention, barely stopping myself before I saluted Dwight.

He shook his head as if he didn't know what to do
with me. "Philomena, I asked you how you're doing
with the homework."

"Homework?" Shit. What did he want us to do? And
God, did I need to pee. "I'm doing well. Thanks."

He exhaled a long-suffering sigh. "Do you remember
what the homework was?"

I glanced at Matt, who sat next to me, willing him to
give me a clue. He shook his head at me too. I told him
with my eyes that I was going to start interviewing for a
new best friend.

Then I remembered. "Oh, yeah. The homework.
Right. I'm doing well."

There were a couple of snickers from the lower belts.
I took notes so I could properly beat—um, instruct them
on respecting their betters later.

"In what way have you practiced?" Dwight asked, waiting for me to hang myself.

I'll show him. "Just by being more aware when possibilities present themselves."

"What opportunities have shown themselves to you?"

Rio was the first thing that came to mind. I needed
someone to help me get back Barry and there he was,
right in front of me. Though I couldn't tell Dwight that.

Of course, it didn't quite work out the way I'd meant
it to. I'd pretty much forgotten about Barry the last
several days. Hell, I'd barely thought of him at all. But
Rio . . .

I went mushy on the inside. I really liked him. A lot.
The kind of like that makes you queasy in the gut.

I frowned. I'd gone out with Rio because of Barry, but
maybe Rio was the real opportunity here.

The lightbulb flicked on bright.

But my parents . . . The light dimmed a little. They
were still expecting Barry at the party. I felt a moment of
panic. Then I remembered the feel of Rio's hand in

mine and how he felt holding me from behind as he whispered in my ear. Not to mention how glowing I felt after spending time with him.

I blinked. I loved him.

"Doc," Matt whispered sharply. He jerked his head toward our instructor, who was studying me with a quizzical expression.

"I have to go." I jumped up and bowed quickly to Dwight. "I have an opportunity I need to grab."

I rushed out of class, snatched my bag, made a pitstop at the bathroom, and headed for my car.

The guy at the front desk looked up when I burst through the gym doors. "Hey, there. How can I help you tonight?"

"Is Rio still back there?" I pointed to the studios, already heading in that direction.

"Yeah." His welcome smile turned knowing. "Go right on back."

"Thanks." I ran down the hallway to Studio 3, but he wasn't there. A trill of panic coursed through me, but I told myself he had to be here—I just knew it—so I started looking in all the glass-enclosed classrooms.

I found him in the last one. His back was to me and he was sparring with someone. It took me a few seconds to recognize that his opponent was Barry.

Taking a deep breath, I pushed open the door and stood there, waiting for them to take a break.

Barry must have caught sight of me out of the corner of his eye, because he dropped his hands and said, "Mena?"

"Barry, don't—" I winced as Rio popped him a solid one on the chin "—drop your guard."

To his credit, Barry didn't go down. He did look pretty dazed though.

Rio stopped weaving and bobbing. "You okay, Barry?"

"Uh, yeah. Sure."

He didn't sound sure, but I wasn't going to point that out. I needed Rio to myself.

"Why don't we call it a night," Rio suggested to Barry, though his eyes were on me. "You should ice that."

"Uh, yeah." He staggered in the direction of the locker rooms, shaking his head the whole time.

Taking off his gloves, Rio waited till Barry was out of earshot before he said, "This is a surprise."

I couldn't tell from his neutral tone whether that was a good thing or bad. Might as well assume the best, so I smiled. "I was in the neighborhood."

He just stared at me with his blue eyes. I couldn't read any emotion in them, and that freaked me out. I came here to hand over my soul to him—why was he watching me dispassionately?

I was tempted to back out of the room, but that would have been the coward's way out. I scowled. I'm no coward.

Damn it, I came here to give him an answer and I was going to give it regardless of what he did with it. I knew what I wanted and I was going to seize it.

Narrowing my eyes, I strode up to him till I was toe to toe. His expression never changed.

I lifted my chin and said the only thing I could think of. "I came to fight you."

There was a flicker in his gaze. When he didn't say anything, I thought I'd imagined it.

But then he said, "Are you sure?" and I caught a hint of something that sounded an awful lot like hope and desire.

Emboldened, I dropped my bag and pushed it aside with my foot. "More sure than anything."

He studied me as if gauging how serious I was.

"What? You scared?" Probably not the wisest to goad him, but if something didn't happen soon I was going to snap with tension. "Think you can take me?"

"I can take you," he replied softly, tossing his gloves aside. "The question *is* can you handle it?"

"I want to handle it," I told him seriously.

His smile was a slow, erotic bloom, kind of like those Georgia O'Keeffe paintings. "Good."

Then he rushed me.

It surprised me, but I ducked left. As I went under his arm, my elbow grazed his ribs, then I immediately whirled around and punched his kidney (lightly, only so he'd feel it, not so he'd piss blood for the next week).

He retreated out of my striking range and appraised me with renewed respect. "Impressive."

I shrugged and kept an eye on him. He was out of my range, but he could still kick me (did I mention how his legs were strong and lanky?). Not that I thought he might kick—boxers wouldn't think of doing that, since it was against their rules. In Kung Fu, there were no rules, so I had the advantage. The only advantage he had against me was his smile.

He dropped his weight, lifted his fists, and bobbed from foot to foot, doing his boxer's thing.

See, I didn't get all that fidgeting around that boxers did. Granted, Rio didn't expend a lot of energy doing it; I had the feeling he did it just enough to try to psych me out, to distract me.

He threw a couple of jabs. I faded back and slapped them away, measuring the length of his arms. Fortunately, I was used to working out with Matt, who also had long arms, so I wasn't intimidated by his reach. I just needed to slip in and he'd be mine.

I *so* wanted that.

I thought I'd play with him a little myself. I set my weight and circled him to the left. "Is that all you've got?"

"I'm taking it easy on you." He didn't sound winded, even though he'd been sparring with Barry.

I liked that. "I think you're scared of being beat by a girl."

"I might be if I actually thought you'd beat me." He threw a right hook.

It was lightning fast and I almost got caught by it, but I managed to duck under, striking up to his nose (I only tapped it). I was going to use it to leverage his head back and push him to the ground, but there weren't mats in the studio and I didn't want to hurt him. So instead, I twisted his head to the side and stepped behind him.

I pulled him down till my lips were against his ear. "Do you know how to go down?"

His lips curled, slow and evil. "Try me."

Shiver. I'd love to.

Before I could reply, he twisted around, grabbed my arms, and kicked my foot out from under me. I breathed out as I went backward (it helps take the sting out of the fall), but at the last moment he twisted.

"Oof," he huffed as I landed on him.

"That's what you get with chivalry." I climbed on top of him and hooked my feet under his knees to keep him from reversing my hold. As I hindered his arms, I tucked my head in the crook of his neck. It was tactical (gets your head out of striking distance), but I used the opportunity to inhale him.

God, he smelled good.

He struggled to get his arms free. He was much stronger than I and without my causing him any pain I knew he could overpower me, but his struggle was half-hearted. Really, to me it seemed like he was just rubbing himself up against me, but that may have been wishful thinking.

"Next time I'll know better," he said, testing my hold.

I lightly bit his neck. "Next time you won't get the chance."

He bucked his hips and flipped us over, reversing my grip and pinning my arms over my head.

I paused. Mostly I just wanted to luxuriate in the feel of him stretched on top of me. Unfortunately, he wore a cup too, so I didn't get the full effect.

Even though I couldn't feel his package, I could see how turned on he was by the look in his eyes as he stared at me. His gaze dropped down to my chest. My gi top had opened, and under it I wore only a white athletic bra, soaked with sweat. It had to be transparent enough to show the outline of my nipples, which hardened shamelessly under his gaze.

And to tell the truth, the way he had me pinned turned me on. A lot. A new feeling for me, because fighting was always just fighting, not foreplay.

I arched my back. Using everything at your disposal was the first commandment in Kung Fu. "Like what you see?"

His grip tightened on my wrists even as he casually replied, "It's intriguing."

I was about to take advantage of him being distracted when he dipped his head and set his teeth around my right nipple.

I gasped. "Oh, that's playing dirty."

He nuzzled me. "I haven't even begun to get dirty yet."

I wanted to ask why the hell not, but I got lost in the bite and release of his teeth on me.

With the last vestiges of sanity, I crossed my arms over my head, broke his hold, and tugged both his arms to one side. Quickly, before he could react, I straightened his leg by burrowing my knuckle into a pressure point, flipped him over, and sat on top of him again. His arm still in my grip, I trapped it in a figure-four leverage.

"Do you give up?" I panted. From excitement, not exertion.

He smiled slowly, his lids half-lowered. "Are you sure you won the round?"

"I think it's a safe assumption." I torqued his arm the tiniest bit to remind him that I had him trapped. No way was he getting out of this hold, at least not without a broken shoulder.

"Didn't your parents teach you about assuming?" he asked.

"Yeah—" I grinned "—but some situations are outside the realm of change."

He cocked an eyebrow. "Are they?"

I applied a touch more pressure on his arm. "Aren't they?"

He reached up with his free hand, wrapped it in my ponytail, and brought my face down to his, his mouth a breath away from mine. "You sure about that?"

Gulp. "You may have a point."

His nose rubbed mine. "Are you going to let me go?"

With his lips (the lips I'd been coveting for what seemed like eons) so close to mine, I was already losing my grip, in more ways than one. But I couldn't concede so easily. Not without knowing what I was getting in return. "What's in it for me?"

"I should think that's obvious."

"Um—" I shivered as his cheek rasped against mine. "I need clarification."

His tongue flicked my lower lip. "How much clarification?"

I almost fell off him, I was so shocked at the shooting sparks the lick caused. I felt it all the way down to my toes and back up to the tips of my breasts.

My hold slipped. I'd thought he would muscle his way out of it, but then I realized he wanted me to surrender to him. Willingly.

I don't know why I found the thought sexy.

"How much clarification?" he repeated with another flick of his tongue.

Clearing my throat, I said, "The terms need to be completely outlined."

"Okay."

I narrowed my eyes at how easily he agreed. "Okay?"

His grin was pure mischief. "I have no problem outlining the terms."

"You don—oh!" I gasped as he ran the tip of his tongue along the outside of my lips. I moaned and tried to capture his tongue in my mouth.

"Agree first," he panted, withdrawing from me.

At least he was as affected by our game as I was. I pressed my leg against his cup, which had started shifting. "You drive a hard bargain."

"Phil."

I swallowed. This was it. No turning back. I had to be sure this was what I wanted. Gazing into his eyes, I read all the need—sexual and more—and I knew.

I let go of the leverage and wrapped my arms around his head. "I agree."

He stared at me, as if making sure I was on the same page as he. It took him all of two seconds to see this meant exactly the same thing to me as it did to him.

But just in case he didn't *really* get it, I said it out loud. I needed to say it out loud. "I love you."

He ran a finger down my cheek. "Phil," he murmured like it was the most beautiful word in the English language. "I love you too."

And then his lips lowered.

Chapter Seventeen

Best Kisses I've Ever Had: The Top Three

3) *Brian Anderson, kindergarten, on the playground*
2) *My dad, when I caught an Indra Swallowtail butter-*
   fly for his collection
1) *Rio—at least I think it will be if it ever happens*

Finally I was going to know what his kiss was like, if it was worth abandoning my plan to get Barry back and make my parents happy in the future. I let my muscles ease and puckered my lips invitingly.

A door slammed down the hall. Both our heads jerked up. Someone was coming. Rio quickly rolled us to sitting and grabbed his shirt.

Damn it.

We'd both just gotten off the floor when Barry poked his head into the studio. "I'll see you Wednesday, Rio."

"How's your face?"

I looked at Rio, impressed. By his calm question you'd never have suspected a moment before he'd been flirting with ecstasy. I, on the other hand, probably looked thoroughly despoiled. I glanced in one of the mirrors. Yep. Totally.

Barry shifted uncomfortably, like he could sense the undercurrent flowing back and forth between me and Rio. "Mena, do you need a ride home?"

A week ago I would have jumped at the chance to be alone with Barry. The better to convince him to get back together. Now . . . I gazed at Rio and shook my head. We had unfinished business to take care of. "No, thanks."

"Uh, okay." Barry gave us an odd look. "I guess I'll just go then."

"Okay," I said with an impatient smile.

He started to leave and then turned around again. "By the way, Cindy wants to get together again. All four of us. Maybe Friday?"

He didn't sound enthusiastic. And by the look on his face, the prospect seemed to rank right up there with going to the dentist. But I didn't care. I wanted Rio alone—*now*—and it seemed expedient to agree. "Sure. Great."

"I'll tell Cindy then." He edged out of the room again.

I waited to see if he'd come back, but he stayed gone so I turned to Rio.

"I'm sorry," he said before I could utter a word.

"What for?"

"For earlier." He ran a hand over his short hair. "I shouldn't have lost control like that."

I frowned. "Yes, you should have."

"Anyone could have walked in."

"I know." Shiver.

He eyed me sharply. "Are you turned on by that?"

I pursed my lips. "Would that be bad?"

He gaped at me. Then a glorious, sexy smile spread across his face. "No. I guess it wouldn't."

"Good," I said, returning his smile.

"Come on." He grabbed my arm and dragged me out of the studio.

"Where are we going?"

"My place."

Finally, some action. I let him hustle me past the receptionist, who looked intrigued by the determined way Rio rushed by. There'd be gossip about it tomorrow, but I didn't care. One, I didn't work out there. Two, it was kind of nice having a man want you this bad.

As he propelled me toward his car, I hesitated. "But I drove."

He stopped. "Would you feel better if you had your car with you?"

"Yes." If he bombed in the sack (ha!), then I'd have an out.

Seriously, what if all the hype didn't live up to the actual act? What if the fireworks turned out to be duds? Best if I could make a quiet getaway.

Rio didn't question my decision. He just nodded. "Follow me."

Like I'd lose him now.

Five minutes later we pulled in front of an old warehouse. I frowned. The building itself wasn't so bad—like a huge brick box with lots of big windows—but the neighborhood left a little to be desired.

I locked my car and joined Rio. "Is my car going to be safe here?"

"Yeah." He unlocked a side door and held it open for me. "I have a deal with the local thugs."

I couldn't tell if he was serious or not, so I let it pass and entered. He led me to an industrial-sized elevator. He yanked the outer doors shut, rolled down the inside gate, and flipped the switch and got it moving.

"Ever played out any Fatal Attraction scenarios in here?" I asked idly.

"Not yet." He glanced at me. "But the first time I kiss you, it's not going to be in an old freight elevator."

I leaned against the wall and crossed my arms. "So you're going to kiss me?"

"I'm going to kiss you all over." The elevator jerked to a stop. "Very soon."

He opened the doors and walked out into darkness. He reached along a wall and a bank of soft lights came on behind him.

"Oh, wow." I'd been so focused on what we'd do when we got here, I didn't think about what "here" would be like.

I stepped out and did a slow turn to take it all in. The room was huge and looked simple but expensive. I wondered if he saved his money until he could buy what he wanted instead of settling for cheap stuff. The kitchen was off to one side.

But the most impressive feature was the view. The bank of windows overlooked the river and downtown Portland. At night, like now, it looked like Disneyland. "You live here?"

"Not what you expected?" He moved up behind me and circled his hands around my waist.

I shook my head, partly in wonder, partly because he was numbing my mind by nuzzling on my neck.

He turned me around to face him. "We need to talk."

Forget talking. I wanted sex. I leaned into him. "We need to get undressed."

His eyes glinted in the low light. "Okay." He picked me up, fireman style, and hauled me off.

"That was easy," I said, smacking his ass.

"I seem to be easy where you're concerned."

"Thank God for small favors." I held out his waistband to get a peek inside.

He smacked my hand aside. "Behave."

Pout. "That's not what you were telling me a minute ago."

"We're almost there," he reassured me as we went behind a partition I didn't realize was there. It'd looked like a wall from the living room. He turned a knob and soft lighting lit the room.

"Wow," I said again, trying to see around him.

It was his bedroom. Along the wall was another view of the city, which was incredible, but what really attracted me was the raised platform in front of it with the low, big bed on it.

The bed was *really* big. If we got in on opposite sides, it would have taken days before we met in the middle. And it had a cushy white comforter on it with fluffy pillows.

"Nice bed. I didn't know they made them that big."

Rio tossed me in the middle and stripped off his shirt. "I like space."

"Seems like there's plenty here." I spread my arms out and rubbed them over the cool cover, like I wasn't swooning over my first uninhibited gander of his chest, which, by the way, was *excellent.*

"I like how high the ceilings are too." I'm sure the effect was spoiled because I didn't bother to look up to see exactly how high they were. In my defense, the eighth wonder of the modern world was standing before me. "Makes the room seem even bigger than it is. Though it's got to be, what? Five hundred square feet?"

"Phil, are you sure you want to discuss architecture now?" He tugged at the drawstring on his shorts.

My mouth went dry. "Um. No."

"Do you need help?" He knelt at the foot of the bed and leaned over me to undo my gi pants.

"Maybe I should take a shower first." I gave him my sultry look. "You could take one with me."

He shook his head and pulled my pants off. His hands trailed down my legs. "I can't wait. We'll shower after. I promise."

Thank God I shaved today. "Uh, but I'm kind of sweaty."

"You smell fantastic," he said, running his face along my calf.

I smelled like Ron, the guy I'd worked out with this evening, but the way Rio was rubbing his face against my skin reduced my mind to mush, so I didn't have it in me to argue.

He moved up between my legs and flicked my cup with a finger. "We need to get this off."

I grinned as I pushed the waistband down. "It doesn't turn you on?"

"To be honest, no." He fingered the lacy panties I wore underneath. "These are more my style."

"Good to know. I'll remember that at Christmas." I almost moaned when his finger slipped under the leg of my underwear and ran along the outer lip of my private red-light area. I thought he was going to slip in and take me where no man had in forever (I hoped, I hoped) but instead, he pulled the panties out of my crotch and settled them the way they were supposed to be.

Rio forestalled my question. "I just want to see what it looks like before I take it off."

Okay. I could deal with that. While he was admiring my underwear, I decided to take off my gi top. And then I needed to take the bra off—it wasn't exactly sexy.

After I tossed it aside and settled back onto the bed, I noticed he'd sat back on his haunches and was studying me. I grinned. "Irresistible, aren't I?"

"You don't even know," he said reverently. His shorts, cup, and whatever else he had on came off in one smooth movement and he lunged to cover my body with his before he flipped us over so I was on top.

I automatically put my arms around his neck and arched my hips into his impressive-feeling package. "Happy to see me, huh?"

He loosened my hair from my ponytail and ran his fingers through it. "More than you can imagine."

I sobered at his serious tone. Looking into his eyes as his thumb rubbed my jaw, I lost my breath.

"Are you ready, Phil?" he whispered huskily.

This was it. This time I knew without a doubt he was going to kiss me.

"Um." I panicked for a split second. What if he had a flabby kiss? What if he slobbered? I *so* didn't want that.

By this time my lips were practically against his, so close I felt him smile. "Do you trust me?" he asked in his dark bedroom voice.

"Yes," I answered without thought.

"Good." His hand tightened in my hair and he drew me down the next few millimeters to meet him.

Our mouths glanced, once, twice. His teeth nipped my lip and my eyes flew wide open at the electric shock that coursed through me. I opened my mouth, intending to say "Whoa" but he swooped in for the attack. He skillfully teased me with small flicks, making me want more but not giving it.

We rolled again so he was on top. His hand went to my ribcage, just below my right breast.

I moaned as I tried to capture his tongue, and I shimmied at the same time to get his hand to move up to where it'd do more good. He resisted, luring and teasing until I thought I was going to explode out of my skin.

"Enough," I declared. I grabbed his head with both hands and brought his mouth down for a full-on kiss.

Mistake. Big mistake. Not because it was terrible, but because it was so glorious I thought my heart was going to explode into a million pieces. Of course, at that same second he moved his hand to my breast.

I screamed—or I would have if he'd let go of my lips. But he clung to them, sucking and licking until I could feel it in regions down below.

I came up for air. "Take my goddamn underwear off."

His grin was wolfish. "Are you sure?"

"Yes!" I grabbed his ears, pulled his face down, and glared. "And you better have condoms or you're going to be in serious trouble."

"I love a woman who knows what she wants."

I don't know how he did it, but he had my panties off, a condom on, and was back between my legs in one movement.

"I always thought you were talented." I gasped as the tip of his hard-on slipped just inside me.

"Thanks for the vote of confidence," he said with some trouble as he pulled out of me.

Nice to know he was as affected as I was. I moaned as he rubbed himself up and down before he slipped into me again.

I pouted, at least as well as I could under the circumstances. "I can't decide."

"What." It was more a grunt than a question.

"Whether I should be pissed that you haven't touched me more—" gasp as he pushed higher into me "—or die of intense pleasure now."

He nipped my lip. "Why settle?"

Without warning, he slid out of me, turned me over, and slipped his arm under my waist to pull me to my knees. Holding me against him, I felt him position himself from behind and slowly—painfully so—glide into me. The stretch was both painful and erotic, and I didn't know whether I screamed because I hurt or because I was in ecstasy.

Then he bit my neck and said, "Remember. This is what you wanted." And he slid his hands down till they were buried deep between my legs.

Another scream.

Intense.

Blinding.

He barely moved his fingers, just a soft caress right

where it counted. My hands on the mattress for balance, I pushed back to meet his deep strokes.

Inside me, I felt him swell and grow even harder. The change in the way he felt triggered something inside me. I screamed his name and came harder than I'd ever thought possible.

Rio's hands tightened on me and he gave a triumphant shout as he rolled against me one more time, forcefully. Then we collapsed into a panting heap on the bed.

Hours must have gone by before I had the strength to elbow him. "Off."

"Sorry," he mumbled as he rolled off my back.

I took a deep breath and opened my eyes. Rio lay on his back next to me, eyes closed, one arm flung out, the other resting on his chest.

I grinned. "Trouble breathing after that brief workout, huh?"

He cracked open one eye. "Brief?"

Shrugging, I turned onto my back and pretended to study the ceiling. "It was over pretty quickly, don't you think?"

He gripped my chin and forced me to face him. "Are you saying you weren't satisfied?"

I hadn't known such satisfaction could be achieved on this plane of existence, but I wasn't going to tell him that. So I shrugged again and said, "It was a good start."

His beautiful blue eyes narrowed and he came up on an elbow. "A good start."

"Though I guess for someone your age you lasted pretty long." I blinked in what I hoped was an innocent fashion. "I've read it's only downhill from here."

He rolled over onto me, trapping my arms over my head. "Already talking trash about my performance, huh? I guess I'm going to have to prove myself."

Shiver. "Yeah, I guess you will."

He bent his head and sucked half my breast into his mouth (it's small so it's possible—trust me).

"Oh!" I almost bucked him off me I jerked so hard.

He grinned against me. "Not bad?"

"It's acceptable," I said breathily.

"Hmm." He licked around the areola like it was a Tootsie Roll Pop before he gave the other side the same treatment.

I grabbed his ears and held him to me, arching my back so he could take more.

"Like it?" he whispered.

"Oh. My. God."

"I can move on if you want."

"Yes. No." I frowned. "Yes."

He let go of my nipple with a pop and grinned up at me. "Which is it?"

"Well—" I pursed my lips "—can I reserve the right to come back to this?"

"Of course." He smiled like a dark angel and slid down my body. "But you won't want to."

Ha! Right. He didn't know how intensely wonderful this was!

"Oh, my *God*," I screamed as I felt his tongue lick into me.

"Told you."

I started to tell him gloating didn't become him, but he did it again and again and again until I couldn't think and all I knew was the velvety feel of his mouth against my most private parts and the sharp tingles his tongue caused as it explored me.

I closed my eyes and gripped the covers in my fists, trying to ground myself, but everything spun faster and faster until I exploded in a fiery burst.

Rio lifted away from me. If I could have formed a coherent thought, I might have asked him what he was doing. But he settled between my legs a moment later so I assumed he'd gotten another condom.

Gasping, I came to when he pushed himself into me. "Sensitive?"

"Deliciously so," I reassured him. I opened my eyes to find him gazing down at me like I was the center of his universe and he couldn't think of a better place to be.

I smiled. I couldn't think of anyplace better either.

"You want to stop?" he asked tightly.

"Are you kidding?"

He grinned. "Good." He sat up and pulled me so I straddled his lap. It put my chest at the right level for his mouth, which he fully took advantage of.

I sighed and let my head fall back. "Oh, this position is *nice*."

He chuckled and I savored the feel of his breath against my skin. "Have I proven myself yet?"

"Um—" I bit back a moan as he did a particularly naughty swivel with his hips "—maybe soon."

"Soon?" he growled against my neck, nibbling that sensitive spot just below my ear.

"Very soon. I think."

He gripped my butt and ground me against him. "I guess I'll have to try harder then."

"Harder is good." I gasped as he hit a sensitive spot inside me, over and over until I was on the brink again. I held on to his shoulders for dear life.

"Come for me, Phil."

The low gravel of his voice was all I needed to fall over the edge. I came again—not as hard as the other times, but in an undulating, long wave. He cried out moments later, his hands holding me in place.

I wished I had the energy to open my eyes and watch him come. I wanted to. The thought would have whipped me to a frenzy if I hadn't been wasted and wilted against his chest.

Carefully, Rio lifted me in his arms and settled me under the covers. He kissed my forehead. "Be right back."

I nodded and snuggled into the down comforter. His bed was so comfortable.

I heard a toilet flush, a faucet running, and then the soft padding of bare feet on the cement floor as Rio made his way back to bed.

He slid under the covers all the way across the bed until he scooped me tight against him, spooning me from behind. Brushing my hair with his fingers, he whispered in my ear. "Phil?"

"Hmm?" I groggily wiggled till his package fit perfectly against my butt and slipped his hand up so it rested on my breast. So we'd be ready for later.

"Stay the night."

"Okay," I agreed readily. It felt right.

He pressed a kiss to the nape of my neck and snuggled in.

I sighed happily and fell asleep, safe in his arms.

Chapter Eighteen

"*It's really nice to wake up in your own neighborhood, and not have to worry about going to work, no plans. Just being able to ease into the day.*"
—MacGyver, "The Prodigal" Episode #9

I startled out of sleep, my heart pumping.

Something was weird.

Someone stirred behind me and I froze. Who the hell was in my bed?

I looked down. Where the hell was my bed?

A hand snaked around my waist and tugged at me. "What's wrong?" the muffled voice said.

Rio. Right—I was at his place. I relaxed into his embrace and slid back under the covers. "Sorry."

He tucked me into his side and nuzzled my neck sleepily. "What for?"

"For waking you up."

"It's okay." He pressed against me and I noticed just how okay it was.

I smiled, slow and lazy, and slid my hand down to cup his hard-on. "I don't know about this. I'm surly in the mornings before I have my coffee."

He rolled me on top of him so I straddled his hips. "This is much more effective than caffeine."

"Is it?" I swooped down to lick his nipples. I'd found out last night that they were as sensitive as mine.

He speared his fingers into my hair and held me close. "Guaranteed to put you in a great mood all day."

"That's a big promise," I murmured against his chest. I wiggled to tease him a little, but only ended up breathing harder myself. "A day is pretty long."

He gripped my butt and surged against the outside of my womanly parts. "Good thing the day is almost half gone."

My hand had just gotten a grasp of the situation (if you know what I mean) when I realized what he said. I sat up, his erection in my grip. "Half gone?"

Nodding, he covered my hand with his and squeezed. "It's past ten."

I groaned, both from what we were doing and the fact that it was so late. "I have to go to work."

He nuzzled my neck. "Stay. Just for a little longer."

"I want to, but I can't." It came out a plaintive whine. I jumped off the bad and scrounged for my clothing. "I'm late. Even for me."

Leaning on his elbow, Rio half-sat, half-reclined. "Will you be missed?"

"Yeah. My intern will freak out and raise a search party." I picked up my athletic bra. Ripe. I wrinkled my nose at the smell and decided against putting it on. Then I sniffed myself. I smelled like Kung Fu and sex and Rio. I couldn't go to work smelling like this. "Can I use your shower?"

"It's through there." He nodded toward an opening I hadn't seen.

I paused a moment, caught in the regret on Rio's face. Such a contrast to seconds ago when he looked ready to eat me alive (sexually speaking). I wanted to kiss him and apologize and promise we'd continue later.

Ugh—I didn't have time. I had to get to work. I knew he had a fairly flexible job, but not everyone could flit through life just being a boxing instructor. I had a serious career.

With a sigh, I rushed to the bathroom (also huge). I turned on one of the biggest showers I'd ever seen and waited for hot water.

I was rinsing my hair when the shower door opened suddenly. I gasped as Rio stood in the doorway.

"I came to help." He stepped in and closed the door behind him.

The shower didn't seem so spacious with Rio standing in it. "I've done this a lot. I think I can handle a shower on my own."

"Can you?" He reached around me to grab a dispenser of soap and squeezed some into his hand. Without any ado, he set his hands to my breasts and lathered them up.

"I already washed that part," I protested weakly.

He nodded but didn't stop. "I'm sorry I let you oversleep. I didn't know you had to be at work at a specific time, otherwise I would have set an alarm."

I winced at the mention of an alarm. "I try to get there by ten." I almost groaned and his hands rubbed down my sides to my back. I leaned against him, slippery and wet and turned on.

"We'd better make sure you're clean all over then," he said against my neck. His finger slipped between my legs from behind.

I let him soap me all over. They say cleanliness is next to Godliness, and that morning I was definitely in heaven.

* * *

When I finally arrived at work, I may have been in yesterday's clothes but I was, in short, euphoric.

I was in love.

I strutted down the hall to my cube, Starbucks cup in hand, grin permanently etched on my face. I slid into my chair and greeted the guys. "Good morning, gentlemen. Beautiful day, isn't it?"

The couple who heard me over their headphones and pumping music stuck their heads around their cubicles and scowled at me.

"She must've gotten laid," one of them muttered.

I had. Gloriously so. But I just gave them a Mona Lisa smile and let it flow over me.

Today, I felt good. Relaxed. Thoroughly sated.

It was a new experience for me. Who knew? I didn't. I had no idea sex could be like *that*. I wrinkled my nose. Someone should have told me. I picked up my phone and called Matt at work.

He answered on the third ring. "What?"

He sounded alert, if peeved, but I ignored that. "Why didn't you tell me about sex?"

"Doc?"

"Who else would it be?"

"I don't know. I get people calling me all the time asking about sex."

If he were in front of me I would have punched him, but he wasn't so I did the next best thing: I pulled out the whistle from my desk and blew it loudly.

"Doc!"

At the same time, there was a yelp from the peanut gallery and a dull thud. I looked up in time to see one of the guys startle right out of his chair and fall on his ass. I grinned. It was the same one who said I must've gotten laid, so I didn't feel bad.

"What the hell is your problem?" Matt snipped at me.

"I've got no problem. I'm perfect today." I beamed as if he could see it.

"I don't have time for this," he grumbled. "I have a deadline to meet."

"Then answer the question."

"What question?"

I rolled my eyes. "Why didn't you tell me about sex?"

"Didn't you go to junior high? They covered all the basics."

"Exactly!" I nodded. "It's the *other* stuff I'm talking about."

"What other stuff?"

I opened my mouth to tell him and immediately flushed crimson. A crimson, I'm sure, that was so dark I looked purple. I certainly felt purple.

I couldn't tell Matt. That'd be like going home and reporting to your mom.

Ick.

So I said, "Never mind."

There was a pause and then Matt said, "This is revenge for some imagined thing that I've done, isn't it?"

"No." How could I explain I really needed someone to talk to about the shattering (literally) revelations I had last night? "I'm sorry I bothered you. Go back to work. I'll call you later."

I hung up as he was sputtering indignantly. He'd get over it.

What I needed was a close woman friend to talk to. Someone to confide things. Daphne? I made a face. Not Daphne. Someone wise about sex. Someone who'd understand.

I snapped my fingers. Magda.

"Mena."

I whirled around and hit my knee on my desk. "Ouch. Damn it. Johnny?"

He leaned across my desk, his hands gripping the edges. "I haven't heard from your sister yet."

"So?" I scowled and rubbed my knee. Then I actually looked at him and noticed the slightly panicked, slightly distraught expression lining his face. "Johnny, are you lovesick?"

He sighed dramatically and wilted (I swear). I had to bite my lip not to grin.

"Is it something I did?"

I shook my head. It was something I did—or rather, didn't do. Like give Daphne his phone number. But I wasn't going to tell him that. No telling how he'd react. He looked like he might attack.

So I said, "I think she was just busy this weekend."

He looked stricken. "With other men?"

Ha! That'd be the day. "No, we did some, um, sister things. You know, bonding and stuff."

"She didn't like me, did she?"

"No. I mean, yes, she liked you." I sighed and covered my forehead. "Look, I forgot to give her your phone number."

He blinked. "You did?"

Counting to ten, I waited for him to charge. I counted a couple of extra numbers (just in case) but nothing happened, so I glanced up at him.

It was pitiful, as if someone had handed him a brand new computer with dual processors and a terabyte of storage.

"Look," I said, not able to take his sorry state any longer. "I'll give it to her tonight when I get home. I promise. I'll even make her call you."

"Okay." His grin was goofy but somehow endearing. When he walked away, he had a skip in his step.

I shook my head. Pathetic. I squinted and tried to imagine him as a brother-in-law.

Nope. Couldn't do it. But stranger things happened in the world, I guess.

"Daph!" I slammed the front door closed and took the stairs two at a time, heading for the kitchen to get an emergency snack. I'd been starving all day. Must have been all the exercise I got yesterday.

Daphne looked up from the vegetables she was chopping and frowned. "Why do you keep doing that?"

"What?"

"Calling me Daph when you know I don't like it."

I opened the fridge and rummaged. There was more food than usual. My sister must have stocked up. Problem was, none of it was edible. "What the hell is this?"

She glanced at the package I held in my hand. "Tempeh."

I poked at it. Blech. I put it back and searched for something normal. Fortunately I found a package of hot dogs in there.

"How would you like it if I called you—" Daphne's brow wrinkled in thought.

"Mena?" I offered helpfully as I pulled out a frying pan.

"I was thinking more like Phil."

Rio called me Phil, and I didn't mind it one bit. In fact, I liked it a lot. "You're right. I'd hate it."

She frowned at me. "Then why are you smiling?"

I shrugged as I rotated my frying dogs. "Maybe it's a tic."

"You're strange, did you know that?"

"You're one to talk. You buy foreign substances that they didn't even feed to astronauts in space." I rolled the hot dogs off the fryer and onto a plate. Instead of sitting at the table, I leaned against the sink and watched

Daphne as I blew on my food to cool it. "What are you making?"

"Stir-fry." She glanced at my plate. "There's enough for both of us if you don't ruin your dinner."

"With this? This is barely a snack." I took a bite, chewed it happily for about one point three seconds before I gagged and spit it out onto the plate. "What *is* this?"

Daphne looked at me like she wanted to say *duh*, but being Daphne she'd never do that. "Tofu dogs."

"Gross." I did a residual gag, stepped on the garbage can, and tossed the pseudo-dogs in the trash. "Why didn't you warn me?"

She shrugged and continued chopping.

I narrowed my eyes at her. If I didn't know better, I'd say she looked satisfied. "You aren't going to put anything weird in the stir-fry, are you?"

She blinked innocently. "I was thinking of tofu dogs, but maybe I'll leave that out."

I gawked at her. "Did you just make a joke? Am I in an alternate universe?"

She rolled her eyes as she poured oil in a pan and started adding veggies.

Smirking, I got out a couple of plates and silverware for the two of us. "Guess who I ran into today?"

"Who?"

"Johnny."

She dropped half a dozen zucchini pieces onto the floor. "Johnny?"

"Yep. He misses you."

"He does?" The disbelief in her voice made me grin harder.

I nodded. "Bad."

"Philomena Donovan." She glared. "It's not nice to tease people."

"God, you sound like Mom." I crossed my eyes at her

as I reached around her to get napkins. "And I'm not teasing. Johnny's in a bad way for you."

She gaped at me.

"Yeah, I know." I shook my head in wonder. "I don't understand it either."

I waited for her to say something more, but she just stood woodenly at the stove and stirred the food. I sat down at the table and kept an eye on her, afraid she'd set something on fire in her trance-like state.

She brought the pan to the table and dished food onto both our plates. I was surprised it smelled so fantastic. Not that I'd admit that to her. Besides, it was probably because I was starving.

I dug in. It tasted as great as it smelled. I don't know why I was surprised—what *didn't* Daphne excel at?

As I shoveled more food into my mouth, I realized she wasn't eating. She sat there staring at her plate.

My first thought was she poisoned the food to get rid of me (I don't think she was ever thrilled to have a younger sister), but I decided against it. If she wanted to off me, she'd come up with something more scientifically interesting, like blowing my atoms apart or something. "Something wrong?"

She looked up with a puzzled frown wrinkling her forehead. "I don't know what to do."

I waited for her to expound, but she didn't so I had to ask. "About?"

"Johnny."

"Call him." Can we say duh? "Invite him to your party."

"But—" She frowned at her plate.

"But what? Just tell him you want to be his love slave and let nature take its course." It wasn't rocket science.

Actually, what Rio did to me last night had to have required advanced education. I grinned. I'd have to ask to see his credentials.

"I don't have his phone number," she said plaintively, pushing her food around.

I speared a mushroom with my fork. "No biggie. I told him I'd give it to you."

The way she stared at me made me uncomfortable. It was as if she didn't know what to say, like she was stunned I'd do something like that for her.

I fidgeted in my seat. I didn't know why it was so unexpected. I wasn't completely a sucky sister. I cared.

I did. Really.

"Do you know where my cell phone is?" I asked after we finished dinner.

"On the coffee table. Next to that magazine with the red cover."

Of course Daphne would know exactly where it was. Good thing for me—it saved me the half-hour it would have taken me to find it.

I flipped it open and searched my call logs. Aha. Phone still open, I went back into the kitchen and handed it to my sister.

"What's this for?" she asked with a frown.

"Johnny's number. Call him while I take a bath."

She gripped my arm as I turned to go. "Thank you."

"I told you, it's no biggie." Wrinkling my nose, I shrugged off her hold. You'd think I saved her kitten or something. I escaped into the bathroom right as I heard her tentatively greet Johnny.

"Made his day," I murmured as I ran the water and tossed a handful of lavender salts in. By the time I stripped, it was half-full so I got in.

Yeah, I was eager for a bath. I'd wanted one all day—I was sore all over, not only from my Kung Fu workout but from the one Rio gave me too (grin). And I needed some time to think things through now that I didn't have that cloud of lust hanging over me.

Okay, I admit, maybe I still had a miasma of lust clouding my mind. I couldn't be blamed. Rio would have that effect on even the most shriveled-up virgin.

"You know," I told myself, "forget thinking. There's nothing to figure out." I was in love with Rio and he loved me. If my parents didn't like him—almost guaranteed to be the case—well, it wouldn't be the first time I'd let them down.

It would have been so great to have them dote on me just for the one day though.

I sighed.

But I needed to keep my eye on the ball. I knew in the end being with Rio was the best thing for me.

"Don't you think, Mac?" I leaned back and rested my head on the rim of the tub to look up at the MacGyver poster overhead.

Only he was gone.

I gasped. Someone kidnapped MacGyver out of my bathroom.

Daphne.

"Daphne!" I debated staying in the bath—I'd just gotten in, after all—but I didn't think I could enjoy it knowing she took down *another* MacGyver poster. After I made it clear what I thought about that.

Water sloshed over the edge of the tub as I surged out. I yanked the door open and, at the last minute, decided to grab a towel, though at this point I don't know why I cared about my treacherous sister's sensibilities. "Daphne!"

I strode into the living room. She was curled on the couch, phone to her ear, casual as could be. Like she wasn't a MacGyver assassin.

She blinked at me. "You're dripping on the rug."

"To hell with the rug. Where is it?"

"Don't swear." She turned her attention back to the phone. "Johnny, could I call you back? Mena's having an episode." She smiled at something he said. "She *is* a little high-strung."

I stamped my foot. "I am not high-strung. I was fine until you started messing with my most prized possessions."

"Thank you. Goodbye." She closed the phone and faced me, one eyebrow cocked. "What was so important it couldn't wait until my conversation was finished?"

"MacGyver," I shrieked, waving my arms.

She crossed her arms. "You know, this obsession you have with a fictional character really isn't healthy."

Teeth clenched, I said, "The poster in the bathroom. Where. Is. It."

"I took it down." At my growl, her chin jutted. "The mold growing on it was unsanitary."

I'd show her unsanitary. Hands outstretched, I advanced on her.

Her eyes widened and she gasped. "You wouldn't."

"Try me."

She huddled closer to the arm of the couch. "You'd have to explain it to Mom and Dad."

I froze midstep. She was right. Damn.

With another growl, I turned on my heel, marched to my room, and slammed the door. Real adult, I know.

"Just a few days," I muttered to myself. Just a few more days and Daphne would be out of my hair. And the next time she asked to stay with me, I'd say it was already occupied, even if I had to find a homeless person to move into the spare room.

I pulled on my robe and was pacing my room when Daphne knocked softly on the door. "Mena, there's a call for you."

I was about to tell her what she could do with the call when she said, "It's someone named Rio." I threw open the door and snatched the phone out of her hand. "Hello?"

"Phil."

The one syllable turned my insides to mush. A warm glow replaced the tension I'd been feeling.

"You're welcome," Daphne said, firmly closing the door behind her.

I stuck my tongue out at her and then turned my attention completely to Rio. "Hey."

"I missed you all day."

God, his voice was sexy. Caused tingles all over. "Me too. Missed you, that is."

"What are you doing now?"

I grinned. "What do you have in mind?"

"I could come over."

"My sister's here." Somehow I felt funny about bringing a guy to my room with her staying here. Which was wrong since it was my home and I should have been able to do anything I wanted in it. "You're so lucky you're an only child."

He chuckled. "I always thought it'd be nice to have a sibling."

"Not one like Daphne."

"She seems nice. Though I don't know much about her except that she likes Sexual Trances and does a mean striptease."

I pursed my lips. "You think she does a mean striptease?"

"I'm not an expert on stripteases—"

"I'm sure you're not," I said dryly.

"—but hers seemed adequate." There was a tinge of humor coloring his words. "Of course, I'd be much more interested in seeing you perform."

My lips quirked. "Would you?"

"Definitely." Pause. "I have a boombox and some music if you're interested . . ."

I grinned. "Are you a good tipper?"

"Baby, I can guarantee you won't complain."

Shiver. "Well then, get the music ready. I'll be right over."

Chapter Nineteen

Lessons Learned from MacGyver
#56
Imagination is the most important thing the human mind
has.

If Rio wanted a striptease, a striptease he was going to get. À la Philomena Donovan, which meant I had to gather a few things before I headed over to his warehouse.

He was waiting for me downstairs by the elevator, leaning against a wall with his arms crossed, when I arrived. He wore a soft-looking T-shirt, jeans that sat low (real low) on his hips, and no shoes. Who knew bare feet could be sexy?

He watched me with his hawk-like gaze, not moving a muscle as I approached. "I was beginning to think you'd changed your mind."

"No." Like I was idiot enough to change my mind. I stopped right in front of him. "I had to decide which outfit to wear."

He did a slow perusal of my body and then fingered the lapel of my robe. "You didn't find anything?"

I grinned as provocatively as I could. The robe was tactical; what was underneath was going to make his eyes explode. "Oh, I found something. I think you'll like it."

"I like this robe." His finger slipped inside the collar. I got goosebumps as the back of his finger brushed my skin. "It's soft."

I pushed his hand aside and sauntered into the elevator, extra swing in my hips. I turned around, leaned against the back wall, and crooked a finger at him. "You're wasting time."

He stepped in, closed the doors, and came at me, his weight low like a predator's. My heart drummed rapidly but I didn't back down. He put his hands on either side of my head and leaned his body into mine. "What's in the little bag?"

I glanced down at the bag I carried. "You'll see."

"I'd like to see now."

Catching the double entendre, I grinned and slid my hand down between our bodies to cup him. "Impressive."

He dropped his head and nibbled his way up the column of my neck. "Maybe we should skip the striptease."

"Oh, this isn't something you want to skip." I ducked under his arms to operate the elevator controls. Surprisingly, he stayed where he was, gazing at me with a combination of amused tolerance and desire.

I grinned. I loved power.

When we got to his loft, I rolled the doors open and walked into his living room. I didn't have to look to know he followed; I could practically feel the heat of him moving toward me.

Setting down the bag, I looked around for a chair suitable for the striptease. I decided to use one from his dining room set because it had a slat in the back. I picked it up and set it in the middle of the living room. "Sit there," I instructed Rio, refastening my robe.

He lifted an eyebrow. "The couch would be more comfortable."

"You'll be comfortable." Deliciously evil grin. "I promise."

"Why does that worry me?"

"Where's the music?"

"I'll turn it on." He went to a low end table that had a monster remote on it and pressed a button. Suddenly there was soft music surrounding us.

"You have the place wired with hidden speakers?" I asked, unable to repress the techie in me.

"In the walls."

"What kind?"

"Homemade. A friend of mine tinkers with sound systems. He set me up."

"They sound great. Maybe I can talk to your friend sometime."

"You need speakers?" he asked, sitting in the appointed chair.

I set my bag down on the table and rummaged through it. "Matt's been looking for speakers. He's picky about sound quality though."

"I'd like to meet Matt."

I glanced up, frowning. "Why?"

He smiled. "He's your best friend. I thought women always wanted to introduce their new boyfriend to their best friend. Isn't it some kind of ritual we men have to go through to prove our worthiness?"

I pictured Matt and Rio meeting.

Yikes. I grimaced internally.

"Well?" he persisted.

"Yeah. Maybe," I answered evasively. I pulled out the handcuffs I'd been looking for and hid them in the pocket of my robe.

"You don't think he'll like me?"

I tried to remember the last guy I dated that Matt liked. Nope. There'd never been one. But I ducked my head and said, "How could he not like you?"

Silence. I snuck a glance at Rio. He didn't look like he bought that last statement. I really needed to work on my acting skills. I wondered if that was something I would have learned if I stayed in college.

I was going to change the subject but he beat me to it. "Is the music okay?"

Oh yeah—the music. I tuned in to it. "Alicia Keys?"

He nodded.

"It's great." It had the perfect rhythm to grind my hips to. I just needed to get back into the groove of the striptease. Mentioning Matt threw me off.

But I knew what would get me back in the mood really quickly. "Take your shirt off."

He cocked an eyebrow, but didn't question my command. He pulled it over his head and casually tossed it onto the nearby couch. "Anything else?"

I glanced down at his jeans and wondered if I should have him undo the fly. No, I wanted to do that myself. I shook my head as I advanced on him. "You're exactly how I want you."

Almost true, but he didn't need to know what I had in store for him.

I checked out his chest completely. Every other time I'd seen it I was too close to him to really get a good look. From a couple of feet away I had the perfect vantage point. But in reality, it looked just as good as I remembered it.

I pointed at his pecs. "How do you get such definition?"

"Working out and clean living."

I smirked. He wouldn't be living too clean tonight.

"You have that look in your eye."

I pursed my lips. "What look?"

"The one that says you're up to no good."

I took a couple of steps so I stood between his legs. He spread them so I could move in closer. I leaned down and whispered in his ear, my fingers trailing down his arm to his hand. "You don't really want me to be good, do you?"

He grinned. "Either way I think I'll be just fine."

"Damn right." I quickly pulled the handcuffs out of my pocket, pushed his hand behind the chair, and snapped it on his wrist.

Rio jerked but before it occurred to him what was going on, I passed the other end of the cuffs through the chair and clasped his left wrist too.

I straightened and grinned at the perplexed expression on his face. "What's the matter?"

He tugged on the handcuffs as if they'd give. As if I'd have cheap handcuffs. These babies were regulation. I'd bought them online from a superspy store a while back when I had an intense curiosity about, well, let's just say about uncharted seas. And tonight that's exactly where I was setting sail.

"Phil, I don't know about this." He tried to scoot free.

I pushed him back in the chair with a hand on his chest. "Do you trust me?"

He stopped moving and stared into my eyes. "Yeah," he said without hesitation.

Oh, that was nice. I smiled, open and bright. "Good."

He yanked on the hardware. "But I don't like this."

"You will," I promised. I grabbed the remote from where he'd tossed it on the couch and turned the volume up a notch. Then, my gaze on his, I slowly undid the sash on my robe. Holding it closed, I waited for the right beat and then let it pool on the floor at my feet.

He inhaled sharply.

That's right. I ran a hand down my torso and grinned knowingly. "You like?"

"It's not bad." But the huskiness in his voice was admission enough.

I tried not to gloat. I knew I looked good; I'd picked my outfit especially. But hearing it in his voice was like a shot of Stoli to the bloodstream. Maybe two shots.

"Do you have more underwear like that?" His eyes caressed their way down my body.

I shrugged casually. "Maybe."

Actually, it was the only real lingerie set I'd ever bought. I didn't wear cotton briefs like Daphne, but I didn't go all out like I did tonight with garters and stockings and everything.

It was damn expensive too. I'd read about the launch of Agent Provocateur's online store and I went to check it out. I'd never heard of them before, but I immediately found this set and I couldn't resist. The black merry-widow made it look like I had boobs and the stockings made my legs look long and sleek. I wore the high heels because I figured guys really liked them. Didn't they all have fantasies about having sex with a woman who wore nothing but high-heeled black fuck-me shoes?

He cleared his throat. "When does the striptease start?"

"Eager, are we?" I gave him a coy smile and started shimmying to the music. I caught the beat and began to really strut my stuff.

I swiveled my hips around in a belly dancing type of move (thank God for Shakira videos) turning a circle until my back faced him and he had a clear view of my butt undulating. I ground my hips a little more, my arms in the air. Turning to look at him over my shoulder, I asked, "How're you doing there?"

He swallowed and nodded, but didn't say anything.

I ducked my head to hide my grin. Perfect.

Lowering my arms to circle around my head, I swiveled around and did a Beyoncé move right up to his legs. With a surreptitious glance, I checked out his package.

Yep. I had to stifle my gleeful giggle. Totally engorged, um, I mean, engaged.

His legs opened again, slowly as if he had no control over them. I ignored the invitation and danced where I was, dangerously close yet so far away.

Rio cleared his throat again. "When does the stripping start?"

"Anxious?" I looked pointedly at his fly. "Or worried?"

"You know, payback's a bitch."

I knew my smile had to be über-cocky. "As Pat Benatar said, hit me with your best shot."

I think he growled, but I couldn't be sure because the music spiked for a moment.

Because I wanted him completely frenzied, I shrugged my shoulder in such a way that the strap of my merry-widow fell. Then I did the same with the other side.

This time he did growl. He jerked his arms forward, like he wanted to grab me, but the handcuffs brought him up short.

With an outstretched arm, I pushed him back into his seat and straddled his hips. His head strained forward, and because I still had clothes on (if you could call the scanty underwear clothes), I let him nuzzle his way down my chest. I should have known better though, because he unerringly latched onto my nipple through the lace.

I pushed him back again. "This is a lap dance. I can touch. You can't."

The way he looked at me, like I was toying with a jungle cat who was a second away from mauling me, almost made me reconsider. Almost. Worst-case scenario, his revenge would drive me insane. How could I mind that?

Rio respected my rules though. He sat back, his eyes feral, and let me continue.

"Good boy," I said because I like to live on the wild side. Then I ground my hips over him like there was no tomorrow. Every now and then, I'd bump his hard-on. I could feel its twitching through the jeans.

The problem with the striptease (or just tease, because I hadn't begun to strip yet) was that as much as I was torturing Rio, I was torturing myself as well. I felt creamy and hot and swollen to the point where I just wanted to settle on him and drive us both to oblivion.

He read it in my face too. His lids were half-lowered, making his grin look that much more lazy and sinister. "Backfiring, isn't it?"

In response I reached behind me, undid the tight little row of hooks on my merrywidow, and deliberately let it fall to the floor. The song ended, and the sudden silence before the next song started punctuated the unveiling.

"That was well timed," he said, straining forward to touch my breasts.

"I meant it to be." Complete lie, but he didn't need to know that. I leaned back a little and began to gyrate again. "You don't really think I'd let you have them that easily, do you?"

He shot me a sheepish grin. "Had to try."

Men. But there was part of me that liked that he wouldn't give up trying to get at me. It made me want to show him what he was trying to get.

So I stood up, shimmied till my back was to him, and eased the lacy thong down my thighs. With another wiggle, it slid the rest of the way to the floor. I kicked it off my feet and looked over my shoulder to make sure Rio was still paying attention.

Attention—ha! He was practically drooling, his eyes glued on my butt. So I shook my ass some more before I turned around and gave him something to really goggle at.

"I think you proved your point."

I grinned at the hoarseness in his voice. "What point?"

"That you're better at stripping."

"Ah." I'd forgotten about that. It'd become so much more than that to me. I sidled up to his legs again, kneeling in front of him. I pushed them apart and wriggled my way between them. I did a couple sinuous moves against his belly, deliberately brushing against his arousal. He groaned and arched his hips into me.

Yes. I had him at my mercy. Grinning, I eased myself down his abs to the waistband of his jeans. On impulse, I licked the skin right there.

He gasped. "Jesus, Phil."

I glanced up. "Hmm?"

"Enough playing." He jerked at the handcuffs again.

"Careful. You'll scrape your wrists raw." Next time I'd get fur-lined cuffs. I lapped at the tight skin of his belly again.

"Phil," he moaned.

There was a world of pleading in his voice, and because he'd been such a good boy, I decided he deserved more. So I unbuttoned his fly and opened the zipper slowly with my teeth.

His cock sprang out like it had a life of its own. Eager and flushed, if it could speak I knew it'd be begging me too.

I gave the tip a lick. I liked the way it leapt under my tongue so much, I gave it a few more. Then I figured I might as well go all the way, so I took him in my mouth as deep as I could.

Rio groaned. I knew he was a breath away from coming so I released him with a pop. "Not yet."

He stared down at me, his cheekbones flushed. "You want me just as badly."

I couldn't deny it—it was in the tenor of my voice, the hardness of my nipples, and the wetness on my thighs. But that didn't mean I was going to give in. Not yet.

I backed off and went to rummage in the bag again. I found a condom and the jar I wanted. I unscrewed the lid as I sauntered back to him.

"Peanut butter?" he asked with a raised eyebrow.

I grinned. "Yummy and full of protein. For endurance," I said with a wink. I quickly slipped the condom on him before scooping peanut butter onto a finger.

"Actually, I was trying to be imaginative. Chocolate sauce is so overdone."

"You aren't really—" he swallowed audibly "—I guess you are really going to smear that on me."

I grinned but concentrated on covering his nipples. When there was a thin coat on each peak, I set the jar down, straddled his hips, and worked the tip of him just barely into me.

We both moaned, but I had plans so I tried to keep my head. Sliding down on him, I steadied myself on his shoulders and bent to lap at one of his peanutty nipples.

"Phil."

My name was a rumble in his chest that I felt more than I heard. For variation, I kissed him, hard with lots of tongue, before I attacked his other nipple. But I was impatient for more, so I straightened to concentrate on what was going on down below.

"You have some peanut butter on you." The next thing I knew he'd leaned forward and grasped my nipple between his lips.

"Rio." I grabbed his head to hold him close. I yelped as he bit me, then moaned as he sucked the pain away.

My hips began to grind against him in their own rhythm, fast and frenzied. I wanted to slow down, but my body wouldn't listen to my mind. I let my head fall back and my eyes shut as I got close.

Rio's groan muffled against my breast. He drew more of it into his mouth and thrust up with his pelvis. The two sensations together sent me over the edge. I screamed and held onto his shoulders. Distantly I heard him shout too, but I knew he orgasmed because of how he felt inside me.

I collapsed against his chest, breathless and light-headed, my head cradled in the hollow of his neck.

"Phil?"

I grunted.

"Think you can uncuff me now?"

Chapter Twenty

"If you try hard enough and make the best of a situation,
the situation won't get the best of you."
—MacGyver, "Birth Day" Episode #36

Wednesday evening. Daphne was going out with
Johnny (yes, miracles do happen), so I'd arranged to
have Rio meet me at my place after his boxing lesson
and my Kung Fu class.

One problem I didn't foresee was getting rid of Matt,
who gave me a ride home.

Usually it was no big deal. If we weren't going out for
a pint, he'd drop me off at home and race off to get
something to eat. Tonight, for some reason, he'd parked
his car, followed me up the steps to the porch, and
slouched against Magda's door with his arms crossed.

"I can make it in on my own." I gave him a look over
my shoulder as I unlocked the front door. "See?"

"Maybe I'll come in for a while." He unslouched and
started for the doorway.

"No!" I coughed. "I mean, I'm kind of tired. I thought
I'd take a shower and hop into bed."

That wasn't a lie. Not really. I did plan on taking a

shower and hopping into bed pretty quickly. I just didn't plan on doing it alone. Or sleeping any time soon.

Something on my face must have given me away, because Matt's eyes narrowed. He studied me for an uncomfortably long second before he said, "I'll come up and make you a snack before you go to bed."

"No, really, Matt—"

But he'd already pushed his way past me and was skipping up the stairs.

Grr. I ran up after him. What time was it? Maybe I had enough time to humor Matt before Rio got here.

Eight thirty-five according to the DVD player. Shit. I told Rio to be here at nine.

"You want a peanut butter sandwich?" Matt called from behind the refrigerator door.

I almost choked. "Um, peanut butter would be great."

"Although I could make just about anything."

I walked into the kitchen to see him close the door with his foot because his hands were full. I glanced at the clock on the oven, hoping I'd misread the DVD clock, but it read eight thirty-six.

He dumped everything on the counter and took out a cutting board. "I can't believe you went grocery shopping."

"I didn't." I hopped up on the counter and tried to resign myself to eating a sandwich when the only way I wanted peanut butter was if it was smeared on Rio.

"Oh, right. Daphne's staying with you. I wondered why there was healthy food in there and not just candy bars." He opened a drawer and frowned. "Where's the bread knife?"

I blinked. "Huh?"

"Never mind." He opened another drawer and apparently found what he was looking for.

Matt knew his way around my kitchen better than I did. I had no clue where anything was or even what they were called, much less that you used a special knife for bread.

But who cared about any of that? It was eight thirty-eight, for God's sake. I tapped my foot against the cupboard. "Hurry up."

He glanced at me as he ever so carefully spread peanut butter across the slices. "Hungry, huh?"

"Starving." But not for food.

He smirked like he could read my mind. Hell, he probably could.

I turned beet red. Because the thoughts in my mind were X-rated. Maybe worse than that. Was there a Z-rating?

He held up a piece of bread. "I have to start over."

"Huh?" I looked at the bread to see what was wrong. Mold?

"Look." He held the piece close to my face. "The peanut butter is uneven. It's thicker on this side, and in trying to even it out I tore the bread."

I squinted to see what he was talking about, but I couldn't. I shook my head. "Where is it torn?"

"Here." He poked a finger at a spot that looked perfectly normal and punched a gaping hole in it. "Oops."

I glared at him. "You did that on purpose."

"Me?" Matt blinked his eyes like an innocent baby.

I didn't buy it. Through gritted teeth, I said, "Hurry *up*."

"That hungry, huh?"

"Matt!"

"I'm making it. Jeez. You can't rush genius."

Bastard. I was about to tell him unequivocally to forget the sandwiches and that he had to leave when I heard the front door open and voices at the bottom of the stairs.

Shit. Daphne. And Johnny.

"Looks like you have company," Matt said casually.

I scowled at him, hopped off the counter, and went to

head off disaster. I met my sister and her beau at the top of the stairs. They had their arms around each other (gross) and were laughing.

I narrowed my eyes at Daphne. "I thought you were going to be out tonight."

"I was." She batted her eyes innocently. Only with Daphne it wasn't an act. "But I forgot a sweater, and I wanted to show Johnny my room."

"Hi, Mena." Johnny gave me a jaunty little wave. "Didn't know you were going to be here."

I caught the look they exchanged, like I was the one intruding. Delusional. And I wasn't going to let them get away with it. I held my arms out to keep them from entering the living room. "You can't stay."

"I live here," Daphne said slowly, as if I were retarded.

"No, you're just visiting. And you said you were going to be out."

"We were. But we're making a stop here first." She gave Johnny a look that clearly asked him to excuse her insane sister.

But I wasn't insane, I was horny. "Look—"

"I'm just going to show Johnny around." They brushed by my outstretched arms. "Oh, hi, Matt."

I stood at the top of the stairs, grinding my teeth while Daphne introduced Matt to Johnny. As I headed toward the kitchen, I checked out the clock again. Eight fifty-seven.

Please, *please*, let Rio be late.

"Want me to make you guys a peanut butter sandwich?" Matt asked Daphne and Johnny.

"No, thanks. Johnny and I went to this great restaurant close by. Hurley's. Have you ever been there, Matt?"

I choked on spit.

They glanced at me before going back to ignoring me. Then I noticed the top Daphne had on. "Hey!"

All three of them gave me various looks of exasperation.

As if I cared. I was more concerned with the tank top she stole from me. Even worse, it looked better on her than it did on me. "What's up with the clothes?"

"Do you like it? I got it 'specially for Johnny." Her eyes widened and she blinked rapidly.

I frowned at my sister. "Are your contacts dry?"

"I don't wear contacts." She blinked a few more times, but what got the message across was the pleading look she gave me.

Oh. *Oh.* She didn't want Johnny to know she wasn't as hip and happening as he thought she was. This was going to cost her. (I couldn't help it—I think it's a gene younger siblings inherit.) Then the doorbell rang.

Oh, shit.

"Doc, that was the door."

Matt, ever the helpful best friend. I glared at him and walked down at a snail's pace to the front door. Wishing it was a homeless person come to crash the party, I threw open the door. But I knew I wouldn't be that lucky. "Rio."

His smile was slow and sexy as he stepped forward to circle my waist with his arms. "Phil."

"Listen, there's something I need to tell you . . ."

He bent down and laid the most passionate, hungry kiss I'd ever experienced on me. His arms tightened and next thing I knew I was pressed against the length of him—the very hard length of him—lost in his mouth. Finally, we came up for air and stood, staring into each other's eyes, breathing like we'd just sprinted a mile.

Rio pushed back a strand of my disheveled hair. "There was something you wanted to tell me?"

I blinked. "There was?"

He grinned and began to move me toward the wall. "If there wasn't, then maybe we can get on with—"

"Doc, you okay down there?"

Oh, shit. I looked up at Rio, who looked back down at me with a frown. "Who's that?"

I grabbed the collar of his T-shirt. "Listen, things haven't quite gone according to plan."

"Doc," Matt called from the top of the stairs. "You okay?"

"Fine," I squeaked, my hands tightening on the shirt.

Rio's gaze cooled and his arms loosened from around me—a little, but I could still feel it. "If you're busy, we can reschedule."

"No! No." I shook my head vigorously. Then I grimaced and dropped my head against his chest. "All I wanted was an evening alone with you and then everyone showed up and I can't get rid of them and I don't know what to do." I lifted my head as inspiration struck. "I can throw them out the living room window."

Rio chuckled and gripped my waist. "That might be extreme."

"An explosion would make them leave." I pursed my lips. "One time MacGyver made a bomb out of weed killer."

"Doc?" Matt's heavy footsteps clacked on the wood steps. "Oh. Sorry. Didn't mean to interrupt."

Yes, you did. I pulled out of Rio's arms and glared at him.

Matt ignored my obviously peeved expression, skipped down the rest of the steps till he was on the landing with us, and held his hand out. "I'm Matt. Philomena's best friend."

I sighed at the challenge in his statement and waited for the usual male posturing.

Surprisingly, Rio just smiled and accepted the proffered hand. "Rio McKenna. Good to finally meet you. Phil's told me a lot about you."

"Funny, because she hasn't mentioned a thing about you."

I elbowed Matt and turned to Rio with a gritted smile. "Matt's making peanut butter sandwiches. Would you like one?"

Rio's eyes went sultry. "I'd love one."

This time I whacked my forehead for real.

Matt stared back and forth between us, finally giving Rio an approving nod. "I think we'll get along just fine."

Peachy. That was all I needed.

But at the moment, there was nothing I could do but go along with this whole farce of an evening, if I wanted to get Rio alone anytime soon. So I sighed and trudged up the stairs with them.

"Barry!" Daphne cried with a smile.

Oh, God—not Barry too. I looked around the living room. It wouldn't have surprised me if he was hiding under a cushion or something.

She walked out of the kitchen, Johnny hot on her tail. "It's nice seeing you again, Barry."

Shit. I plopped onto the loveseat with a groan. I forgot about that.

Matt looked around. "Barrington is here?"

"Barrington?" Daphne frowned briefly before understanding hit. She turned to Rio. "I didn't know your name was Barrington."

"It's not," he said with a kind smile.

"But—" She looked at me and then back at Rio.

I had to speak up. It was a matter of self-preservation more than anything. I had to keep my sister from blurting something potentially damaging. "His name is Rio, Daphne. Though you may not remember because you were so out of it that night."

Her forehead creased. "But I thought—"

"Rio, can I get you anything to drink? A beer?" Matt asked loudly.

Oh, you are a good man. I tried to tell him with my eyes that I owed him big time. The way his lips quirked told me he knew and was going to milk it for all it was worth.

"A beer would be great, thanks." He strode to me and sat down next to me, his arm slipping around me to cuddle me to his side. It was almost enough to distract me from this fiasco of a rendezvous.

"Doc? A beer?"

"Maybe a glass of water." I shrugged at the questioning look he shot me. I had to keep my wits around me.

"It's so funny," Daphne said as she dragged Johnny by the hand to the couch. "I could have sworn your name was Barry."

"Barry was the other guy," he replied, toying with the rubber band in my hair.

Matt came back, handed Rio a bottle, and perched on the end of the other couch, opposite my sister and her date. "So."

"So you forgot my water," I said peevishly. Not because of the water either.

Rio started to rise. "I'll get it."

"No, you sit." Matt waved him down. "I'll get it for her."

The doorbell rang. Again.

"Maybe it's Jehovah's Witnesses," Johnny offered helpfully.

"No way. They'd go to a Satan worshipper's house before coming to Doc's." Matt hopped up. "I'll get it."

Fine. Whatever. How much worse could it be?

"Look who's here," Matt said when he returned a couple of minutes later. "Barrington and his lady friend."

Of course. Now if only my parents would arrive, the night would be complete. I quickly rescinded that statement in case there *was* a supreme being who was actually listening to me at that moment. Didn't want to give him any ideas.

"Mena!" Cindy shrieked as she cleared the stairs. She threw her arms out wide and headed straight for me.

Because I was afraid she'd tumble down on top of both me and Rio, I jumped up to intercept her. "Cindy. What a surprise. *Oof.*"

Her hug squeezed the air out of my lungs. Over her shoulder Barry gave me a sickly smile, which said plain and clear this was the last place he wanted to be.

Ironic, wasn't it? Now that I wanted Rio to myself, Barry kept popping up.

"Barry said that Rio told him he had a date with you tonight and I told Barry we *had* to stop by and say hi because we were on our way to dinner at Hurley's, which is my absolute *favorite* restaurant, isn't it, Pookie?"

A pale pink flushed Barry's face. "Yes it is, Sweet Blossom," he replied dutifully.

Gag. I looked at Rio and wondered what kind of name I should call him.

His responding look said: *Don't even think about it.*

I smirked.

"Mena, you should offer your guests some refreshments."

Scowling at my ever-proper sister, I turned to my supposed guests. I didn't want to offer refreshments; I wanted everyone to leave. "What can I get you?"

"I'd love a Cosmo. The pink goes with my shoes." Cindy stuck out a long leg to show us all.

"Sorry, I don't have vodka. How about a beer?"

She tipped her head and pouted thoughtfully before she finally said, "I'll just have water."

"Okay." I glanced at Barry. "Beer?"

"Yes. Thank you," he said without looking up from Cindy's still outstretched leg.

I rolled my eyes and went to do my duty. I had my back to the living room when I felt steely arms clasp around my waist. Rio. I melted as I felt his lips nuzzle my neck.

"Get rid of them," he whispered as he settled himself against my butt.

Yum. He was already firming up. I started to push back to encourage him when a horrible idea occurred to me. I whirled around and glared. "That better not be the effects of seeing a certain pair of legs capped in pink heels."

"Actually, I got aroused seeing you in your gi." He trapped me against the counter and fingered the opening of my top as he pressed his lower parts against mine. "And you know how much your cup turns me on."

I laughed. Then he bent and gently bit the base of my throat. Gulp. I stopped laughing.

"Get rid of them," he murmured again.

Right. "Right." I turned around and poured the beer I just uncapped down the drain. The water followed. "Wait here."

I strode into the living room, hands on my hips. Everyone looked up when I entered. I faced Cindy. "I ran out of beer and water."

Matt shook his head. "I hate it when the tap goes dry."

I gave him a menacing look before I faced Cindy again. "Sorry."

"It happens," Cindy said philosophically.

Barry stood up and held out a hand to his girlfriend. "We should get to the restaurant anyway."

Just then, I could have kissed him, slug tongue be damned.

I glared at Matt and Daphne. Matt made a big production of picking lint off his gi, but he finally got up when I walked over and pain-punched his ribs.

"Ow!" He rubbed his side and frowned at me.

I turned my glare on Daphne, who hopped up before I moved an inch toward her. "We should go too. Come on, Johnny. Let's go for a walk."

Johnny didn't have a chance to do much more than squeak before Daphne jerked him to his feet.

Fine with me. I didn't care as long as everyone left. I

escorted them all to the door and went through a flurry of hugs (mostly from Cindy). Before I could lock the door, Daphne turned around and leaned down to whisper. "It's a good thing Barry isn't the one you're taking to my party."

I frowned. "Why?"

"Because he's in love with that perky girl." She nodded toward Cindy. "There would have been no hope for you there. Anyway, Mom and Dad are going to love Rio."

"They are?" She was shitting me. This was her way to pay me back for throwing her Folgers away.

"Of course they are." Her brow wrinkled like she couldn't imagine any other scenario. "You're obviously in love with him, and he is with you. What more could they ask for?"

Oh, I don't know—perfection, maybe? But I didn't get a chance to respond because she turned on her heels and skipped down the steps to Johnny.

"Don't wait up for me!" she called over her shoulder.

No chance of that. I locked the door and ran up the stairs.

Rio stood in the kitchen, arms crossed, leaning against the counter. "Impressive. There are generals who can take tactical training from you."

I untied my gi top. "There's only one type of training I'm interested in right now."

He grinned and pushed off the counter. "Lead the way."

Chapter Twenty-One

Lessons Learned from MacGyver
#16
Secrets have a funny way of getting out.

"I don't want to go."

Rio smiled at me and tugged my hand. "Barry and Cindy are expecting us."

I let myself be pulled an inch and then I dug my heels in. Because he was so strong, I held on to the doorframe too. "Let's stay home. Daphne's out. We'd have my place to ourselves."

He shook his head. "Phil."

Time to change my tactics. I pressed against the length of his body and shrugged my shoulder so the strap of my little dress fell. "Or we could go to your place. We definitely wouldn't get interrupted there."

"You know I'd love to," he said, his hands circling my waist. "But we already made plans."

I batted my eyes. "I'll bring a jar of peanut butter."

"Now how could I resist that?" He chuckled, stroking my hair, which I left down. "Tell you what. We'll go for just a little bit and then head over to my place."

Pout. Still, it was better than nothing. I sighed, long and heavy. "Fine."

"You're awfully reluctant," he said as I locked the front door.

I was. It wasn't about hanging out with Barry and Cindy together. Actually, I kind of liked Cindy, in a weird, other-dimension kind of way. She had to be doing something right because, from the little I'd seen, Barry worshipped the ground she walked on.

Still, I felt off, like there was something looming around the corner that I should avoid. Dwight would say avoiding it would only close me off to any opportunities that could come from it, because in strife there was always the possibility of good. Although I would never say this to Dwight, sometimes sticking your head in the sand was just plain easier.

I sighed again and let Rio lead me down the stairs.

"You act like you're going to the firing squad." He lifted my wrist to kiss it. "We won't stay long. I promise."

I would have sighed one more time, but I saw Magda coming down the block. I squeezed Rio's hand. "Have I introduced you to my tenant?"

He groaned. "Phil, I know what you're doing."

"No, she's right here." I smiled brightly at her as she approached the house. "Hey, Magda. How's it going?"

She looked at me suspiciously and her answer was hesitant. "Okay."

"This is my—" What did I call Rio? My boyfriend? That sounded so juvenile. And lover sounded too tawdry. "My friend, Rio. Rio, my tenant, Magda."

"We need to get going." Rio gave me a look I couldn't decipher. "It was nice meeting you."

"Same here." Magda nodded at him politely, gave me a look too (also undecipherable), and jogged up the porch steps.

"What did you think of her?" I asked when we'd settled in his Mustang.

He shrugged. "What was I supposed to think of her?"

I shrugged back. "I don't know. Did you find her attractive?"

He glanced at me as he pulled out of the parking space. "Is this a test?"

"No." It wasn't, really. And the thought of distracting him from going to Barry's by proposing a threesome with her was only fleeting. "She's a hooker, you know."

"A hooker?" He raised his brows.

"A high-priced call girl."

He chuckled.

"She is." Frowning, I turned to face him. "Does that make her more enticing?"

"No. And I doubt she's a call girl."

"Oh?" He sounded so sure it made me suspicious. "Know all the call girls in town, do you?"

"Hardly. She didn't look like one."

"That's because she's not your ordinary, everyday, run-of-the-mill hooker. She's high-priced."

He didn't say anything, which was the loudest reply he could have made.

"I have proof," I declared.

"What?"

"She carries around a big black bag that's filled with her sex toys."

"You've seen inside it?"

"Well, no." Minor detail though.

He put his hand on my leg, just under the short hem of my dress, and squeezed my thigh. "I love you, you know."

I froze, surprised by how easily he said it. I liked it, so I smiled wide and put my hand on top of his. After a moment, I said, "Does that mean you still don't believe me about Magda?"

He didn't dignify that with a response.

All too quickly, we pulled into Barry's driveway. It was my reluctance that made me wait in the car until Rio came around and opened my door. I sighed for the millionth time, set my shoulders, and decided to just get the evening over with. My feeling of impending doom was probably hormones or something.

We walked to the door hand in hand. I was about to ring the bell when it flew open. "Hey, guys! I'm *sooo* happy you're here."

Cindy engulfed us in her flowery embrace. I coughed discreetly at the powdery floral scent of her. I grinned at the look on Rio's face when she launched herself at him. I thought for sure he'd sneeze, but he held back somehow.

"Come in, come in." She dragged us through the door and slammed it shut.

It sounded so final. Like there was no going back now.

Rio put a reassuring hand on my back and pushed me forward.

"—already making drinks. I hope you like them." Cindy looked at us imploringly.

I smiled and said, "Oh, yeah. Cool."

She beamed happily and pointed us to the living room. "Sit down. I'll go see what's holding up my Pookie."

I perched on a loveseat and Rio reclined next to me.

"You had no idea what she was asking, did you?" he asked with a grin.

"Nope. No clue." I looked around. "Do you think she and her pukie are going to join us soon?"

"Her Pookie, not pukie."

"Same difference," I mumbled.

He pulled me back into his arms and gave me a thoroughly lingering kiss. "Play nice."

"Oh, look, Pookie! Aren't they *sooo* cute?" Cindy squealed as she and Barry entered the room.

Barry grunted but didn't say anything. Probably trying not to spill the loaded tray he carried.

I tried to sit up, but Rio tightened his hold on me. I brought my elbow up, intended to jab him in the ribs, but he slipped a couple of fingers in the top of my dress, at the side so his fingers glided against the outer swell of my breast.

I stilled, not able to breathe at the tingles his touch caused. If I angled my torso just right . . .

"Here you go, Mena." Barry held out a pink beverage.

I tried not to grimace as I took the drink. Cindy must have picked the alcohol selection tonight. I opened my mouth to ask if I could have a beer instead, but then decided to deal with it. Really, I wanted to watch Rio drink his. Smirk.

"Isn't this *sooo* cozy," Cindy gushed as she sat down. She patted the seat next to her, giving Barry a come-hither look.

I had to look away from the adoring gaze he gave her as he did her bidding. Gross.

Okay, it *was* sweet. Just a little though.

"Mena, that dress is so cute on you." She gave me an appraising look. "Did you get it from Betty's Closet?"

"Yeah." How did she know? I lifted my arm discreetly to see if I'd left the tag on.

"I thought so." She gave me a knowing nod. "They're the only store in Portland that carries that designer."

"Um. Oh. Really?" Fascinating. Who knew?

"I love the color palettes she uses. Her designs are so bold."

"Um. Yeah." I smiled politely, elbowing Rio surreptitiously when I felt him snicker.

Barry's cell phone rang (I recognized the James Bond

theme) and he got up to answer it. A moment later he came back, phone in hand. "Sweetie, it's for you."

"Excuse me a second, you guys." Cindy hopped up and accepted the phone. Before she left the room, she kissed the tip of her manicured finger and pressed it to Barry's nose.

I hid my smirk in my drink.

Barry eased back in the seat, a martini is his hand (why didn't he get a pink drink?), and asked Rio, "How's business going?"

"Great. We started a new marketing campaign with the matrix you provided." He turned to me. "Barry helps out with PR for the gym."

"That's nice of him." I glanced at Barry, wondering why he did it. The kindness of his own heart? Maybe he did it for Rio, since they were good friends.

"I appreciate it." Rio speared his hand into my hair and rubbed the base of my skull.

I frowned, partly because I didn't get why he cared if Barry helped and partly because his caress made it difficult for me to concentrate.

There seemed to only be one reasonable explanation. "Is the gym in financial difficulty?"

Both the guys gaped at me, but Barry was the one who burst into raucous guffaws. Rio just chuckled as though he were charmed and simply said, "The gym's doing okay."

"Okay?" Barry managed to choke out. "The gym's doing great. You're opening the tenth facility. You have facilities all along the Pacific Coast."

Rio shrugged and sipped his beverage.

"You're so modest, man." Barry shook his head. "When you told me you wanted to open a gym, I thought it was just going to be a hobby."

The gym was *Rio's*? I goggled at him. "You *own* the gym?"

He shrugged again. "It's a hobby. I like doing it."

"Hobby?" Barry snorted. "You have the start of an empire. You could be right up there with Gold's if you wanted to. You're just stubborn."

"If we had growth like that, we'd lose what makes us stand out."

Barry waved his hand. "That's what you're always saying to us investors."

Empire? Investors? I stared at Rio. "You're an exercise mogul?"

"He's a financial genius," Barry corrected. "And not only that, but he does a fair amount of work with at-risk youths."

Rio's brow furrowed. "You didn't know I owned the gym?"

"No." Why was that surprising? I was always the last to know. "You work with kids?"

"We have a nonprofit division for troubled kids and teens. We sponsor classes and bring in athletes for motivational talks." He frowned. "Does it matter?"

"No." Hell, yeah, it mattered. If I knew this from the start, I wouldn't have tried to get Barry back. "But it would have been nice to know. We're kind of seeing each other, you know."

He brushed his thumb against my lower lip before kissing me. It tasted apologetic. "I'm sorry," he whispered against my lips.

I shook my head and lifted my hand to cup his face. "It's okay."

Actually, it was better than okay. My parents would love Rio. Successful, a homeowner, helped kids. Except for his military background and gas-guzzling car, but not everyone was perfect.

What a relief. I could tell them I was dating him and not Barry. I'd planned on doing it (um, kind of) and living with the fact that they'd be less than enchanted by the turn of events. But now the timing wouldn't matter. Even if I told them tonight, I'd still shine because Rio was better than Barry—his success was earned on his own, not on the coattails of his family.

"You're grinning." Rio traced the outline on my mouth.

"I'm just happy." Maybe I could even ask him if he wanted to go with me to the party. "Tomorrow nigh—"

Cindy stomped into the room. "I can't believe you would do this to me, Barry!"

We all looked up, but Barry was the one who spoke. "What's wrong, Sweet Blossom?"

"This!" She swiped at her cheeks, which were streaked with mascara, and waved the cell phone manically. "Did you think I wouldn't find out?"

Frowning, Barry got up and reached out to her. "I don't know—"

"That's the first truth you've said—you don't know." She shoved him so he tumbled back onto the couch.

Impressive. I gazed at her with renewed respect. She'd do well in Kung Fu.

Barry gawked at her like he'd never seen her before. "Honey—"

"Don't you honey me." She had castration written in her eyes. "You two-timing—" she sputtered "—jerk!"

"Hon—uh, Cindy. I don't know what you're talking about."

"This." She threw the phone so it hit him smack in the middle of his face.

Ouch. Rio and I both recoiled. Good aim.

"My call disconnected and I needed to know what Sheri was wearing tomorrow so I could coordinate, so I went to the call log to pull up her number and there was the list of calls you made." She glared.

Oh, shit.

Barry shook his head, his face bewildered. "So?"

"So?" she shrieked. "*So* who are Susan and Melissa and Allison and Michele?"

I groaned and clapped a hand over my eyes.

"Listen, Swee—" he cleared his throat when her eyes narrowed "—Cindy. I don't know what you're talking about. I don't know these women."

"I may not be as smart as some of your friends, but I'm not dumb either. I can tell you've been cheating on me." Her face livid, she advanced on him. "That's why you stood me up those two times, isn't it?"

"No!" He retreated as far as he could cornered on the couch, hands raised to ward her off. "No, of course not. I told you, it wasn't on my calendar."

Wince. Guilt stabbed me in the gut, and I heard a voice that sounded suspiciously like Matt's whisper, *that's what you get.*

"I love you, Sweet Blossom," Barry said with more emotion than I'd thought he'd be capable of.

"Ha!" She kicked him with the pointed toe of her strappy shoe.

He grimaced and rubbed his shin. "Sweetie, listen—"

"You're a bad man, Barrington Wallace." Tears started to trail down her cheeks again, but I didn't think she noticed because she was so intent on Barry. "I loved you with every fiber of my being and you treat me like this."

"I love you too!" he protested, his heart in his eyes.

"Liar," she spat.

Something in my chest lurched sickeningly. What had I done?

Barry suddenly looked panicked, like it hit him that this was actually happening and that he was losing his Sweet Blossom. He started to get up, but Cindy whirled and headed for the door.

"Wait!" I said.

Everyone paused and turned to look at me.

I flushed. I couldn't let Cindy and Barry end like this.

He'd found what I found in Rio—a soulmate. It wasn't right that they'd break up because I'd had a less than brilliant idea.

Matt had been right. (I hated that.)

The weight of their combined stares made me fidget. Shit. How was I going to fix this?

I cleared my throat. "There has to be an explanation for this."

Cindy harrumphed as Barry said, "Yes." She arched her brow in disbelief, crossed her arms, and scowled at me. "What explanation?"

Like me sabotaging Barry to get him to come to my sister's party with me. I winced. Put bluntly like that, it really did sound mean.

Cindy tapped her foot impatiently and huffed a couple of times.

"Okay—" please, let inspiration strike now "—maybe Barry let a friend use his phone."

Oh, excellent comeback, Philomena. I mentally patted myself on the back. I smiled triumphantly at Cindy.

She didn't look convinced. Glaring at Barry, she said, "Did you?"

He frowned. "No, the only person I lent my phone to lately was you, Sweetie."

She turned to me, eyebrow raised and foot tapping.

I gave Barry an irritated look. I'd handed him a perfect way out of this situation and he didn't take it. What an idiot.

But I needed to fix this, so I tried again. "I bet those are just work calls he made. You know, women at the office he has business with."

I think I heard Cindy mumble, "Yeah, monkey business," but I figured I was wrong. I widened my eyes at Barry, imploring him to collaborate with my story.

He shook his head. "I don't work with anyone named

Allison or Melissa. And the only Susan I know is the girl who brings us bagels from the bakery down the street."

I rolled my eyes. Another great excuse down the drain.

"That leaves Michele. If he did work with her—" Cindy sniffled and swiped at her cheek impatiently "—then it'd explain why he stays late so often. And when he stood me up he said he was at work." She took a shoe off and beaned him in the middle of his forehead. "Jerk!"

Rubbing the end of my nose, I wondered what to do as she took off her other shoe and chucked it too.

"Wait!" I shouted before she picked up something heavier to hit him with.

Everyone looked at me again.

I had no choice. I had to come clean. I couldn't let Barry's life get screwed up because of a seemingly brilliant plan that was actually Waterloo in the making.

I gazed at Rio to gauge his reaction. He looked puzzled but not necessarily alarmed. Which meant he still had no clue what was going on. How would he react when I admitted everything?

He'd be okay, I reassured myself. He'd remember I loved him. It'd be okay.

And if I kept telling myself that, I might believe it.

"I appreciate what you're trying to do here, Mena, but it's not going to matter. Barry obviously doesn't love me like he said." She stifled a sob with her fist and started to flee the room.

"Wait! It was all me."

This time when everyone gawked at me, the looks of confusion were exponentially greater.

I took a deep breath. "I did it. I planted those calls on his cell phone. I changed his calendar so he missed your dates."

I waited for that feeling of relief you're supposed to get when you unburden your soul. Didn't happen. If anything, I felt more wretched. I figure the look of betrayal on Cindy's face was a big contributor.

"But why?" she asked faintly.

I winced. "That's a long story."

"I don't think we're going anywhere," Barry said with obvious relief now that the heat was off him.

"Um. Well." I took a deep breath. "My parents never paid attention to me. But then they did, only it was because of Barry. Except I didn't find out until I broke up with him. So I thought I could get him back and they'd notice some more. There was one problem. He'd started dating you."

Mouth gaping and eyes riveted on me, Cindy eased herself onto the edge of the couch, still away from Barry but at least she wasn't throwing things at him anymore. Barry's entire being was focused on her.

I nodded. This was the right thing to do, even if it caused some trouble between me and Rio. "So I thought I could break you guys up and then snap him up again." I cleared my throat. "I'm so sorry."

Cindy frowned. "But you love Rio."

"I know." I glanced at him again, willing him to see I meant it.

His face was closed and his eyes stony. "Why did you agree to go out with me?"

Damn. I grimaced. Figured he would ask me that. "Because I was attracted to you?"

"Or were you playing a game?" he asked coldly. "To make Barry jealous."

I cleared my throat again. I supposed lying when you were coming clean wasn't a good idea. "I might have briefly considered that, yes."

"I see." He stood up and turned to Barry and Cindy. "I'll take Mena home and leave you two to work things out. Okay?"

They both nodded mechanically, as if not believing what was happening.

Rio came to stand in front of me, his beautiful eyes staring at me like I was a stranger. "Let's go."

My heart cracked, enough that it shot piercing pain through my chest. But I nodded and followed him out of the house. In the car, when it was just the two of us, I'd make him understand.

Somehow I managed to wait until we were both buckled and the car running before I twisted in my seat and said, "I can explain everything."

"You already have." His voice was flat and his hands gripped the steering wheel like it was a lifeline.

Not a good sign. "No. Well, yeah, I did, but you don't understand—"

"I think I got a pretty good idea of what happened." He pulled out of the parking space, driving extra carefully. I think I would have felt better if he were driving like a maniac, to tell the truth. The overly careful driving, and the way his jaw was gritted, showed me just how angry he was at me.

Like I said before, not a good sign. So I tried again. "It's not like how you think. I—"

"Which part?" he asked. "The part where you used me or the part where you lied?"

"I never lied to you."

He glanced at me with one raised brow.

"I didn't." I banged my fist on the dashboard. Then I realized what I did and rubbed the console, silently apologizing for any damage I might have done. You can't treat a thing of beauty callously. Ironic, since that's exactly how I treated Rio. "I never lied to you. Every second I was with you was genuine."

"You still used me. What makes it worse is that I told you about Lisa, the girl I chased to Portland, and you still did it."

I winced. "Maybe just a teensy bit in the beginning." I held up my hand to forestall what he might say. "But it was just the first time or so that we went out. I kind of forgot about Barry after that."

"Kind of forgot," he repeated slowly. "That's really reassuring."

The sarcasm in his voice cut to my heart. "Don't be like that," I whispered.

"Like what, Mena? What shouldn't I be like?"

Everyone called me Mena, but it sounded like a slap coming from Rio. I would've given anything to hear another *Phil* out of him.

Oblivious to my inner turmoil, he ranted on. "I shouldn't be hurt? Because I am. I thought we were special."

Ouch. "We were. I mean, we are—"

"Bullshit," he said bluntly, staring ahead. "You deceived me. You thought I could serve your purpose and you manipulated me until you had all the pieces of your chess game in the right place to go in for the win."

I wanted to argue with him, but he was right. "Okay, I admitted it. In the beginning I was going to use you. But that was only in the beginning. Once I got to know you, I couldn't do that. And even in the beginning, I couldn't keep my plan firmly in my mind around you—"

"That's a real consolation," he muttered bitterly.

"You're not giving me a chance."

"Give you another chance so—what? You can cheat on me? Lie some more?" He shook his head. "I should have listened to Barry."

I blinked. "What?"

His hands tightened on the steering wheel. "Barry warned me not to trust you. I thought he still had feelings for you that would fade when he got closer to Cindy. Guess I should have listened."

My reply was silence. What could I say to that?

Staring unseeingly out the windshield, I rubbed my

nose, which tingled with the tears in my eyes that I was trying to hide. I would *not* cry. I would not. No matter how much I wanted him to stop the car, take me in his arms, and tell me he forgave me. No matter how unlikely that was at this point.

He pulled over and put the car in park.

My heart beat so hard in my chest I thought it was going to burst out. I put a hand over it to calm it and turned to Rio expectantly. The hope that he'd give me another chance was almost painful.

Then he said, "We're here."

I looked up to see my house, lit brightly from within, and hope died in my chest.

I slumped against the seat. "I can't believe you're doing this."

"*The trick is learning to live with it,*" he mumbled.

I whirled to face him. "Did you just quote MacGyver?"

He heaved a sigh and rubbed his face. "Just go, Mena."

The tears I tried so hard to suppress broke free. I swiped them as I pointed at him. "You may be mad now—"

"*Mad?*" His laugh contained no trace of humor. "That doesn't even cover it. Try livid. And more than disappointed in you."

I'd had people disappointed in me all my life. Rio saying it shouldn't have fazed me, but it hurt more than I could have imagined. I wanted to lash out at him and tell him to take a number and stand in line, but my tears choked the words in my throat.

I threw the door open, scrambled out, and slammed it shut. Head high, I walked slowly up the walk to the porch steps. I got all the way to the front door with my key in the lock before I heard his engine rev. I turned around in time to see him race off down the street.

My heart broke. I swear it did. I felt the already

slightly cracked pieces shatter and crumble inside me as
he drove off. The only guy I'd ever truly loved in an all-
consuming, man-woman kind of way—my soulmate—
and I'd messed it up.

I looked up at the light shining in the living room
window. It was Daphne's fault.

Shoving open the front door, I yelled up the stairs.
"Daph! Where the hell are you?"

"The living room," she called back.

I stomped up the stairs—or at least I tried to. My heels
made it impossible to make any kind of satisfying noise
so I had to pause halfway up to take them off so I could
make enough of a thump.

Daphne was curled on the couch with a *Cosmo*,
wearing a pair of my pajamas. "You made enough
noise coming up the stairs. I'm surprised your tenant
doesn't complain."

For a moment, the incongruity of the scene—what happened to the science digests and wool slacks?—distracted
me. I gawked at her, sitting there speaking calmly when
the world was falling apart.

She flipped another page. "And I told you to stop calling me Daph."

But that snapped me out of my stupor. I dropped my
shoes and pointed at her. "You are the Antichrist."

"Excuse me?" She looked up from her magazine and
blinked at me.

"This is all your fault." I pointed at her.

She frowned. "What?"

"All of this." I waved my arms around. "You've ruined
everything."

"Have you been drinking?" she asked, narrowing
her eyes.

"That's not the point here, Daphne," I yelled. "The
point is you're an albatross around my neck."

"What does a bird have to do with anything?"

"A bird has nothing to do with this!" Grr. I paced across the living room and back. The woman was absolutely clueless. "The only thing that has to do with anything here is that you've ruined my life."

Her brow wrinkled. "Because I came home early last night? I already apologized for that. You need to learn to forgive."

"Daphne." I snapped my fingers. "Focus for a change on something other than yourself."

"I don't understand what you mean."

Of course she didn't. "Aside from the fact that you've totally disrupted my life since you've been here—"

"I've tried to keep out of your way, and I think I've done a good job," she said, straightening indignantly.

"Ha!" I barked. "Like when you took apart my office? Or when you took out MacGyver? Or, wait—maybe when you raided my closet without asking?" I looked her up and down.

She huddled defensively. "I didn't think you'd mind."

"That's the problem with you, Daphne. For someone who's so smart, you don't think."

"I resent that."

I stopped pacing to spear her with a look. "Give me a break. Did you pause to consider how I felt lying to Mom and Dad? You know they're going to blame me if they find out you were here."

"They won't find out."

"Ha! Mom always finds out, and I take the blame."

"Please." She rolled her eyes. "Mom and Dad never expect anything from you."

"Because they never even pay attention to me. And I have you to thank for that."

She frowned. "What are you talking about?"

"YOU," I yelled, pointing. "All they ever talk about is their precious little Daphne. They don't even know I exist when you're around."

"You exaggerate."

I felt years of resentment bubble up and overflow out my mouth. "Exaggerate? Right. Like when they forgot my birthday because you finaled in the science fair? Like when they took you with them to Africa but left me at home?"

"You were starting college," she said defensively.

"And you weren't in school?" Now that I started I couldn't stop. I felt years of rage seep out of my pores. "Even after you moved away, all I heard was how brilliant you were, how giving you were for deworming orphans in Somalia—"

"It was Rwanda."

"—and why wasn't I more like you." I stood over her and glared. "You know what? I'm sick of it."

She stood up, shaking. I would have thought it was with repressed emotion, but I doubted she was capable for feeling that deeply.

"You know what? I'm sick of it too."

"Huh?" I blinked. I hated reverse psychology.

"You think it's easy being me?" She scowled at me, her hands on her hips.

Was this a trick question?

"It's not," she yelled.

I recoiled, trying to remember Daphne ever raising her voice, even when we were kids. Nope. She was the calm one. I was the one who whooped and screamed.

"I'm sick of all the expectations." She started to pace, her arms wildly flying around her. "I'm sick of having to be perfect."

I was so shocked, I toppled onto the couch as she swept by me. "Daph—"

"DON'T CALL ME THAT," she screeched. "And don't interrupt me."

I sat back and shut up—that's how freaked out I was.

"I'm so *sick* of being the example," she ranted. "Why

can't I be free like you? Why do I have to have all the pressures of performing? Do you know how hard that is?"

I opened my mouth to reply—

"Don't say anything," she said, glaring at me. "I'm not done."

My mouth clamped shut.

"All my life I've done the right thing and *I'm damn tired of it.*"

Daphne cussing? Okay, now I was *really* worried.

"I didn't want to be a research scientist. I didn't want to be so responsible. But does anyone listen to me? NO." She stamped her foot. "I'm always expected to be perfect."

"But—"

"I said don't interrupt me!" she screamed, beating her fist against her thigh.

Oh, hell—she was going off the deep end and I had no one to help me.

"I'm fed up with having to be perfect. I want to be like you." She glared at me like I had stolen her favorite toy.

"Um." I waited for her to yell at me, but when she didn't, I decided to go for it. "What do you mean, you want to be like me?"

"I mean I want to do what *I* want, not what other people expect me to do. Like dance on a bar."

I wrinkled my nose. "You want to dance on a bar? For a living?"

"You never listen! None of you ever listen." She growled, huffed off to her room, and slammed the door shut.

I stared after her. Even in misery she had to over-shadow me.

Then I remembered the look on Rio's face as he drove off and tears filled my eyes again.

What did it all matter? It was too late. I'd royally screwed up.

Chapter Twenty-Two

Five Reasons to Be an Only Child
1) *No one to boss you around.*
2) *Sole rights to the bathroom.*
3) *No sharing your clothes.*
4) *Privacy.*
5) *Parents' undivided attention.*

Rrr-hha-r.

Rrr-hha-r.

I peeked an eye open and glared at the alarm clock. What the hell? It was Saturday.

Rrr-hha-r.

Oh yeah. Daphne's birthday party. Mom wanted us there early to help out.

Rrr-hha-r.

I lifted a hand to whack it silent but, in a rare moment of lucidity, decided against it. I wasn't sure the plastic I'd made and molded to repair the body would hold up to any more abuse.

Using the tip of one finger, I delicately pressed the button to turn the alarm off. Unfortunately, the bare amount of pressure was still too much for the clock. I heard the crisp snap of my pseudo-plastic and a ping when it hit the floor.

"Damn." I covered my head with the comforter and wondered if anyone would notice if I stayed there all day. My parents would be all about seeing Daphne; they wouldn't notice if I danced naked around the birthday cake. And I had no one else that'd care one way or the other what happened to me. Except Matt. Maybe.

An image of a dark-haired, Irish–Puerto Rican stud came to mind and I forcibly pushed it out. I would not think about him. Not at all. If he was narrow-minded enough not to give me another chance, fine. I wasn't about to waste my time weeping over him either.

"The bastard," I mumbled into my pillow.

But then I inhaled and caught a whiff of his scent on my sheets from when he spent the night, and I realized how empty my bed was. I wondered if he was sniffing his sheets and missing me.

"Bah!" I shoved the covers aside and got up. I needed coffee. A lot of it, if I was going to have any chance of making it through the day.

I picked my robe off the floor, put it on, and did a zombie stumble to the kitchen.

Daphne was at the counter already. Of course. She had a mug in her hand. I looked around for evidence of that vile crap she called coffee, but didn't find anything.

I ignored her presence and reached around her to fill the kettle with water. Slowly I started my press pot ritual, using it as a meditation to clear my mind.

It worked until Daphne slammed her mug down on the counter. "Aren't you going to say anything?"

Startled by the uncharacteristic show of aggression, I glanced at her. She didn't look too violent though, so I willed myself to find nirvana and returned to the rhythmic cleaning of my coffee grinder.

Hands on her hips, she huffed in frustration. "So we're just going to ignore this."

"There's nothing to ignore." I wound the cord of the grinder around the body and put it back in the cupboard. I caught a glimpse of a tin of General Foods International Coffee (I use that term loosely) in the very back corner, semi-hidden behind a can of cocoa. I was tempted to throw the tin away but I didn't have the energy. She'd just buy more—what did it prove?

As I shut the cabinet and poured hot water over the grounds, I heard Daphne murmur, "Why do I even bother?" and stomp out of the kitchen.

I shrugged. Whatever her deal was, she'd be gone once this damn party was over and then everything would go back to normal. Except for my heart, which would still be terminal.

Sigh.

After my coffee was ready, I doctored a mug and took it to my room to wallow in self-pity.

Unfortunately, Matt called and interrupted my pity fest. "Hey, what's going on?"

Just my life in shambles around me. "Nothing."

Pause. "What's wrong?"

I scowled. "Why do you have to be so astute?"

"It's my fatal flaw. So what's wrong?"

What wasn't wrong? I had no desire to list everything for him. He'd just tell me he said so. And he'd be right.

"Doc? Come on. Tell me."

"Why can't I just have my coffee in peace?"

"This doesn't have to be difficult. Just tell me what happened and I'll help you fix it."

I scrunched my nose in an effort to stem the tingly feeling that signaled the onslaught of tears. "You'll tell me I deserve what I got."

"Probably, but I'd still help you fix it."

I laughed, though it sounded hollow and weak even to my ears.

"Is this about Rio?"

My heart constricted at the mention of his name. "Do you ever wish you were an only child, Matt?"

"I *am* an only child."

Oh, yeah. "God, you're *so* lucky."

Matt chuckled. "You know what you need to do?"

"What?"

"Resign yourself to the fact that you have a sister and build a relationship with her."

I frowned at the phone. "That's the brilliant advice you've got for me today?"

There was a shrug in his tone of voice. "It's the best I can offer you. Except for a ride to your parents."

"I've got to go over there early."

"That's okay. I told your mom I'd help too."

What a relief. At least I wouldn't have to ride over there with Daphne.

"Daphne can come along too."

"She said she was going to walk because she needs the exercise."

"Doc."

Shrug. I tried. At least I wouldn't have to ride with Daphne alone, I amended. "Fine. Pick us up at eleven."

"See you in an hour."

He hung up before I could ask him to call back and tell Daphne he'd pick her up too. Which meant I had to talk to her myself.

Blech.

I downed my now lukewarm coffee and went to the kitchen for a refill. The door of her room was still closed. I debated posting a note for her on it, but quickly vetoed that idea. If she didn't see it and missed Matt's ride, she'd blame me. No, I had to tell her in person.

Hell.

I took a deep breath, strode to the door, and knocked on it once. "Daphne, Matt's picking us up in an hour."

Before she could open the door and initiate conversation, I scurried back to my room and enclosed myself in its safety. No, I wasn't a coward—I just wasn't interested in striking up a conversation similar to last night's right before going to our parents'. Mom had Spidey sense where we were concerned and I didn't feel like hashing everything out as guests were arriving to celebrate Daphne's birth.

Speaking of which, I needed to figure out what to wear. Black seemed appropriate. In terms of celebrating Daphne's birth, in any case.

Opening my closet, I scanned the contents to see what I could find. Now that I knew Daphne had been raiding my stuff, I noticed the signs of intrusion; clothes hanging funny and in general disorder. Some (Daphne) might argue that my clothes were already disorderly, but I maintained that I had a system.

I didn't know how long I stood there pushing hangers back and forth, but it had to be a long time because I heard Daphne start and finish her shower and I still hadn't picked something to wear.

"As if it matters," I mumbled. Closing my eyes, I grabbed a hanger and pulled it out. I shrugged when I saw it was a black long-sleeved dress I didn't particularly like. Who'd care? It wasn't like I had anyone to impress. If Rio were coming with me—

"Bah!" I scowled and threw the dress onto my bed. He wasn't going to be there. He was never going to be there. I blew it.

I swiped at my eyes (I wasn't crying—it was just excessive moisture) and tried to work up the energy to go take a shower when all I wanted to do was huddle in my bed.

But Matt was coming and my mom wouldn't have let me out of the party. Not unless I were in ICU almost dying, and even then it was a toss-up. So I bucked up and got ready. Halfheartedly, but at least I was dressed. I skipped makeup—too much effort—and put my hair in a tight bun à la Daphne.

As I slipped on a pair of black pumps, I thought I heard voices so I left the sanctuary of my room to investigate. Sure enough, Matt and Daphne were in the kitchen talking.

They looked up when I walked in. While their jaws didn't quite fall to the floor, they looked a little puzzled.

"Are you going to a funeral after Daphne's party?" Matt finally asked.

I shot him a dark look. "Are we going or what?"

They exchanged a look but, wisely, neither one said anything. Daphne gathered a wrap—not mine, but I did notice she had on one of my cute Betsey Johnson dresses. She looked like she might pop out of the low neckline, but it showed off her longer legs nicely, as loath as I was to admit it. The scarlet print flattered her too, but then our colorings were similar so that wasn't a surprise.

I locked the front door and followed them to the car. Because I wasn't in a social mood, I climbed into the back seat. The better to avoid conversation.

I was aware of the random glances they both gave me. Matt's were puzzled, like he was trying to figure out how he could help me. Daphne's were pissed, like I had no reason to be angry with her. Or maybe she was trying to gauge when to start yelling at me again about how I ruined her life by being born.

We got to our parents' house forty-five minutes later. I could tell Matt was relieved to arrive. I couldn't have cared less, and who cared what Daphne was thinking?

Usually, I loved coming home. My parents lived in the same farmhouse-ranch that we grew up in. It was just outside Portland in the rolling hills that are so popular for vineyards these days. This time of year was my favorite too—all the fruit trees loaded, you could walk out to the orchard and eat whatever you wanted. There wasn't anything like it.

Today I got out of the car and silently walked into the

cool darkness of the house, not checking out the bushes next to the driveway for blackberries or considering climbing a tree to grab an apple. I barely even paid attention to Matt and Daphne's low voices behind me.

I set my purse and sweater down on the chair in the foyer.

"Daphne, is that you, sweetheart?" Mom called from the kitchen.

I made a face as I walked into the kitchen. "It's me."

"Where's Barry? And Daphne's with you, isn't she?"

Sigh. It was going to be a long afternoon. I ignored the first question and answered the second. "She's here."

Mom craned her head to look behind me.

When Daphne walked in, I swear the room brightened. "Hi, Mom."

Mom dried her hands on the apron she wore and gave Daphne a tight hug. "Oh, sweetheart, it's so good to see you."

I needed a drink. Opening the fridge, I pulled out a couple of beers, uncapped one, and took a swig.

"Is that for me, Doc?" Matt gestured at the other beer in my hand.

Actually, I'd gotten them both for myself, but I handed him a bottle.

"Thanks." He flipped the top off and pulled straight from the bottle too.

"Philomena, get Matt a glass," my mom chided with a frown in that tone of voice that implied I had the manners of a barnyard animal.

"It's okay, Mrs. Donovan." Matt gave my mom a lazy smile. "I prefer it this way."

Mom turned her frown on him. "Have you lost weight, Matt?"

He grinned. "I *am* a little hungry."

"Come here and I'll fix you a plate."

He happily went over and put his arm around her

shoulders while she dished him some food. He always could play her like a fiddle.

"What time are people due to arrive?" Daphne asked.

"At one." Mom handed Matt a plate overflowing with food and did a double-take as she actually noticed me. "What are you wearing, Philomena?"

"A dress." I looked down to see if it'd morphed into pants or something when I wasn't paying attention.

"You look—" she frowned "—somber."

I heard Matt chortle and shot him a dirty look before I turned to my mother. "I like this dress."

"It's rather formal for you, isn't it?"

"I bet if Daphne had worn it, it would have been perfect," I muttered, wondering if I should trade my beer for a couple of fingers of vodka, straight up.

"You should have worn something with color, like your sister. Doesn't she look nice in her red dress?"

Instead of pointing out it was my red dress, I shrugged and picked up a platter of vegetables. "I'll put these on the table."

But Mom was already fawning over Daphne so I slipped out. I went to the dining room and set the plate down just like I said I would. I heard my dad's voice greeting Daphne in the kitchen and knew I couldn't go back there and watch them exclaim how great my sister was, so I went out back to our old treehouse.

Dad had built it when Daphne was four and I was three. Because Daphne had reigned supreme even back then, it was kind of girly. At the time it'd been pink (Daphne's favorite color), but the years had eroded the paint and no one had bothered to redo it.

My sister had grown out of it by the time she was six, but I still visited it whenever I came home. Last year Matt and I had even refurbished a few of the wooden boards that were rotting.

Now, I kicked off my shoes at the base of the tree and slowly ascended the ladder (so I wouldn't spill my beer).

I pushed open the trapdoor and waved an arm around to break any spider webs before climbing into the house.

Because the shutters were closed, it was dark inside. Just as well. It suited my mood.

I closed my eyes and sat there in silence, taking occasional sips of beer. Rio would have liked it up here. It was peaceful. I imagined him climbing up the ladder—after me, so he could peek up my dress. And then when we got to the top, he'd pretend to be interested in the view for a minute before he pressed me against the floorboards and kissed the breath out of me.

I scowled and tried not to think, but somehow that's impossible when you're in a dark room by yourself. Especially when you miss someone as much as I missed Rio.

There was a knock on the trapdoor. "Doc?"

Because I knew he wouldn't leave me alone, I scooted over and opened the door.

Matt eased his body through the opening and looked around. "Hasn't changed much, has it?"

"Nope."

Slouching because of his height, he walked over to the window and stared out. "It has a great view of the orchards and valleys though."

I frowned at him. "You came up here to look at the view?"

"No, I came to see what was wrong." He crossed over, sat down next to me, and took my hand. "You gonna tell me?"

I pouted. "What good will it do?"

"I'll help you fix it."

He couldn't this time, but it was awfully sweet of him to offer. Tears clogged my throat so I just shook my head.

"Mena!" Daphne called from below. "What are you doing up there? People are going to start arriving soon."

I scowled down at her. She returned it with a scowl of her own, her hands fisted on her hips. I crossed my eyes, stuck my tongue out, and slammed the door shut.

"Mature," Matt commented.

Before either one of us could say anything else, the door banged open and a livid Daphne crawled through. "You little brat!"

Matt took her arm and helped her into the treehouse. The traitor.

He shrugged. "I couldn't let her fall. I'd have to answer to your mom."

Small point.

"And this is an excellent opportunity to straighten things out between the two of you," he continued. "You're sisters. You should be best friends."

Both Daphne and I snorted at that.

"Daphne! Philomena! Are you up there?"

Great. Mom.

I scooted over to give her room as she entered the treehouse. Matt gave her a hand too.

I wondered about the weight capacity of the old boards, but if Matt was helping Mom inside he figured it was safe, and that was good enough for me.

Mom looked around. "It's rather dusty up here, isn't it?" When no one answered, she said, "You could use some curtains too."

I grimaced and said "No way" as Daphne nodded and simultaneously said "I always thought so." Then we glared at each other.

Mom sat down cross-legged, facing us. "How about you two tell me what's going on?"

Matt started to get up. "Maybe I should give you some privacy."

"No, sit, Matt." Mom waved him back. "I might need a witness."

He grinned. "Your daughters *are* fairly fierce."

"And determined." She eyed the two of us. "Though other adjectives might be more appropriate."

I snorted. Daphne didn't do anything but look miserable. Which set me off. "What's your deal? You have no right to look like that. You're the one who ruined my life."

She sneered—at least as much of a sneer as she could manage. "Grow up, Mena."

"Enough," Mom said in her stern listen-to-me-or-else voice. "Tell me what's going on right now."

Might as well kick off the discussion. "Daphne's ruined my life."

Mom frowned. "What did she do?"

"She was born." I gave her an evil glare.

Daphne rolled her eyes. "Like I said, Mena. Real adult."

"It's true." I turned to my mom. "You and Dad *always* paid more attention to her than you did to me. Don't try to deny it," I said when she opened her mouth. "You guys never include me. It's always Daphne-this and Daphne-that. Well, I'm sick of it."

Just thinking about it was working me up. I got up and paced. Sure, I was hunched over, but you work with what you've got. "All I ever wanted was for you guys to ac-knowledge that I'm just as valuable as Daphne. But I've never done anything right. Until I dated Barry. How frickin' screwed up is that?"

"Language," Mom said with a frown as Daphne said, "Don't curse, Mena."

I chose to ignore them. "With Barry, suddenly *I* was the ex34p5ample. Do you know what kind of rush that was?"

Guess I said it a little bit too forcibly, because they just gawked at me with wide eyes.

My laugh didn't have an ounce of humor in it. "It's too bad I didn't know how you and Dad felt before I broke up with Barry."

Mom gasped. *"What?"*

I nodded grimly. "Barry and I weren't right together. So I broke up with him. Then when I tried to get him back, I fell in love with his friend, an ex-military boxer who drives a gas-guzzler."

Mom shook her head. "Philomena, only you'd be able to turn life int34p5o a soap opera."

Of course she'd criticize me. I plopped down on the floor, away from their cluster.

"You should be thanking me," Daphne said, her nose righteously in the air. "You found Rio because of all this."

"I lost Rio because of all this." I dropped my head to my knees and tried to breathe through the pain.

"What?" everyone gasped at once.

"He found out I started going out with him just to make Barry jealous." I looked up defensively. "But that was only part of the reason I went out with him that first time, and it wasn't even in my mind after. I really, really liked him," I said miserably.

Silence.

Then Daphne sniffed indignantly. "Well, you ruined my life too, if it's any consolation."

I snorted. "Right."

"You did. Do you know how much I hated having to be the good example for you?" Two red spots colored her cheeks. "I'm sick of it."

Mom frowned at her. "What are you talking about?"

She gazed at Mom and said evenly, "I never wanted to go to all those science camps growing up. I never wanted to be a research scientist."

That was news. Even I thought she loved science. She was always such a geek. It didn't occur to me until then that we had that in common. Different fields, but basically the same outcome.

"I'm sick of it," she said tentatively, as if she were afraid of what Mom would say. "I decided to go on sabbatical until I figure out what to do."

"What?" Mom exclaimed.

"Is that why you've been camping out with me the past two weeks?" I asked.

Oops. I mentally slapped my forehead at the look Daphne gave me. I glanced at Mom. I didn't mean to spill the beans. Really.

Mom frowned. "You've been here the past two weeks?"

My sister scowled at me before answering. "I didn't tell you because I needed some time to think."

Mom rubbed her forehead. "I could use a gin and tonic."

I considered offering to go get her one, but the look she flashed me warned me to stay put.

"You girls have impeccable timing. The guests are due to arrive any moment. But we're going to sort this out right now. Philomena."

I started at the way she barked my name. She should have gone into the army—she'd make an excellent commander. "Yes, Mom?"

"Come here."

She wouldn't spank me, would she? I got up hesitantly and crawled to where they sat.

She took my hand. "I'm sorry you felt like you weren't loved enough." She pushed back a strand of my hair that had escaped from the tight bun. "You were such an independent thing, right from the time you were born. So capable. So we gave you the space you needed. We gave Daphne more attention because she was more delicate than you."

Daphne blinked. "Excuse me?"

"Huh?" I frowned. Daphne? The woman who was on the verge of finding a cure for childhood diabetes? Delicate? Ha!

Mom took Daphne's hand in her free one. "You were always so unsure of yourself as a little girl. That's why we pushed you. To accomplish what we saw in you."

Daphne opened and closed her mouth a couple of times before she finally said, "How horribly unfair."

Ouch. I winced.

Mom's spine stiffened and her chin jutted higher. I

prepared for an onslaught, but was surprised when she only nodded. "We did the best we could. Neither of you can deny you've turned out well. You're successful, beautiful women. Both your father and I are proud of you."

She let go of our hands and started to ease up to her feet. Matt immediately jumped to help her up. Patting his hand, she smiled at him before turning back to us. "Don't hide up here too long. We have guests."

We watched her negotiate the ladder in silence. When she was out of view, Daphne and I stared at each other. For the first time I saw her not as the invincible, perfect older sister, but someone who was more messed up than I was.

I cleared my throat. "Sorry I let it slip that you've been here."

"It's okay." She frowned. "Were you telling the truth about Rio?"

I nodded. Tears filled my eyes again. "Damn allergies," I said with a sniff.

"Oh, Mena." She took my hand and squeezed it as Matt came to my side and put his arm around my shoulders. "Did you try apologizing?"

"I tried everything. He won't listen. The bastard." I rubbed my nose, willing the tears back. "He couldn't have loved me like he said if he won't give me another chance, right? We should go down," I said, wiping my eyes.

Daphne grimaced. "This is one birthday I'm never going to forget."

"Look at the bright side," Matt said after we were all on the ground and walking back to the house.

"What?" Daphne and I both asked at once.

He put his arms around us. "You just lost an enemy and gained a sister."

Daphne and I looked at each other around Matt. Maybe he was right.

Chapter Twenty-Three

Lessons Learned from MacGyver
#83
When something's broken, it's easiest to throw it away and forget about it. But if you step back and take a look at what you've got, you find a totally different way for it to work.

I hit redial and waited. Four rings later, Rio's answering machine picked up.

Again.

I sighed and clicked off. I'd already left a bunch of messages for him over the past week. One more would have tipped the balance from *anxious ex-girlfriend* to *stalker.*

Sighing again, I dropped my head back against the couch and stared at the ceiling. Another woman might have wondered where he was or who he was out with. But I knew I didn't have to worry about any of that. Rio wouldn't have found a new girl a week after we'd unofficially broken up. He was too loyal, too good a guy. He was just nursing his wounds.

Not that the bit of knowledge made it any easier on me.

I had to do something. Only I couldn't figure out what.

Daphne walked out of her room, yawning, and headed for the kitchen.

"Morning," I said from my spot on the couch.

She shrieked and whirled around. "Mena! What are you doing here?"

"I own this house," I reminded her.

"That's not what I meant." She frowned, hands on hips. "It's six o'clock. On a Sunday morning. What are you doing up?"

"Couldn't sleep." I fidgeted under my sister's shrewd gaze.

"Did you call him again?" she asked wisely.

Only like five hundred times.

"Do you know what I think?"

Oh, God. "Do I have a choice?"

"I think you need to see him face to face. Apologize and work this out."

"I did apologize." I grimaced at how childish that sounded, but it didn't stop me from huddling even more into the corner of the couch.

"Philomena Donovan," she said in her best stern older sister tone, "are you pitying yourself?"

I stuck my tongue out at her.

"What happened to my spitfire little sister—"

"I'm only thirteen months younger than you," I interrupted.

"—who would take on the world to get something she wanted?"

"I'm not like that, Daph."

She didn't even bat an eyelash at me calling her *Daph*. "Yes, you are. Remember that time you wanted that expensive Erector kit? You hassled Mom nonstop for three weeks before she broke down and bought it for you."

"Big whup." Oh, for those Erector days.

"And the time you wanted to join the science Olympiad in school, but they said you were too young. You argued with the teacher for days till he finally let you on the team."

I made a face. "You remember that?"

She sat down by my feet. "Don't you want him, Mena?"

Want him? I was shriveling up inside at the prospect of being without him. "*He* doesn't want me."

"Then make him want you," she said decisively. When I didn't say anything, she sighed and continued on to the kitchen.

As loath as I was to admit it, she was right. I needed to go see Rio. But I could guarantee he wouldn't see me if I went to his home or the gym.

I needed a different plan. I needed to get him on neutral territory and make him listen to me.

There was only one way to do that.

I picked up the phone and dialed. "Pick up, pick up," I urged.

"Hello?"

"Barry, *don't hang up*," I rushed to say. "Just give me one minute. I need your help."

"*Mena?*" His voice was sleep hoarse, and I heard sheets rustling. "Do you know what time it is?"

"Barry, I need to win Rio back. I know I screwed up, and I know he's angry but I thought if you talked him into giving me a chance to explain—"

"*You've got to be kidding.*" He gave an incredulous chortle. "I'm not going to help you. He's better off without you. I wouldn't subject an enemy to you, much less a friend. I can't believe you're asking."

I gritted my teeth and reminded myself I had no choice. If I wanted Rio back, I needed to grovel big time. "Please, Barry. I just want to talk—"

"No."

Grr. "Barry—"

"No," he said more forcibly.

Forget groveling—I was going to be myself. "You owe me."

"Excuse me?"

"You owe me. I saved your ass with your sweet blossom."

He sputtered incoherently before he finally said, "You're the one who messed things up in the first place."

God, he was so detail-oriented. "Does that mean you aren't going to help?"

"Damn right—"

There was some static, a little fumbling, and more rustling. I heard a muffled feminine voice and Barry's in response, but no matter how hard I strained I couldn't hear what they said.

Then, "Mena?"

"Cindy?"

"Barry will help you," she said firmly.

"Listen, Cindy, I don't want to cause trouble between you two—"

"There's no trouble with me and Barry. We're perfect. In fact, he proposed to me. Isn't that right, Pookie?"

I wasn't even tempted to gag at her saccharine tone. "That's great. Congratulations."

Cindy lowered her voice to a whisper. "I owe you. I don't think he would have proposed without the scare from you."

What could I say to that? "Um. Cool."

"You'll be one of my bridesmaids," she said enthusiastically. "I'm thinking of pink dresses."

I imagined fluffy pink cotton candy dresses and felt nauseous. Guess I deserved the harsh penance though. "That sounds super. Listen, Cindy, about Rio—"

"Tell me what you want and I'll have Barry do it."

I outlined my plan twice, to make sure she got it, and then another time just to be sure. When I was confident she understood what I needed, I got off the phone and made another call.

"'Lo?"

"Matt, can I borrow your beach cabin?"

"Doc? Do you have any idea what time it is?"

"Time is relative," I answered philosophically. "Can I borrow your cabin? Just for the day. And maybe the night." MacGyver said you've got to be more optimistic. Dwight always said you had to speak what you wanted into reality.

"What's the urgency?" But Matt's no dummy, so two seconds later he said, "This is about Rio, isn't it?"

I made a pouty face even though he couldn't see me. "Is that a yes?"

He sighed. "You know it is."

Yes. "You're the best."

"I know."

"So be over here in half an hour, okay?"

"Wait a minute. You never said anything about me going along. I have soccer today."

"Please, Matt," I whined pathetically. "I need you with me." To help tie Rio down in case he wasn't willing to stay and listen.

Matt sighed, long and suffering. "I'll see you in a bit."

"Twenty minutes," I said quickly. "Make that fifteen."

He snorted and hung up.

"Yes." I hopped up. It was all coming together. I pulled up short when I saw Daphne leaning against the kitchen counter, watching me.

"Seems like you have a plan." She lifted her mug of Folgers to her lips.

"I do. Get dressed. We need to get going."

She frowned. "We?"

I frowned back. "You didn't think you weren't going?"

"Uh—" Lowering the cup, she blinked a few times. "I guess not."

"Good. I'm taking a shower." I headed to the bathroom. "Don't dawdle."

"You should take a bath instead," Daphne suggested.

I glance suspiciously over my shoulder. She was up to something. I couldn't resist going to the bathroom and seeing what it was.

I noticed it the moment I stepped in and turned the light on. Gasping, I climbed up on the bathtub's rim to get a closer look.

"I had it laminated."

I turned to see Daphne in the doorway, gazing up at the poster of MacGyver that was back in its rightful place.

"It was disgusting how much mold was on it." Daphne's perfect nose wrinkled. "You should clean it more often. And get off the bathtub before you fall and break something."

For once I did what she asked without comment; shock does weird things to a person. "I think I'm going to take a bath."

She nodded, a pleased smile slowly curling her lips. "Great idea."

"How much longer?" I asked, kicking my foot against the back of Matt's seat like a little kid. You might say I was a touch impatient the whole ride there.

"Half an hour, I think," Matt replied. "And quit it. I'm driving."

Daphne tapped her lips with a long finger. "That's cutting it close."

Matt frowned. "I don't like this idea, Doc. Why can't you just do what normal people do and send him an email?"

"He'd probably just delete it without reading it."

"Dealing with relationship issues over email is wrong," Daphne said.

I frowned at her. "You say that like you have experience."

When she glanced back at me, I could see she was in

full big sister mode. "Do you know what you're going to do when he arrives?"

It was on the tip of my tongue to correct that to "if he arrives" but I remembered MacGyver and Dwight. So instead I said, "I'm going to tell him I love him and throw myself on his mercy. If that doesn't work, I'm going to tie him up and give him oral sex till he breaks down and takes me back."

Daphne gasped and covered her ears. "I didn't need to know that."

Matt chuckled.

We pulled onto a gravel road so bumpy I had to anchor myself or be tossed up against the ceiling. Finally Matt's shack came into view. Truthfully, it was more like multiple shacks smashed together to form a house. Of sorts.

"Here we are." Matt grinned at the two of us.

"Nice beach chalet," Daphne said dryly as she hopped down.

"Thank you," Matt replied modestly.

Inside, it was a completely different story. The wooden floors were polished, the walls were white with seaside watercolors lining them, and the entire space was open and airy. Matt kept it sparsely furnished, but it was perfect for a getaway.

I hoped it'd be perfect for an intervention too.

Rubbing the tip of my nose, I walked down a hall to the master bedroom. Fluffy down comforter on the bed, dozens of pillows in various shades of blue, and white curtains that billowed open to reveal glimpses of the ocean. I added a couple of candles from my bag on the bed stand. "Perfect."

"Wait." Daphne walked in, rummaging in her purse. She took out a box and set it next to the candles. "Now it's perfect."

"Daphne! Where did you get that?" I flushed beet red

when I saw the humongous box of condoms. I was optimistic, but that was plain physically impossible.

"I brought it with me from California. Just in case." She shrugged. "You'll need it before I ever do."

Matt chuckled. "Now it's perfect."

"What about Johnny?" I asked.

She wrinkled her nose. "I'm not going out with him anymore. He wanted me to dress up like a Catholic schoolgirl."

We all froze as we heard a car on the gravel driveway. Rio was here.

Daphne glanced at me and then left the bedroom, Matt close on her tail. I stayed, trying to calm my suddenly frantically beating heart. "Now or never," I told myself and then went to greet them.

As I walked into the living room, Rio turned around from the front window and frowned at me. A deep, never-forgiving kind of frown. I stalled, hopelessness tingeing my previously upbeat outlook.

Then I heard a shriek and was engulfed in a sweet floral embrace that could only be one person.

"Ohmigod, Mena! I can't believe you're here." Cindy held me tighter and jerked me around so my back was to the room. "Barry's thinking of buying a beach house and his real estate agent told us we really needed to look at this one. What a coincidence!"

Excellent coverup. I stared at her with new respect.

"Isn't it fantastic?" she gushed. She let go of me and grabbed Barry's hand. "Show me the outside. Do you think I can have pink roses around the house?"

Barry grunted and escorted her out, but not without shooting one last glare at me. I read the message loud and clear. *Don't mess with my friend.*

I wasn't messing around here. I lifted my chin and turned to Rio, whose gaze was devoid of emotion. Gulp. "Hi."

"What's going on?" he asked flatly.

The sounds of two cars rolling down a gravel road registered. I followed Rio to the window to in time to see both Matt's jeep and Barry's BMW disappear, leaving only a cloud of dust.

Then I realized how close I stood to him. I really wanted to lean closer, but I forced myself to step back. I needed to do this right. "I'm glad you're here."

He cocked a brow. Arms crossed, he leaned against the wall. "Are you?"

God, he had sexy biceps. I ignored his sarcasm and nodded. "I wanted to apologize."

"Apology accepted."

"Really? You forgive me?" Because he didn't sound like he forgave me.

"Forgive you?" He laughed without humor. "Hell, no."

I cleared my throat and tried again. "I'm sorry. Things got a little out of hand, but I love you and I want to make it up to you."

Rio said nothing. He just stared at me with that dead gaze.

I didn't know whether to scream or cry. My hands fisted of their own accord. "That kind of attitude isn't going to help us."

He stared down at me with conquistador haughtiness and, God help me, I wanted to kiss him. So I settled for the next best thing: I yelled at him. "Why can't you just listen to me when I say I didn't mean to hurt you?"

His brow wrinkled but his voice remained low. But it was barely controlled. "You used me to make my friend jealous. How am I supposed to feel?"

He had a point. "Hurt," I conceded. "But I fell in love with you. The deep, all-or-nothing kind of love. Do you honestly think I faked it the whole time?"

"Didn't you?"

I gasped. "Of course not."

"How am I supposed to know what was real and what wasn't?" He gazed at me like I was a stranger.

And I didn't like it. At all. So I did the only thing I knew how to do and hooked his leg with my foot and leveraged his head back to take him straight down.

I landed on him (he only made a small *oof*) and tied his arms up with mine. "Admit that I love you."

"Fine way you have of showing it."

At least the fire was back in his eyes. I tightened my hold. "Admit it."

"Phil, this isn't—"

"Aha!" He called me Phil. It was silly how that small thing made my heart leap with joy. "I knew it."

He frowned. "What did you know?"

"You still care about me."

He sighed. "This isn't about how I feel."

"Yes, it is, because if it were up to me we wouldn't be like this."

He bucked his hips, flipped me over, and straddled my hips, my hands held tightly over my head. "I gave you pieces of myself I'd never given anyone else. You. And for all I know you were just using me. How can I trust you again?"

Even if I didn't hear it in his voice, his anguish filled his eyes. I bit my lip to keep my tears from falling. "I'm so sorry," I whispered. Then I cleared my throat and said it again more forcibly. "I'm sorry. I know what I did was wrong, and I can only plead temporary insanity. But if you don't let me make it up to you, you're even worse than I am."

He looked disbelieving. "How do you figure?"

"You're willing to throw away something great between us, because it was great and you know it can be again if you let it. And you're doing it only out of pride and not because that's what you really want."

Silence while he studied me. Then he asked, "What do I want?"

I lifted my chin. "Me."

Okay, I wasn't so sure that was true, but what did

I have to lose? If he laughed in my face, then I'd only be back to where I was—miserable and lonely. But if he said yes . . .

I tried to project supreme confidence as he held me pinned to the floor, studying me with his turbulent gaze.

Finally he spoke. "I'm not playing a game."

I nodded solemnly. "I'm not either."

Long, searching silence then finally, "It'll kill me if I find out this is another lie."

"I'm not lying," I said fervently. "I promise."

"Because I was serious about this from the beginning." His beautiful eyes told me exactly how serious he still was.

Fortunately, I was on the same page. "Tell me you're still serious."

The wait while he considered the answer nearly killed me. Finally, he nodded. "I am."

"Good." Hooking my leg around his knee, I brought him down so he was pressed fully against me and gazed at him. "Marry me."

He brought his face down till his nose touched mine. "Why?"

I didn't hesitate in my answer. "I love you," I answered simply, because I knew he'd appreciate that most.

His fingers tightened on my wrists. "I love you too." He lifted his head and kissed me.

Kiss was such a weak word for it though. It was more like a starved mating.

But first things first. I broke away from him, panting. "Is that a yes?"

As corny as it sounded, his slow smile was like the sun coming out after weeks of rain. "Make me."

I grinned. That was a challenge I was up to.

Epilogue

"It's occurred to me that some friendships are like a good game of hockey. The right balance of teamwork and smooth skating generally adds up to a winning combination."
—MacGyver, "Easy Target" Episode #81

"Fight me."

Rio cocked an eyebrow and calmly unwrapped his wrists. "Didn't you go to class this morning? I'd have thought you would have worked your aggression out of your system."

The slow, deliberate unveiling made a shiver crawl up my spine. And every inch of skin was mine. I grinned fiercely as I advanced on him. "Oh, baby, this isn't aggression."

He put his hands on my hips and held me away when I reached him. "I'm sweaty."

"I like you sweaty." I tried to wiggle closer.

"But you're dressed." He fingered the thin strap of the little dress Cindy made me buy. "Is this new?"

"Yeah. Cindy wanted a pink bachelorette party." I wrinkled my nose and slipped my arms around his shoulders despite his protest. I wasn't happy about the dress, even if the style looked flattering, but she'd insisted it was perfect.

I thought it was too girly—it had little roses and tulle, for God's sake. Oh, the price of friendship.

"I like it." His gaze roved down to my feet and all the way back up. "I like it a lot."

The way his eyes devoured me made wearing the frou-frou dress worthwhile. "It ties in a bow in the back."

He looked down over my shoulder. "I see."

"Doesn't it make you want to unwrap me?" I batted my eyes and pursed my lips.

"Definitely."

Now we were getting somewhere. I stepped forward. I like to be cooperative.

He held me back. "Phil, I'll get you messy."

"That's what I'm hoping for."

He wrapped a hand in my loose hair. "Tell you what. Tonight when you come home, I'm going to take my time unwrapping you."

"Promise?"

He smiled, slow and predatory.

Shiver. "I'll be home by seven-thirty."

Chuckling, he said, "I don't think either party will have even started by then. And before you ask, yes, I have to go to Barry's bachelor party."

"I don't know about this bachelor party thing." Then a horrifying thought struck me. "You guys didn't hire Magda or anything, did you? Because I'd hate to think her next month's rent would be paid with money you'd stuck in her g-string."

"Phil."

I grinned. He insisted Magda wasn't a call girl, high-priced or otherwise. I knew he was right—probably—but speculating was too much fun. In his meanest moments, he threatened to ruin my fun by asking her what she did for a living, but I always distracted him with kisses.

I loved that my kisses distracted him. But his kisses drove me insane, so I guess we were equal.

"What time do you have to pick up Daphne?" he asked, toying with my hair.

I wrinkled my nose. "Five minutes ago."

"Phil." He shook his head. "You've got to stop torturing her. She needs your support. She seems—" he frowned "—lost."

Lost was a good way of putting it. She'd been acting weird lately. Weirder than usual. I was happy letting her stay in my house—I was at Rio's most of the time anyway—but I figured she'd start looking for a new job or something. Instead she just drifted aimlessly from day to day, which wasn't like her *at all*. "But it's so much fun torturing her."

"Phil."

"I know." I made a face. Whenever I asked her what her deal was, she'd remember an errand she needed to run. But I'd get it out of her. I had my ways.

"Maybe you can ask her tomorrow."

"Ugh." I scowled. "Did you have to remind me?"

He laughed. "Dinner with your parents isn't that bad."

No, they'd mellowed out. It was touch-and-go in the beginning, but the more they got to know Rio, the more they loved him. He and Mom had a regular museum date now. Dad even showed Rio his prized Zerene Fritillary butterfly.

"And my parents will be there tomorrow to act as a buffer."

I groaned. "I can't believe we're taking your parents to meet mine the day they fly in from New York. They haven't even met me yet. I hope they won't hold my parents against me."

I knew they wouldn't though. I'd talked to Rio's mom on the phone a lot. She was absolutely lovely. And his dad wanted to go to Kung Fu with me while he was here. I wasn't sure how my parents would react to Rio's dad, who'd been career military, but I figured his mom being an artist made up for it a little.

Rio rubbed my arms. "My parents already love you. But maybe it'd be best if we steered conversation away from anything political."

I laughed. "Okay."

He dropped a kiss on my forehead and then the side of my neck. "I've got to clean up and get to Barry's."

My goodbye was a long, deep kiss that left him dazed-looking and breathing heavy. I patted his chest, stepped back, and flashed him my best seductress smile. "Don't forget you have a gift to unwrap later tonight."

"How could I forget?" He smoothed a lock of my hair. "It's the best gift ever."

I smiled, bright and happy. "You're even better than MacGyver, Riordan McKenna."

He threw his head back and laughed. "I love you too, Phil."

About the Author

When Kate was a little girl, all she dreamt about was moving to France and living in a stone castle while painting the Provencal countryside. To prep herself, she studied French, stocked up on berets in every color, and practiced her shrug for hours in front of the mirror.

But then, because indentured servitude seemed more attractive than eating baguettes and drinking wine, she took a detour into the world of high tech. Eventually, that insanity wore off and she decided to try something more stable. Writing seemed the logical choice.

Unfortunately, she doesn't own her castle yet, but she holds out hope that one day soon she can pull her berets out of storage. Keep tabs on her progress by checking out *www.kateperry.com,* or contact her at *kate@kateperry.com.*

GREAT BOOKS, GREAT SAVINGS!

When You Visit Our Website:
www.kensingtonbooks.com
You Can Save Money Off The Retail Price
Of Any Book You Purchase!

- All Your Favorite Kensington Authors
- New Releases & Timeless Classics
- Overnight Shipping Available
- eBooks Available For Many Titles
- All Major Credit Cards Accepted

Visit Us Today To Start Saving!
www.kensingtonbooks.com

All Orders Are Subject To Availability.
Shipping and Handling Charges Apply.
Offers and Prices Subject To Change Without Notice.